the water underneath

the water underneath

Kate Lyons

ALLEN & UNWIN

First published in 2001

Copyright © Kate Lyons 2001

This project has been assisted by the Commonwealth
Government through the Australia Council, its arts funding
and advisory body.

Allen & Unwin
83 Alexander Street
Crows Nest NSW 2065
Australia
Phone: (61 2) 8425 0100
Fax: (61 2) 9906 2218
Email: frontdesk@allen-unwin.com.au
Web: http://www.allenandunwin.com

National Library of Australia
Cataloguing-in-Publication entry:

Lyons, Kate.
   The water underneath: a novel.

   ISBN 1 86508 418 2.

   I. Title.

A823.4

Set in 11.5/14 pt Adobe Garamond by DOCUPRO, Sydney
Printed by Australian Print Group, Maryborough, Victoria

10 9 8 7 6 5 4 3 2 1

For my family

contents

prologue

They dragged her out of the lake at dawn. No jaw, one eye socket, like some strange fish. The water was closing and closing, the centre blank as the tissue of a scar. Then, in a place a thousand miles from the ocean, they found something which might have been a seashell but which they knew was not.

The lake gave birth regretfully, washing her up in slow burps.

The lake at dawn is pale pink, the sky pale blue reflected, the trees islanded and bony and wearing birds' nests like funereal hats. You come to it on dirt road red and rutted, tracing a swollen kidney of water, through mangrove grey and knotted as an old fist. Now and again, trunks unclench, giving you water in a gasp. Dust skitters you sideways, as if earth would like to shrug you off.

Early light is kind here. Heat is a hum in the hollow of a rock. There are white Darling lilies blooming on the

river bank and the water by the roadside is the colour of
pearl. But by midday the sun will beat down, turning the
earth back to parchment, chiselling cracks in the mud
where you could almost expect to find the skull of a cow.
It will wither all the flower gardens in front of the caravans,
peel the paint from the toy picket fences and fade the
cartoon colours on the painted parking stones: blue for the
Miners' Union, green for the Catholic Workers, white for
anyone in between.

These are the sort of people who are fond of signs:
'Please keep to the paths provided', 'Please park between
the lines'. By eleven the men will be drinking beer and
fishing, the women will knit sweaty wool into bootees, the
kids will float around on blow-up sea monsters and collect
lumps of sand at the crotch. After lunch the kiosk lady will
pull down her shutters, roll up the sleeves of her nylon
tracksuit, fold fat white forearms and go to sleep.

At sunset when the harsh reds have died to blues and
purples, the colour of a bruise spreading, the caravanners
will sit on their banana lounges, these people called Harold
or Faith or Kay. Drink more beer. Comment on holiday
weather. Watch sun set across water's sullen skin.

The slam of the car door starts an echo. A hollow
bounce off dust. It plumbs a distance you could never hope
to comprehend. The indifference of earth. An empty cra-
nium of sky.

You make yourself walk toward it, toward the smell and
shape and feel of it, toward the idea of water, past the
barbeques and the tricycles, the exhausted gardens, the wet
bathers flapping and the grease of yesterday's chops. A man
is snoring in his annexe, a woman is muttering in her sleep.
A wire gate marks the beginning of the foreshore; there's

no fence attached to it and the reeds and scrub grow all round and through it and the water at high tide disregards it completely, lapping up against shower block steps. The sign here: 'Please shut the gate'.

You take a last look at the world of order and boundaries, at this place of pink tracksuits and dried flower arrangements, and you go through the gate, shutting it carefully behind.

The lake has crept back to its private sources. Under its skirts a secret country. Fine-hair plants sketch muscled folds of earth. They are tired of ceaseless water, breathless in sudden air. The earth rises and falls, the little plants are disturbed in their hiding, the lake bed twists in ridges and sinews, like the convolutions of a brain. You can walk and walk here, but even a kilometre into the centre the water is still receding, ever flatter and more secret, more silver as you get closer, then green, then pale brown like the river upstream.

The water isn't cold. It doesn't even feel like water, has a thicker texture, like seal hide or deep suede. It is swarming with fish which have nowhere else to go. They swim round and round a lake bed so flat and shallow the water looks painted, grey-green on red. Now and again nature out of sheer boredom throws up one with three fins, one eye, two tails. Between your toes is a black and mathematical mineral which, if you break it, shatters into smaller and smaller versions of itself.

Far out in the middle, earth falls away. Then there is nothing except flat horizon sinking and the flicker of unnatural fish.

water

chapter 1

She'd travelled you see, since sunset over twenty years before, in fits and starts and long silences, down from the foaming banks, down the strong brown muscle of the river, down from the big weir with the musical name. Her journey was as long as her mother's lifetime. But in the life of a river, in the past and future always present in a river's journey, Lily Cook was just a drop in the ocean. And the ocean was a thousand miles away.

Then, like now, the river was in flood. It was the biggest rainfall the town had seen in fifty years.

In a place like this, rain was always an event. More than that, it was an absolute surrounded by an almost-silence which was the fear of a vengeful God. People talked or thought about rain constantly, its continued absence or rare arrival, and not in the usual way that people talk about the weather, as a time-passer or an icebreaker or an intricate dance of pleasantry standing in for something else. Here, rain was rain. It stood on its own two feet.

People in that place talked about rain in an urgent way,

as if to imprint water on memory before real life drank it up. In the newsagents, at the bowling club, in the supermarket aisles, in the saloon bar at the pub, they rushed to capture it, in inches, days and dam gallons, in the novelty of bogged cars and wet washing and leaking roofs. When they said, 'I've never seen rain like it', they meant it. To exaggerate would tempt fate. When the rain was gone, they tried not to scan the endless sky.

The year Von and Lily Cook went missing had already been remarkable. In his 1967 Collins day-to-a-page diary, Frank Kelly had carefully marked the milestones with headlines cut from the *Daily Truth*. If asked he could have told you that in March a dust storm had moved the town's western border by a quarter of an inch. In April they'd finally installed sodium streetlights in the main street of town. In May the southern sky had been aglow with the aurora australis, and two weeks later the second-last picture theatre burnt down. Of interest mainly to ornithologists was the discovery in September of a black duck from New Zealand, which had flown nonstop for 1300 miles.

Just after Christmas the rain started and Frank Kelly's diary entries suddenly stopped. But the *Truth*, no matter how soggy when it slapped against the front doorstep, continued to record, without fear, favour or much sense of proportion, the trajectory of town events. The day after Boxing Day two men drowned in the Three Mile Creek. By New Year's Eve and the annual town dinner dance, the North Mine Marching Band was in full swing.

New Year's Day, 1968, and it was still raining, had been for ninety hours straight. Not just ordinary rain, but buckets of it, great big sheets of it, far too much for dry land to absorb. Something longed for had become almost overwhelming; the reservoir full, the flat earth resisting the shock of it, townspeople forced to cross the main street on wooden duckboards in the absence of proper gutters and kerbs. They flapped their trouser cuffs and held their new umbrellas awkwardly, as if they had just discovered an extra limb. Their skins exclaimed with moisture while they cursed the gluey mud.

But secretly they were one with the river. They were waking from a long dry dream. They liked the feel of water on skin and, if propriety allowed, would probably have danced around in it, bareheaded, shoeless, with barely disguised lust: housewives in Woolworths shifts, men in sticky thongs and singlets, matrons soaked to flabby curves under all that terylene.

And the river was remembering, all of it, not just the well-known broad sweep of it but the long slow whole of it, to the solitary drop and vein. It rushed furiously down dry scars and arteries, reclaimed ancient capillaries and amputated limbs. It carried nearly all before it, churning, vindicated, living finally, in a sort of muddy anguish, until it reached the deep red wounds the lake had made a million years before.

Mavis Kelly's niece was the only witness to what happened. But although the police took notes and the *Truth* printed her picture and the name of the town appeared in the city newspapers, causing a brief flush of civic pride, no-one took much notice of anything Mona Kelly said. Everyone knew that Kelly girl was a bit touched in the head.

As if to lend credence to this, there was Mona on New Year's Day. When any sensible person was inside playing Scrabble, Mona was sitting out in the pouring rain. At the lake people had gathered just inside their annexe flaps, sticking out a palm to gauge the size, potential and heft of the drops. They sat with a beer or a shandy, guessing at the exact number of inches and how much it would take to top 1927's record fall. A few beers later and they were betting matchsticks on the maximum capacity of the Five Mile Dam. A few beers after that they had agreed a barbeque was out of the question and were tossing a coin for who'd nick back to town for fish and chips. But no-one did. Only a fool would go out in this.

Mona Kelly didn't mind a bit of rain. In fact she liked it, the way this new element had washed away nearly all the straight lines of which that town was constructed, so that housework, homework, teatime, ten o'clock Mass were rudely ignored. Even the town streets, usually so rigorous, were blurred at the edges now, dissolving a little as bitumen washed away. It meant Mona could disappear and no-one would even notice, so intent was everyone on the sky. She'd already ridden her bike six miles up from the lake, her strong leg muscles working tyres which kept sinking into mud. She'd torn her dress on the barbed-wire fence they'd strung to stop someone just like her climbing out on the lip of the weir. At the top was a sign jointly sponsored by the Rotary and Lions Clubs: 'Dangerous when river in flood'. Mona sat right below it, hair plastered and dripping, dangling bare feet and a fishing line over the drop.

On one side water was brimming nearly to the top of the sheer concrete wall. It was frightening, that water, its usual brown treacle now bloated and yellow, running like a living bruise. It was as if a family pet had turned rabid at the end of its chain. Mona tempted it, almost sneered at it, leaning backwards as far as she could go, until she could taste the sheer blind anger of it, the stink of rotten mud. They'd opened the sluice full bore and a mash of dead things were vomiting through: tractor tyres, broken-necked maggies, belly-up fish. There were kero drums bobbing happily and tricycle wheels spinning and old Frigidaires fully stocked with jetsam and bilge. There were even a few stiff-legged sheep, floating upright as if out for a punt.

Mona wondered whether to move on down to the lake and see what happened when all this death arrived there. Whether it would be a mass of dead sheep and birds. But the lake was miles away and her legs ached and the road was flooding and her pushbike had a flat.

Now and again, and regularly, as if to some inner alarm clock, Mona scanned the horizon, hand cocked as if to shield eyes from the sun. But it was just habit, that way of looking into distance. There was no sun, no glare. It was something she'd copied from Frank. The rain kept pouring. There was no reason to expect him but in Mona's experience, if you sat and watched and waited long enough, things usually happened along.

Partly she was waiting for Frank. Partly she stayed because there was something irresistible about the river's angry boiling yellowness and the dead floating things and the sign saying 'Danger'. The largest, dullest and most stubborn part of Mona believed she would catch a shark.

'A man threw something in the water' is what the police reported the Kelly girl to have said. The story was on the front page of 1968's first edition of the *Truth*. It drove off the church fete and the council elections and even the town's parking dilemma: parallel or rear to kerb. When questioned, the girl said there were two objects, all wrapped in white. 'Like mummies,' Mona Kelly said.

'Like your mummy?' asked the thick-headed policeman, whose greatest feat to date had been solving the theft of the school's chocolate wheel. He said it very slowly, because as everyone knew, this Kelly kid was a bit soft in the head.

Mona in turn thought this policeman was more stupid than sheep. 'No, like mummies in Egypt,' she said extra slowly, sticking pretend bandaged arms out in front. One small one, one big, the first one a fair bit smaller Mona reckoned, on the other side of the river, back from the weir and under the bridge. The man worked a lever, the shelf tilted, the things fell in the water, and the sluice gates poured everything downstream.

'What lever, what shelf?' asked the bewildered policeman.

'On the truck!' said Mona, rolling her eyes.

'What truck?'

Mona screwed up her face and picked at her toenails, peeling off strips at the quick. Her lips were too red and hung open wetly, because her adenoids had never been fixed. She was already bored by the cream and green police station, which smelt strongly of those blue cakes used to ward off the smell of piss.

'Anyway, my mum's dead.'

'What else did you see?' asked the other policeman, thinner and smarter than the first one and carefully taking notes. You could hardly say Mona Kelly's mum was alive and well, she was mad as a meat axe, but he'd seen her an hour ago, getting off the Adelaide bus. You couldn't miss her really, what with the way she was singing the Ave at full volume and with that tea-cosy thing on her head.

'Nuthin'. Didn't see nuthin' after that.'

Mona's feet hit the chair rungs with a repetitive thud. After an hour or so of this and the sound of her breathing, the two policemen were glad to take her home.

The policemen's big break didn't come until they were driving back down the main street. The rain had stopped finally. The sun was beating down. Already the mud in the puddles was puckering. A few days from now the town would return to its true element. A square mushroom in flat red dust.

Mona pressed her nose up against the car window, watching the men drinking in front of the curly verandah pub. She was looking for her father, a man last seen with a beer in his hand. But the men were sitting half in the shade, half in the sun, with boots pointed muddily skyward and their faces obscured by the wide brims of hats.

'I think he was wearing a hat.' Mona went on picking her nose.

The thin policeman hurried to write this down in his notebook. The thick policeman later underlined it in red pen. They continued on down the main street of a town where every man, nearly without exception, wore something on his head.

chapter 2

Frank Kelly was a man of many hats. Once he'd been a stockman on a property way out west. Once he was a miner in real desert country, with a proper tin helmet and a lamp. At yet other times he'd been a shearer and a roustabout and an abalone diver, off the coast of Broome. But for most of what people regarded as his proper life, he was a shopkeeper where he wore no hat at all.

Whenever people think of Frank they see a distant stick figure against endless sunset: red earth, black tunnels, blue sky. While in reality he was always in motion—diving deep, riding across, digging through—in their picture of him he refuses to move. In the mind's eye Frank inhabits a dream like a painting where the dreamer is the watcher, as anchored to perspective as the sun or the moon.

In this dream Frank stands very still, looking for something, lost in a long dry sigh of space. Sometimes a road or river cuts the frame, always in directions east and west. These are questions disguised as answers running off into the blue. Sometimes, in the furthest corner, just on the edge of sight, there is the merest hint of mineral or old moisture. It is sheer as babies' eyelids or the stubble on Frank's chin.

With this dream comes the knowledge that he is impervious, to blood, fire, energy, sweat or tears. It's frightening, this strange integrity, the spit image of squeezing blood from a stone. It is as if through sheer determination Frank has made of himself some foreign substance, scoured out by wind and dust and sun. Yet under that skin you can see blood swirling, thoughts dancing like insects in a haze. You can try and try to look for his eyeline, to follow his great expanse of doing and not saying, to plot the deft trail of his silence, faint as smoke or dust or hieroglyphs. But rooted like a tree, weathered by silence, you can only watch him disappear over some horizon. A big man casting a long shadow. Drawing the eye and leading it away.

You might never imagine Frank Kelly penned quietly behind some clean laminex counter. Hatless. Waiting only for time to pass.

By 1967, the year Von and Lily Cook disappeared, Frank Kelly had a whole collection of hats hanging on the hooks in his hallway: terry towelling ones, old Akubras, straw sunhats, even a black pork pie from when he used to go to Mass. But his travelling hat, though faded and tattered and gone threadbare in the crown, hung in pride of place. He wore it for gardening. Because he couldn't bear to throw it out.

In 1953, that travelling hat of Frank's was brand new. A few weeks before Christmas that year he'd put it on— brown hide, broad-brimmed, still smelling of a saddlery but already collecting a fine film of dust—and simply disappeared.

This in itself was not surprising. Frank Kelly was famous for his disappearances, irregular events become so regular you could set your watch by them, like tropical noonday storms. In fact at the age of fourteen and fresh out of the Home of Compassion, Frank had disappeared for ten whole years. But no-one ever forgot him; his memory, like Father Christmas or a stained-glass saint, gave off a dim but sympathetic glow.

In that missing decade people often wondered whatever happened to that nice Home of Compassion boy Mrs Goddard took on. They remembered how he'd carry your bag of groceries without being asked, or wash your car for sixpence and never ask for a bob. How he was always cleaning an old person's clogged-up gutter and how he was the only altar boy who always attended early Mass.

When Frank came back to town for good, he arrived just like Vonnie: one day a hat-shaped hole in the fabric, the next the town moving over to accommodate him, like he'd never left at all. Frank swelled, literally, to fill the space. He had a white-collar job in the mine office, he married Mavis Goddard from out the property, he owned the corner store out south. At least now when he went AWOL he kept to a routine. 'Gone walkabout,' was all anyone offered when someone else said, forgetting it was Christmas, 'Where's Frank Kelly, haven't seen him doing late shift in the shop.'

Where Von Cook came from was also a mystery. One day in 1953 she wasn't there and Frank was off gallivanting while Mavis 'did the church'. The next, Frank was rigging a rope swing on his back verandah while Mavis bought discreet items at the chemist and hemmed a confirmation dress, her mouth thin-lipped with pins.

When people thought about it later, as Bernie Whelan often did after that business down by the river, no-one even knew Von's real name. She was Kelly when she came to live with Frank and Mavis, Cook when she married the second Cook boy and 'That Von' when she went completely off the rails. In fact her Christian name was the only really certain thing about her, never Mrs Cook or Miss Kelly, always Von or Vonnie, which no doubt came from Evonne. It was a pretty name, but slightly foreign sounding to someone like Mrs Whelan, who was reared with lots of Marys, Annes and Bernadettes. And, as Mrs Whelan said later to Vera McNally, with the benefit of hindsight and a few festive season sherries, if Von was only a Cook through dire necessity and a Kelly somewhere back to begin with and God knows what bits of mongrel in between, well, really, what else could you expect?

A few days after Christmas of 1953, Frank drove his Ford truck in on the Sydney road and up the main street. He parked slap bang in front of the cathedral, where parish faithfuls were caught nattering after early Mass. Frank handed Vonnie down like she was the Queen, like she was stepping out of a horse-drawn carriage, like she was a big event. Housewives in the Foodtown stopped to peer over their trolleys, and Mr Marconi stood on tiptoe behind his grapes. But they all looked the other way when Frank caught their eye. Frank strolled hand in hand with Vonnie all the way down the main street, stopping to collect a long overdue suit at Mason's dry-cleaners and to buy the girl a pair of pink plastic sunglasses he saw her ogling in the chemist's shop. They were meant for a much younger child and they made her eyes look too close together but she wore them proudly, teamed with Frank's brand-new hat.

Walking down the footpath in the midday sun, Frank looked somehow naked, with his head of hair springing rudely up. Back then it was still pitch-black, with no touch of grey.

At Whelan's, Frank and Vonnie sat right up at the counter, as proud as you please. Mothers in sensible sandals, men in their best cufflinks and town waistcoats, the clutch of bowls matrons in their Omo whites, everyone turned their heads to look through Whelan's window, like Frank had their chins on a string.

But Frank wasn't looking at them. Frank's own chin was held straight and high. He ordered a lime spider and a jam donut for Vonnie and a vanilla milkshake for himself. He specified a clean plate. Mrs Whelan rankled. But she said nothing except, 'You're back.'

The lass looked about nine or ten, Mrs Whelan told Vera McNally at the hairdressers, and for a girl her age she was dressed in a cobbled together type of assortment—a dress a kiddie might wear to Sunday school or to one of those Eytie christenings, all black velvet ribbons and pink and yellow smocking, finished off with an old striped cardigan and, God save us, big clodhopper boots. 'She looked like a liquorice allsort,' Mrs Whelan whispered. 'Like a walking St Vinnie's.' The women shook their sculpted heads.

The girl fell on the sweets like a starved person, loathe to waste a single crumb. Frank leant easily on the counter, keeping an eye on things in the Hawaiian-style mirror, blowing bubbles with his straw. When he caught Von looking at him there, hatless and framed between a palm tree and a hula-hula girl, he stuck out his tongue. Von sprayed lime spider all down her front. Mrs Whelan frowned behind the Peak Freans. Von's eyes fell to her boots. These eyes were very dark, with green flecks like the vein of mineral in a rock. Her arms against the white puffed dress were a sort of tawny brown.

Part dago, decided Mrs Whelan, and the other part, well, everyone knew a bit about that.

Frank just stared at Bernie Whelan in the mirror, as if daring her to ask.

All he said was, 'Reckon it's been hot.' Mrs Whelan sniffed, because that's about as much as it deserved. But half an hour after Frank and Vonnie banged out the swing door, she was lining up at the counter of Mavis Kelly's shop.

'Saw your Frank just now,' Bernie said, under cover of a half of tank and a tin of baked beans. 'Didn't tell me you had a visitor coming, Mavis. Relative, is she? Come to stay for a bit?'

The women were avid. Stitches were dropped, change left untallied, chops left to blacken and burn.

But Mavis kept mum. 'Family,' is all she would say, then and now. Encouraging an idea of Frank's family that was at once terrible and wonderful and hinted of grim responsibility and things narrowly evaded, if only because of Frank's good heart.

By the next day people were putting two and two together and coming up with five. And over the next few weeks of afternoon teas and shopping expeditions and bingo of a Thursday, Vonnie was knitted into something big and colourful enough to unpick for weeks. Frank Kelly's family multiplied from a garden-variety dead mother and father to something as mysterious and widespread as cancer, with rumours of more than a few black sheep.

Mavis took it all on the chin. And only when she was right at the end of her short tether, and only after wielding a rolled-up *Truth* and then pointing with it to the cathedral towering above her on the town's only natural hill, would she say: 'I'll do it, you mark my words, Evonne! I'll send you to the Home of Compassion! You just ask your Uncle Frank.'

To Von, who'd never heard of compassion and only dimly experienced it, this was a place of terrible hellfire, of swords and maybe whipping, a place where people always 'Did The Right Thing'. In her mind it was written in bold black letters on the front page of the newspaper and started with a capital C.

Frank knew something no-one else did and he kept it to himself. It was a rare coin he fingered, like a shell which echoed the sea. He knew the power of silence. It wasn't an absence like most people thought. It was solid as a load of bricks. When Frank went for a beer down the club of a Saturday afternoon and the regulars on their third schooner said, 'Frank! G'arn, let us in on it! Who's that lass you've got in tow?' he just let them rib-dig each other and chuckle and imagine, thinking in their way of big-hipped women and sly grog and things which fell off the back of trucks.

Frank waited for his silence to catch them, like a net yielding silver fish. He dangled it, hooklike, until it stuck in their throats. After a while the men faltered, shifted on their stools, adjusted their bartop elbows and started talking about which horse was a goer in the two o'clock.

Frank gazed into middle distance from under the brim of his brand-new hat.

. . .

The first thing Von saw of Uncle Frank was that hat. It just appeared without warning around the corner of the Mother's back verandah, between the statue of the Virgin Mary and the stone birdbath, a dusty brim moving of its own volition and wearing like plumage the bright purple of the jacaranda tree. Even when the hat evolved into a person, the only part of him that Von could see under the big blue stuffed dog he was carrying, twice her size and wide as a doorway, was that hat and a pair of steel-toe boots.

Von reckoned she should go and call the Mother. The Mother had been waiting all morning for someone called Uncle Frank.

'Your Uncle Frank's coming,' she'd told Vonnie at breakfast. 'Him that lives Out Back.' The Mother had pointed with her butter knife in the general direction of the Great Dividing Range. 'Finally deigned to make an arrangement has Frank Kelly. Wouldn't credit it, would you? Wonders will never cease.'

The man put his fingers to his lips. He winked, made jabbing movements with his thumb. It looked interesting, so Von sat down on the back step. The man placed the big blue dog on her lap. It towered over her, all lolling tongue and rolling eyes. The man passed over a little bottle of Schweppes lemonade. Von felt the size and weight of that horny hand. It smelt of tobacco and musty clothes and wet hessian sacks. But when he picked her up for a piggyback, the strength of those hands were a comfort. They would never let you fall.

Quietly, with an exaggerated tiptoe, like a cat in a cartoon, the man crept back inside the house and down the Mother's long shiny front hall. Even though he had big clodhopper boots on he didn't make a sound. Von's legs clung like a crab's to the man's belly, arms held tight around his rough red throat. Giggles were bubbling. But the man made a shooshing sound with his teeth.

Through the front wire door they could just see the Mother standing on the top step of the verandah. She made a small stern figure under the arch of bougainvillea. She'd been out there a full hour before Frank was expected. She'd said sixteen Hail Marys and quite a few Our Fathers, she was in the clear for a venal sin. But it was a satisfying penance. She waited so Frank would know he was putting her out. She waited as shorthand for all those years she'd waited to date.

It was raining lightly, so the Mother held a black umbrella over her nun-like dress. The tissue she always kept tucked in her sleeve had travelled up to her shoulder and snarled there like an extra breast. Her limbs held her clothes like a cheap coathanger, her fingers were pale spiders string-ing dry black prayers. Later Von would recognise all those painful angles in Mavis, those arms over which skin was stretched so tight, elbows were a white full stop.

'Watch out, Vonnie! Think I might be drunk!' Frank erupted onto the front verandah, almost knocking the Mother off her pins. The Mother had three legs by then, Von remembered: two white and bluish, one brown and knobbled. A mark of her oncoming death.

Uncle Frank swung Von to his shoulders, lurching and spinning so she saw the world tip and slant, the footpath looming like an accident, all mixed up with Frank's boots and the jigsaw of buildings and the smoggy sky. Things ordinary just a minute ago took on a fairground whirl. Frank laughed and staggered and tilted, mock-tripping over shrubbery, until it was like being tickled in the stomach, an unbearable pleasure you did and didn't want to stop.

All the Mother said was, 'It's time for tea.'

You had to wait for the Mother to turn around on the verandah before you could go inside. It was a slow process involving the brown leg around which the Mother's own sticks rotated, like an insect with an extra limb. This close up, her old lady hump looked enormous. She smelt funny too, like moths. And while the front of her hair was sculpted in a big blue wave, there was a flattened sleep whorl at the back of her head. This knowledge could give you power, intimate and pink through blue-rinse tufts. Even Von knew how to comb her hair.

The Mother was really called Mrs Goddard and no-one ever called her anything else to her face. But looking up at her from a fresh lick and spittle one Sunday, Von had immediately christened her the Mother. Because that's what Mrs Goddard most resembled, that cold and eyeless statue of the Virgin Mary by the back fence. The Mother suited her: generic, graceful, austere. Chilly as the church.

'Mavis sends her love.'

In the kitchen with its white and blue tablecloth and its rows of plates even as teeth, the Mother was cutting up scones. Like everything she did, these were too tiny and too perfect, with sultanas which stuck under your tongue. 'Secret's in the rubbing,' the Mother said, her thin musician's fingers sifting butter and flour until it was fine as seed. The Mother sliced these tiny scones into half, then half, then half again. The intent was dainty but not encouraging. The Mother was on a mission from God.

'Beatrice? Did you hear?'

The Mother continued waving jam at scones as if Frank hadn't said a word. She often did that, just ignored you. Her silence was vast and glassy as her highly polished floor.

But Frank wasn't scared of anything, or so it seemed. He just said it again, much louder this time, like the Mother's hearing aid was low on juice: 'Beatrice! I said Mavis sends her love.' He handed over an envelope on which Von recognised the familiar spiky writing from those letters which came every second week. These always made the Mother frown and say, with teeth gritted, 'The blood money's in.' Von decided Mavis's love must be like the love of God, because it made the Mother go thinner and grimmer and stand up straighter, like she did when it was time to go to Mass.

The Mother scrabbled in her smooth black handbag, yellow nails brittle against the clasp.

'Evonne. Go and fetch the milk. And be quick about it. Kettle's on the boil.'

The Mother's skin on Von's palm felt rare, like rice paper and dead people. And it wasn't even enough any more, milk had gone up. But the Mother refused to believe it. 'That's blue murder,' she always said, and expected Von to argue with the Chinese man down at the store.

Get your own milk, Von thought, scuffing along. She planned to buy throwdowns, those little crackers with the red and yellow swirls. They would hear her coming, bang, bang, bang and crackle, all up the Mother's street. Von picked up some other kid's dead cracker from the footpath; the smell was burnt and delicious and slightly exciting. It cast a faint shadow of old danger. Of danger still to come.

. . .

'Shop was shut,' Von lied. Uncle Frank was digging in the garden. He didn't argue, just winked and walked up the driveway next door. Mr Gillespie's milk was always still sitting there at midday, something which caused the Mother to mutter about the 'demon drink'. Von could never work out what could be so devilish about that bottle of milk compared to their own. But Uncle Frank just nicked it. Just took it straight off the Gillespie doorstep. And put it on the Mother's. Nothing happened. There was no thunderbolt from heaven. Frank didn't go straight to hell.

While Frank dug holes and filled them up again, moving dirt from one place to the other with no particular purpose and spreading far too much blood and bone, he muttered the mysterious names of the plants in Mother's garden, knitting that greenery, so overgrown and wild with moisture, into a shawl of magic words. Azalea, oleander, rhododendron: Frank told those plants like a voodoo rosary, like a ponderous Latin prayer. He transformed dull squat shrubs into foreign exotica with his mysterious spell. His incantation flourished, a murmured lace threading the big verandah with its expanses of wet moss and cold stone. That smooth cool promise ran on and on round endless secret corners, making you want to slide on your bum. But that wasn't allowed.

Frank, digging and muttering, marvelled at greenery, at the damp darkness of Sydney soil. Earthworms he turned up were cut in two by his spade. They died twice over, wriggling back from sun. Von liked the way he wasn't getting anywhere, the aimless nature of the digging, as if the act in itself was enough. She decided she would like to be a man like Uncle Frank when she grew up.

Men like Frank had precise creases in their trousers and a checked shirt and a wide-brimmed hat. When they reached into a pocket for a balled-up handkerchief, they could make rude sounds with it which were somehow allowed. Men like Frank had grizzled noses with large nostrils, sometimes with white hair sprouting out. They had a particular smell, a mixture of tobacco and flannelette and Sunlight soap threaded with something salt and dark. What Von would later recognise as the smell of sex dampened. Like museum lions.

Von pretended that Frank had come to live with her and the Mother and be the head of the house. The Mother would be forced to dig in the garden beside him, inhaling Frank's blood and bone. The Mother would hear first hand the hoiking noise Frank made in the back of his throat. Her fine piano player fingers would be all dirty and calloused. She would wear Uncle Frank's chicken shit under the perfect half-moons of her nails.

'Evonne! Sit up straight! Drink your tea.'

The grandfather clock ticked on and on. Like a heart entombed in a wall. The Mother's grandfather had owned it in England and his grandfather before that. In the hollow voice of dead grandfathers it demanded sacrificial windings, down through many years. Its tick was like bones clicking together down a well.

The ticking of the grandfather was now the only sound in what the Mother called the 'drawing room', although as far as Von knew, precious little drawing went on in there.

All you could do was sit stiff and straight-backed, being careful not to scuff the Persian or scratch mahogany with your Doulton cup. The Mother sat to attention near the tea things. Von clung to an ottoman, trying not to slide off. But wherever Uncle Frank sat he looked comfortable; he was leaning forward easily, tipping his tea into a saucer and drinking it in slurps. The Mother sat up even straighter at each one so that, as Uncle Frank said later, she looked like a piece of four-be-two.

Von knew something had happened in her absence and she was impatient to know it; this made everything, teacups brittle as seashells, weak tea, scones like playthings, seem sinister, out of place. The clock ticked. A cockroach crawled along a skirting board, down the china cabinet, across the Persian and then under the leg of the Mother's chair. Her shiny nun shoes were far too small. Above each ankle rose a small puff of pain.

'So,' Frank said, 'it's decided. Eh Beatrice? We agreed?'

The Mother tapped one foot. She kept Frank dangling in her silence, above the polished echo of her floor.

'She can take that new school dress with her. I suppose Mavis paid for that. But everything else stays here.'

The Mother's voice was strangled in a way that came from too-tight girdles, too-small shoes. She turned away from Frank toward her piano, her whole body moving stiffly, never losing a straight line between waist and skull. 'Imagine a string pulling you to heaven,' she always said. But Von didn't want to go to the Mother's heaven. She just wanted to know what was going on.

The grandfather ticked. Frank slurped. The Mother tapped her feet to faint music only she could hear. No-one said anything. And waiting there, bracing her feet against the floor, Von could hear the Mother talking to herself, almost indecipherable, that frail singing mutter made of no words at all. Her face had gone blank, the skin pale under the beige. Where her eyes had used to glint there was a film of uncertainty, as if she was looking at things through an old and gauzy scarf. She fiddled with dry sheets of music from her piano seat, old skin rasping over black symbols, all the while muttering in a thready whisper, that language just below the level of noise. It seemed the web connecting the Mother to the world had petered, was swinging idly in the breeze.

After long minutes of this, the clock clicking dry bones, the Mother muttering, Frank slurping his tea, Von couldn't stand it any more. Her fingers were curled ready in her pocket. So she smacked the cracker down hard on the Mother's wooden floor. The Mother jumped. She seemed to crumple, get older, look suddenly small.

Frank picked Von up then, took her outside.

'It's alright, Vonnie. You're coming home with me.'

While what was now just an old woman cleared the tea things, they escaped to the garden with the rest of the scones. They stuffed them into their mouths, three or four pieces at a time. Frank tried to whistle with his mouth full, spraying crumbs all over his front. They fed the rest to the birds on the edge of the birdbath. Birds threw shining glints against wet green. To Von this old church font, dreary just this morning, was suddenly an Enid Blyton thing, both wonderful and implausible, like fairies or unicorns. Trees curved more fully down to meet the garden, moss grew more green and vibrant, climbing up and over carved stone grottoes, the cupid seats, the gargoyle fountains by the fence. It flourished beardlike on the statue of Mary at the door.

Von and Frank walked right down to the stone wall where you weren't allowed to go. Frank just climbed over it and carried Von toward the cliffs. Through Moreton Bays, roots rearing so high you could sit between them like an armchair, to the rocking wharf where the 'fairy' came in. Von sensed a wetness, a richness in the air that she had never smelt before. Her nose thrilled to it. Uncle Frank raised his head like a bloodhound and sniffed.

Under the wharf ancient things clung patiently to rocks. Bending down, picking them up, putting them back again, not speaking but holding hands. Green moss and grey waves, the smell of salt and rich earth in the same place, the birds, the water lapping, the crusty pylons. The quietness. It was like the first time Von had ever seen the sea.

'There's a place there where you can see the curvature of the earth.'

Uncle Frank was pointing to a spot on his map, to a tiny black dot he called home. Well he had the map in his hand but he wasn't looking at it. He was heading home now and that feeling of home, etched in Frank's palm, well it didn't show up on any map at all.

They'd been driving all night from the city, where Frank always got lost. He was unused to the freeways and byways of it, the way streets grew on top of each other like fungus gone wild. Stretches of water kept interrupting the land. Things refused to fall into the neat dry grids he was used to, roads all called after minerals and emanating from a single and central idea.

'Mongrel bloody thing.' He was wrestling with his ancient Gregory's, odd chunks of Sydney fluttering all over the car. 'Can't make head nor tail.' That map of Frank's home which Von found in the glovebox had no slabs of green or blue, no cobweb of back alleys, just roads at right angles and white space running off the edge of the page. To Frank this was true wilderness, these twisted turns of city, that tangle of hills and highway and blue ocean, with sail boats scudding along the top. Tall buildings zig-zagged, bearing a crossword of important sounding names. Their heights serrated the eye. They made Frank feel smaller than he ever did in a wide open space. Every now and again he craned his head under the flap of the sun visor, to see a skyscraper swoop. At home nothing was more than two storeys. Here was vertigo in reverse.

Finally he stopped completely and stuck his head out the side window, trying to fix his position in the usual way. But you couldn't even see the blasted sun here, that was the problem. Too much smog.

'Bugger of a thing.' Frank flapped torn pages in Von's face. 'Here, put that Catholic school through its paces. See if you can find the highway. Buggered if I can. Wouldn't hurt them to put up a ruddy sign, would it? Just now and again.'

'What about the Mother?'

'Bit bushed, that's all. Needs to have a rest.'

The old woman had stood on the verandah as they left, frail and bent over her knobbly stick. She looked like she had shrunk, like all the juice had been wrung out of her, like her clothes were standing up by themselves.

'Don't sniff,' she'd muttered, tucking a Kleenex up the front of Von's jumper, spitting on her hankie and cleaning scone crumbs off Von's chin. Part of Von wanted to kiss her. Instead she set her face hard under Frank's brand-new hat. The Mother muttered, 'Who in God's name does she think she is?'

They stopped at a little shop before they hit the highway and Uncle Frank let Von choose what she wanted to wear. It was like Christmas, digging through all the bins filled with odd shoes, hairy jumpers and even a fur thing with a tail. Uncle Frank said this was where the rich people threw away the clothes they didn't want. Von couldn't imagine that someone wouldn't want these black beaded handbags and red swishy dresses, the yellow hats topped off with fruit and feathers, even a pair of black boots just like Uncle Frank's. When she emerged from the change room resplendent in pink and green and canary yellow, Frank called her 'the cat's whiskers'. He stuffed her grey school dress in the bin.

They drove all night, along the highway, stopping once for fish and chips, full of so much grease and salt and vinegar, the Mother would have had a fit. Then it was on and on, past the deserted car yards and the takeaway shops, lit yellow under the flourescents, through flat plains of blackness where Uncle Frank sang 'Road to Tipperary' and 'Roll Out the Barrel' and there was nothing to look at except the green dials on the dashboard and nothing to think about except the lull and hum of rubber on tar. Then up the winding mountain road, in long slow coils like a snailshell, where you couldn't quite tell you were climbing except that Uncle Frank said you were and because your ears blocked and Uncle Frank told you to swallow and they popped, just like he said.

The truck stopped now and then on the verge. Frank stared straight ahead while Von retched up battered shark. Then he handed her his man-size hankie and swung back out into the traffic, he didn't miss a beat. The little truck rounded the final curve on the long climb, semis grunting and heaving and cars all piled up behind them, and Von didn't know people were swearing and sighing and banging their hands on steering wheels, caught helplessly behind Frank doing his slow country miles. Through the back window their headlights strung out prettily, like pearls on a black necklace, 'Like knots on a piece of string,' Von reckoned. Frank smiled. Then, peeping over the shoulder of the highest mountain, the lights of Lithgow twinkled, 'Like jewels on a black carpet,' Frank said, and Von stored this one up.

At the very top he swerved to a sudden stop. He fiddled with something under the wipers, his breath a big puff of steam. He put a blob of something cold in her lap.

'Snow,' is all he said. Von had never seen snow. She was disappointed. In the car light it was not pure like icing sugar but dark grey, running quickly to sludge.

Then they were winding down the other side of the mountain, the road in the mist like a tunnel which would deliver them, to another life, another place, to somewhere else. The car tipped and swerved, planets navigated their ocean, Frank's feet and hands moved in slow syncopation. Like he was swimming underwater. Like he was conducting an orchestra of stars.

chapter 3

Boxing Day 1967 and Frank Kelly as usual was up before the sun. It was the week of the town's annual pilgrimage to the caravans, and at dawn, from his half-painted front verandah, Frank could see neighbours unearthing eskies from garages, removing tennis balls from trailer tows. Even this early sun was beating down hard on the bitumen. By ten a.m. barefoot children would be doing their fastidious hot-tar hopscotch across the road. Which summed up this town in December more than anything else.

It was going to be a real stinker. Frank smiled. He pulled in his stomach, stood up straight, pumped his arms, elbows aloft. There was a lot to do today. But first things first.

By seven a.m. Frank was already well engaged in it, piling on sugar and milk. Porridge rose up well above the rim. He poured and poured, until the milk nearly over-flowed onto the laminex. It bulged and bubbled; the beige mess plopped like lava, sugar rose in a seismic mound. But everything was held there by Frank's strange centrifugal force.

'Frank Kelly! Watch my bloody cloth!'

Breakfast was just one of the habits Mavis Kelly deplored in Frank. She sat opposite with her dry toast bearing a smear of marmalade, sipping plain black tea.

'What we going to do about Vonnie, Frank? And Lil? While we're out the lake.' Frank was still pouring. He liked a lot of milk. 'Gone half past seven already, Frank. Have to make some arrangements. Can't just leave it to chance. Eh? Frank! Do you hear?' It had just gone quarter past. Give or take.

'Y'know, Frank, thith really can't go on.' Mavis had one fingernail stuck between her front teeth, to excise a stray bit of seville.

'Recalcitrant in eight letters?' Frank yelled on a rising inflection, leaning back on the kitchen chair. The steel struts groaned, the chair rocked on its haunches; Mavis held her breath. Frank was a big man and getting bigger. His checkered belly scraped the table, he had rolls of sunburnt neck. As always he had one biro poised above the newspaper and the other leaking into his top pocket. There was a permanent blue patch over the heart.

Mavis worried about Frank's heart. First there was the beer, the long-neck bottle every night after dinner, not to mention the pies, the pasties, the pavlovas, the eleven o'clock sausage rolls. Then there were the slabs of ham fat eaten secretly at Christmas, spread first with Fairy and slapped and rolled between two hunks of bread. Mavis surprised him yesterday hiding behind the pantry door, and not for the first time; he looked her straight in the eye as he bit through layers of white dough, yellow grease, brown skin. He just smiled, wiped marge off his chin and strolled right past her, out to his shed.

'A dodgy ticker' is what he called his heart. Like he owned an interesting but unreliable watch.

'Any ideas, Mavis?' The ash from Frank's Peter Stuyvesant was growing longer and longer, soon to fall unnoticed down Frank's front.

But Mavis was busy wiping Frank's sugar off the table-cloth, worrying about the washing, the lamingtons to ice, the ham to slice for the holiday shift. And as always there was Von.

'Mona! Don't slump!'

'Got it,' said Frank suddenly, swooping down as far as his belly would allow. He pressed so hard on his biro, it bled blue ink. The laminex bore the ghosts of words which had long ago lost their clues.

Frank Kelly usually had skin the colour of warm toast, but when he got out in the sun it turned the boiled red of Heinz tomato soup. His hair under his old travelling hat was black and crinkly, fading to grey. His thumbs were flattened from years of random hammers, but his fingers were lean and knotted as a piece of rope. Those hands knew how to string a fence and how to fix a radiator, how to milk oil from engines, how to test for moisture between hard layers, sense water from below the earth's skin. How to hold dust cupped in one palm and let it blow in the direction of wind.

He scooped up a handful now from under his lemon tree. Sifting it, feeling the exact shape and scope of dryness, the precise amount of lack between each grain. It was drought, no doubt about it, no matter what they said about hot spells and annual averages. Frank knew better. He raised his nose and sniffed. There was weather coming, a lot of it. But it was a fair way off.

Carefully, methodically, covertly almost, Frank unwound the garden hose.

Despite the fact that he was in regular trouble for ignoring water restrictions and received jealous frowns from neighbours as well as stern letters from the town water supply, the only thing Frank was really good at was cactus. He had hundreds of them, the spiked green garden variety as well as more exotic ones a bit like small intestines, pink and fibrous and rearing out of the guts of ceramic swans. The rest of the garden was in the future, existing only in Frank's mind's eye. There were blank plots of ground with illustrations of the flowers he would like to grow, rows pregnant with monstrous pumpkins, stakes where tomato plants would grow heavy with fruit. Everything in this imaginary garden was criss-crossed by small paths of painted stones which made the emptiness gay and promising as a cartoon.

Frank liked his garden precisely because it was exactly like all the rest in this street on the right side of town. He had a butterfly house number and a stone possum climbing the trellis, he had all seven dwarves bar one. There were Grecian stone pillars on his verandah and a tiled front apron which was easy to sweep. He had six rubber tyre bird feeders and two corrugated-iron birdbaths and a row of swan plant holders forming a guard of honour to his front door. The only thing Frank drew the line at was blackfella gnomes.

Right down the back, down a brightly painted crazy path lined with dreams for spinach and potatoes, giant cucumbers and baby squash, Frank had his shed. Mavis wasn't allowed in there and would not have wanted to anyway, afraid of the cleaning she might have to do. Sometimes she ventured too far past the Hills Hoist but, alert to the sudden silence, she crept away.

A good thing too because Frank had rigged up one of his inventions over the door. This collection of old toaster parts had enough volts to kill an army but it was only a precaution: his blueprints for the manure-driven lawn-mower and the electronic dog food dispenser were buried deep under the lemon tree. Frank was no mug, he knew all about the government, those CIA spies.

Nothing concrete ever emerged from Frank's shed. But when visitors came to tea he would use a lull to try out one of his ideas.

'Take cemeteries for instance.' This was dropped into a silence created by plate-bringing controversies. Mavis was head of the CWA. 'Criminal waste of space. And if they burnt everybody, even the Catholics, what do you reckon would happen? What about all those green gas omissions, you tell me that!'

Frank looked triumphantly round the table. The women nodded and went pale. Frank subscribed to *National Geographic* and scientific pamphlets published in Finland, or was it Fremantle? In any case Frank was an expert on these things.

'Know what I reckon? Bury the bastards feet first. Vertical, not flat. Think how many you could fit in.'

Frank folded his hands across his belly. There was a long silence. Then Mavis recited a recipe for fruitcake. After that, no-one ever disturbed Frank in his shed.

Frank settled in now for a good half-hour of watering, ignoring Dawn McGregor's angry curlers wobbling over the

side fence. Now and again he leant down to touch the
hearts of ragged lettuce and finger the leaves of what would
have been a tomato in a better world. But Frank didn't see
things dying; he saw instead bounty and potential, green
things growing where only dust had been before. He imagined life running through his fingers and down the tender
shoots of plants.

At seven thirty precisely Mavis unlocked the shop. 'Corner
store' it said in big red letters on the brick wall above the
awning, along with an ageing ad for Vincent's Powders and
a hand-painted notice, equally indelible: 'No credit given,
don't ask'. 'Milk bread cigarettes' said the portable whirligig
Mavis would later put out on the footpath. No ye olde
this, no metaphors, no clever turns of phrase. Life was too
serious for things to mean what they might not.

The shop itself was whitewashed brick with bay windows, very clean due to Mavis, with gleaming silver meat
cutters and glass Kelvinators full of devon and cheese.
There, everyone called the devon Fritz. They ate it with
tomato sauce on white bread. There were lollies in cardboard boxes, all the old types, cobbers and freckles and
those rubbery pink and white teeth. People called Frank's
shop the deli, but back then it was just a word, like bread
or shop or milk. There were no antipasto jars or smoked
salmon, only packets of White Wings and bottles of pickled
onions and pale pink sausages in strings.

Mavis was slicing lunch meat for the holiday shift cribs.
Bright pink and only vaguely related to ham, it fell in neat
rounds on her greaseproofed tray. Her red and white lino
shone with wax and there was not a crumb or a smudge

or a stray bit of dust to be found on Mavis Kelly's shelves. The fridge hummed, the slicer whined, the sign on the door still said 'Closed'.

Mavis reckoned if by an act of God or an earthquake she failed to open one morning, even on a holiday, there'd be a riot on Bauxite Street. By eight thirty there'd be a queue out on the footpath; the early shift squinting in daylight, women still in their dressing gowns, with sleep-flattened heads and the odd forgotten curler in their hair. They'd shuffle in wearing their towelling scuffs and steel toes and rest their grubby elbows on her just-washed laminex, dropping stray fronds of ash on her lino, wanting their pounds of silverside and their pickled onions and their Fritz nuggets, asking for this thing or the other 'a bit thicker, love'. Demanding a loaf of that new pre-sliced bread.

Pre-sliced. They'd be wanting it pre-digested next.

While Mavis cut and buttered and tsked, she kept an eye on That Mona, who was riding her bike up and down on the footpath, back and forth, back and forth. The Cornflake clips on Mona's Dragster clicked and whirred, faster and faster, an irritating little syncopation, like a dripping tap or a bottled fly. Round and round she went, ribbons on her handlebars streaming, long legs pumping, until she was just a blur of striped T-shirt and brown legs and stringy hair. At the McGregor corner Mona slowed and rode in a wobbly circle, just out of Mavis's line of sight. Mavis's talons tapped a tattoo. 'Mona! Inside!' Mona idled back, her feet dragging furrows in the dust.

That Mona was a worry. Just like her father, always sloping off. There was a lot of Gwen in her too, that aimless amusement in doing the same thing, over and over, until any normal person would just want to scream. When she was little, Mavis used to have to put the girl in a harness and tie her to the Guide Dog moneybox then lash her fast to the Tweety Ride. If you didn't, she'd have every lolly off the supermarket shelf. Shoppers shook their heads and muttered. But then they wouldn't be the ones chasing the little bugger all over town.

Once Mavis even had to call the police.

'Going to find me dad,' Mona told the coppers when they picked her up five mile out on the city road.

Mavis prayed for Mona every night, and she also prayed for Frank and Vonnie; well, she didn't pray for them as much as remind God of her sacrifices with regard to each. She catalogued to God the numerous faults of Mona's mother and Mavis's sister, Gwen, who were the same person, and Mona's father and that bloody Wally Thompson, whom everyone thought was one and the same person but then Mavis knew a thing or two. In bed at night, after apologising for not kneeling—God understood, He knew Frank had never finished the carpeting, and anyway, since that Vatican rubbish, they'd even put felt on the church kneelers and no-one bothered to wear a veil—Mavis reminded Him of the hole in the corner registry, of her borrowed wedding dress that wasn't white. The blank space in the photos where her mother should have been. In fairly grammatical instalments, Mavis brought to His attention how Mona was delivered like a brown paper package from Sydney, in the care of the conductor, would you believe, and with a terse note from Mavis's mother pinned to her cardigan, saying Gwen had to go and 'have a rest'. Now Gwen couldn't be trusted to pay the milkman, let alone look after a child.

Watching Mona go past again—click, click, whirr whirr, eyes slitted sideways, dress scooped halfway up her bum—Mavis let out a silent scream. She asked that wherever Wally Thompson was, God would strike him down dead. Then she paused and crossed that one out, as if with red pen.

Even without high heels Mavis could clacket. It was all that jewellery; the woman was alive with silver, encrusted with gold. Even this early she had on the full regalia: the big Lightning Ridge opals and the silver knuckledusters and those earrings the size of Mr Marconi's best grapes. In those wide dry distances full of empty air, where everything travelled—the fall of a foot, the slam of a broken wire door—Mavis resounded like an approaching tank. Trevor groaned.

Crossing the road took a full minute, even though Von and Trevor lived right across the way. Streets here were wide and lazy as airstrips, the footpaths the size of a decent city road. The space always made Mona want to run and run, down the long fat breath of it, gulping big air and not stopping until she reached the road out of town. But Mavis had a vicelike grip on Mona's wrist. 'Hurry up, you little bugger, for pity's sake. In a minute you'll know just what's what.'

In the bright morning Von's house looked drearier than usual: it was just a lump of yellow pebblecrete on a square of red dirt. There were rusty car parts and old tricycle wheels and empty bottles everywhere, and Von had left the kiddies' pool to sag with water and leaves. The place looked like a tenement, like a council house for wasters and no-goods. And there was no need for it, it was a crying shame. Heels clicked. Rings sparked hurtfully off tar.

Mavis didn't bother knocking; the front door was open anyway, swinging on its broken hinge. Forging down the front hall, noting the dust on hall tables, the furry coffee cups, the overflowing ashtrays, all the time Mavis was fuming: bloody Von, bloody Frank.

The bedroom door slammed. A picture of Our Lady popped miraculously off the wall.

'Trevor! Where's Vonnie? Frank needs to know.'

The baby was asleep beside him, curled up in the nest of what in Mavis's book were dirty sheets.

'Trevor Cook! It's after eight and about to catch it. What on earth is going on?'

It was ten to, give or take.

'Bloody hell, Mavis! What'ya doing in here?' Trevor buried his head.

'Don't you swear at me. Where's Von, and what's happening with that baby? I could hear it crying halfway up the street.'

Of course Mavis hadn't really heard Lily crying but in her indignation she imagined she had heard it; that thin echo penetrating, travelling across the road and through the kitchen windows of neighbours sitting respectably over their toast and tea. This, the unfairness of shame cast like a reflected light upon her, set Mavis's mouth like quick cement.

'I'm not putting that baby on the bottle. I'm telling you now. A rod for my own back. That's what'd be.'

Lil's bottom lip was level with Trevor's eye. She started that small sudden sucking movement. It reminded him of Von's breast. He stopped thinking about that straightaway.

'For Chrissake, Mavis. Give us a break.'

But it was hopeless. Mavis had planted herself like a major landmark at the end of the bed.

Mavis suddenly realised she was in a bedroom with a near naked man. She flared her nostrils; she was smelling the scent of a man in the morning, the special sleeping skin smell only men have. Clothes hung in clots on the dresser, underthings, private things, which shouldn't have seen the light of day: a grimy bra and a pair of blue Cottontails, unwashed no doubt, Trevor's shockingly ragged singlet, and on the side table a masculine scatter of change. Mavis started backing out the door.

'What sort of mother goes out this time of the morning? With a newborn baby to feed. Get her up this minute and make it snappy, I've got a shop and a house to run. Anyway, shouldn't you be at work?'

By this time Mavis was safe in the kitchen, so she was just a shrill mosquito, deadened by dust and carpet and the sliding door.

'It's Boxing Day, you old bag. I'm not on shift.'

In the kitchen Mavis was rousing and pacing, bustling and squirting, forcing water through teats with one expert thumb. Tongue clicking, rings winking, heels ticking furiously across lino, until Trevor thought his head might burst.

'Where's Ruthie? Do you know that much at least?'

'Still asleep. No school.'

Mavis had Ruth up, toileted, face washed with a flannel, and into her dressing gown and slippers before Trevor had lit his first cigarette.

Mavis sat at the head of the table feeding Lily. Trevor cradled his fag. Ruth ate her Cornflakes. Mona kicked Ruth under the table. Ruth stuck out her tongue. The sun

climbed finally through the kitchen window and it made
the little room, with its worn-out lino and breadcrumbs
and grease-ringed stove top, seem even more hopeless than
before. Mona breathed like a steam engine underwater.
Trevor put his head down among the crumbs.

Hunched over like that and shirtless, it was possible to
count every one of Trevor Cook's ribs. They were breakable
as the spines of a cheap umbrella, beneath skin so pale you
could see the blue journey of veins. He looked like a sick
sapling, Mavis thought, like you could just snap him over
one knee.

Trevor's hair was fine as Lily's and standing up like a
toilet brush, matted in a sleepy baby clump. But Lil's was
a different colour. Lil's was pitch-black, not dirty blonde
like Trevor's, not brown-black like Ruthie's, not even red-
black like Von's. It was that blue-black you saw on some
Marconis straight off the boat.

The dark colouring was something Mavis could guess
at, an old pebble surfacing; in fact she knew more about
that particular thing than Trevor and Von combined. But
babies' hair changes all the time, sometimes it falls out
entirely and grows in totally wrong. A black-haired baby
can turn out white blonde, dark auburn or even carrot-top
red. Mavis's hair wasn't really auburn, it was plain brown.
She dyed it herself every month. They charged too much
down at Hair Today. But she always thought of it as
auburn, more specifically autumn russet, which was the
colour on the Clairol box.

Even while she was thinking all this, the whole time,
like a sly and silly tune you can't stop humming, Mavis
could smell baby. It was on her fingers, curling through
her autumn russet, nestling in her chenille-covered breast.

It rose seductively from the funnel of the bunny-rug, hovered like a halo above the fontanelle. That milky sweetness would have made anyone else soften, perhaps even smile. But the thought of babies just made Mavis angry. In fact it made her more angry than anything. And that was saying something, as Frank would have said, putting in his two bob.

It led Mavis to dwell on that supreme injustice, the little packet of pills in her bedside drawer. They nestled right next to her rosary, as if mocking in their shiny compactness the days, weeks, months and years of her clicked-off apologies, the trajectory of her future sin. She counted them off each night with a glass of water. Then, reading each bead in the dark like holy braille, Mavis said her prayers.

Mavis had to ask God to forgive her for this one as well as commend her for it, so the tone was both apologetic and martyred, not an easy feat.

Mainly she asked Him to forgive Frank whose fault these things really were. She was in absolutely no doubt that God would.

Mavis handed Lil back to Trevor like a well-wrapped fish and chip packet, like something he'd left behind. Lil started screaming the moment she left. Trevor paced up and down, from back door to stove to fridge and back again, stopping once to press his nose against the flyscreen and stare without conviction up the road. Lil screamed louder. So he kept pacing, up and down, making tired cooing noises, his overall brace dangling across lino, Ruthie trailing close behind.

. . .

In Frank Kelly's imaginary garden, light still streamed down, the earth rolled flat forever in its bright technicolour glow. If you pissed on that dust, it would turn dark in splotches and be dry before you even did up your fly. And if you travelled along the grid of roads all named after minerals, plodding in their flat-footed fashion past the Anzac cannon, the blond brick Lions Club, the 1950s milkbars, the curly verandah pubs, if you left behind all those neat front fences and the stern-looking churches and those fastidious houses in martial rows, you would come to the truth of the place.

Out there they had turned the stomach of the earth around itself like a sock. On the rag-tag edge of town the houses were still made of stolen corrugated iron and the front gardens were just red dirt. Even further out, miles and miles out, at the place with no name by the side of the river, floorboards had been ripped up for kindling, fires were lit in the middle of lounge rooms and most of the windows didn't have glass.

Out there you could sometimes find the skulls of animals. Baked thin as china, perforated by sun.

Frank never went out that side of town.

chapter 4

Direction in that place was absolute. In fact it was ruthless, an iron-fisted grid. Streets went exactly where predicted. Things had a beginning, a middle and an end.

To the east, north and south there could be cities. People had heard of them, read about them in newspapers, some had even been there, at Christmas or for a holiday by the sea. But across the shimmer of vast distance they had the air of fables, of dubiously too-tall tales. They were exaggerated alright, and far too long-winded, those neck-craning skyscrapers over thirty storeys high.

Country stories were straight and to the point. To the north a mine, to the south a mine, and roads east and west pivoted on their axis, they followed it like the sun. Beyond them there was only desert, stretching on and on.

The RSL memorial marked the exact centre of that known flat world. A tall stone soldier stood there, made taller by a lot of old dead men. And Von Cook stood under it, because it was as good a place to start as any, because most places here looked like every place else.

The digger had been there forever, or so it seemed. His too-big uniform rolled in monumental wrinkles, hung with stern gravity over granite spats. He'd weathered dust storms and mine cave-ins and bird shit, seen the town throw itself together out of scrounged bits of tin. He'd met it all with gun slung and feet planted, a formidable foursquare chin.

By Boxing Day 1967 he'd suffered some war wounds: a chipped buttock, a peace sign on his ankle, nose burnt verdigris by sun. But he still occupied high ground where everything else just went on and on. He seemed to gesture, with eyes and gun and forward thrusting body, to an alternate universe, where men were men and women weighed nothing much at all.

Problem was, no matter where you stood, you could never catch the digger's eye. He was set on a horizon that didn't include you. A flat world of upright deeds. Propped against iron-clad facts.

Four wooden signs sprouted like skewiff feathers from the digger's dusty slouch. They pointed to roads like the poles of a compass. All of them defined town as 'not there'.

One road went to Adelaide. One went to Sydney. Another went to Sydney via Mildura and the border, the long way round. The last went to the airport, then to the river, then to places even more lonely than here. The X where these roads met and where Von Cook was standing described the precise point where this town shouldn't be.

That was the worst of it. You couldn't get out, not really, not on foot. You could walk and walk on one of these roads and a few miles outside the town borders you were nowhere. There was nothing there you could imagine except the absence of here.

It was six of one, half a dozen of another really. Because no matter which road you took, it was hot as hell. Bitumen was burning, glinting, bubbling almost, turning liquid in the heat. Von had to keep hopping from one foot to the other because her dud toe, the one she'd mashed with a house brick one Christmas, bulged like a split sausage out the side of her thong. Everything, the sun, the heat, the dust, the tar welding fast to plastic soles, everything was trying to root her to the spot. All the straight straight streets running straight as a die to meet without surprise on a corner, generating in a grid of dust and glare these hot and boring days. Mornings filled with bright plastic playthings. Afternoons breathless with the gossip of town women. Weaving long and pointless as a child's first scarf.

Von just couldn't stand it any more. She needed a mistake, something to tear this safe pattern from its props. Throw two plains in with a purl and escape through the hole that would eventuate. That's what Von Cook had decided to do.

It could strike at any time, this feeling, like the way Mary Maloney used to chuck a fit. Von could be standing at the Whirlpool or cleaning out the fridge, having resigned herself to a day spent on housework so that Trevor, like any other husband, could come home to find his lino mopped, his chops sizzling, his work shirts pegged out tail to tail. Sometimes she got as far as sweeping the front verandah; but even while she was Doing The Right Thing, Von imagined the big football ground spotlight of town swivelling toward her, like Sister Loyola's eagle-eyed God. That pitiless gaze knew when even the smallest sparrow dropped from the sky. It saw her garbage piling up, the red film of dust on her windows, her washing stiff with sun on the line. When neighbours poked their nose over the back fence, they could nod and shake their curlers and fold their arms quite comfortably across fat flowered hips. 'See? Typical. Well what did you expect?'

That's when the heaviness would hit. From a sky burnished blue and vacant, so you could lose yourself in it, hear only your own blood singing in your veins, a cloud would settle over Von's house alone. It seeped out of walls, that feeling, rose like dust from the carpet. Fell with great weight across everything she did.

As soon as she started walking, beyond the front gate, along the grid of streets, on one of the four roads leading out, the fog lifted. But it never went away. It hovered, invisible as your shadow at midday. You had to keep moving or you could end up like Von. You would be pinned to the bed while the heat slatted through the venetians and sheets went unwashed, potatoes unpeeled, carpet un-Hoovered, Lil screaming blue murder and Ruth sticking her head round the doorway, asking over and over until Von thought she might strangle her: 'Mum? What's for tea?'

Round and round, clockways then anticlockways, like bath water on the other side of the world. Ruth's handlebars lay at ten to four then at twenty to two. She was riding no hands on the patch of dirt Dad called The Front Yard. Not because she was a showoff like Mona but because she had a finger stuck in each ear. Lily's crying had reached that stage where between each sob ran a ragged silence, that gasping panic like a wave about to crash.

Dad had taken the baby back to bed with him and dozed off in dreary stripes from venetians, in the little box house on the corner of Bauxite and Zircon, hot as an oven now in midmorning sun. The sound of Lily crying bounced off scrap iron and torn lino, ricocheted between gyprock and fibro and tin. Trevor's sleep was fitful, alive with whining chainsaws, cats yowling in undergrowth and a woman's breast leaking blue and watery milk.

'Just goin' out for a walk, Ruthie,' Mum said before she left. It was early, just after sun-up, and when she'd stuck her head round Ruth's doorway, Mum's hair was wild, her dress all wrinkled, there were grey rings of mascara round her eyes. 'You head on over to Auntie Mavis later. She'll have a pie and a cake for you at lunch.'

Her mum didn't know this for certain. It could just as easily be a white bread sandwich with that gummy ham off the slicer and some of Uncle Frank's greenish tomatoes, each mouthful of which you had to chew fifty times. Aunt Mavis's doorstoppers made Ruth want to chuck.

When Mum went out walking, Ruth felt vaguely anxious. Mum going walking wasn't just a pause in the pattern. It was a mistake. Like having an extra neck in your jumper. Just didn't make sense.

Mum tried to make it sound like it was nothing much at all.

'Won't be long, Ruthie. Just need to clear the head.'

But Ruth waited for the day her mum wouldn't be back by late afternoon, or teatime, or even by breakfast the next morning. Ruth knew it was coming. That time when her mum wouldn't come home at all.

Training wheels clattered on the footpath. The sun beat down. The shop sign rattled in a rare gust of wind. Nothing else moved.

Ruth walked a bit faster when she got to Uncle Frank's side of things. She could just see his hat there in the driveway, floating suspended between the chook wire with dead sticks on it Aunt Mavis called Our Pergola and Uncle Frank's mysterious back shed.

In the end, Von just played eeny meeny miney, thongs stringing old chewy from tar. She ignored the digger and his cold stone toes. She stared at her own feet instead. Anyway, from this angle, the bloke was a bit crook. His jaw was huge, his head was way too big for his body, like one of those babies with water on the brain. He had little stony jaw muscles knotted in each cheek. Like he was permanently cranky. Like he was Gregory Peck in *The Guns of Navarone*.

Mo fell on the Airport Road. Officially this road had another name, it was called after some mineral or other, some famous piece of rock. But if a road led to somewhere other than town itself, to a destination bigger and better than here, well then that's what you called it, no matter what was written on some DMR map. In the absence of another city, people settled on the nearest available thing. So there was the Tip Road, the Abbatoir Road, the Lake Road, the Airport Road, the Cemetery Hill. Even though there was another town along the Airport Road, after the airport, by the side of the river, it was only a handful of houses and one corner store and the people who lived there didn't really count. Not officially, not in terms of Tuesday's football practice or Woolies of a Saturday or bowls of a Thursday afternoon. Maps showed the river and the windmill and nothing else.

Which road you took didn't really matter, not in the big scheme of things. It was the walking that mattered. That urge to get away. The words were a train chugging, an urgent rhythm carrying Von up the main drag, past the shopping strip and the council baths and the RSL, past the used-car yards and the old goods train depot, toward the bad side of town. Thongs slapped the score. Every two blocks a cross-street, regular as breath. Every three blocks a bus stop, every corner a bench. Every four blocks a traffic light. They all seemed to be red. But you didn't need to look left, then right, then left again. You could see something coming for miles. Everyone pottered at walking pace on the extreme left of a street so wide cars looked like Matchbox toys, all out of scale.

Soon she got the knack of it, she started feeling lighter, the fog lifted, just a bit. She was a good walker, Von was, because although she was skinny she had strong legs with tight calf muscles and her one bit of vanity was to wear her dresses slightly shorter than any girl in town. It wasn't a mini she was wearing by any stretch of the imagination— there were girls in the *Women's Weekly*, at the Melbourne Cup races, with skirts right up to their arse. But this wasn't the city. Things took a while to catch up. Von's dress was short enough that blokes in trucks were inspired to lean out and whistle and honk their horns. Her legs were nice enough that matrons meeting her on a corner stood up straighter, stuck their cross your heart tits out and put their heads together, shaking perms fitfully, like dogs with a single flea.

'Hussy!' It was a familiar hiss, barely audible, like the noise made by spit on a match. The women just kept walking, trailing their little wheely trolleys, chins glued to the horizon, as if not looking at Von meant she didn't exist. They waited until they were well past her and then it started, the tongues going clickety clickety, the heads shaking, the whispers hissing lipstick spit into hands. She could see them now, those matronly heads, as if lined up for Communion in the cathedral, each rising on its powdery dewlap from the same big shelf bosom, tongues sticking out like something rude. All those heads shaking. No, no, no.

Von poked two fingers up at their cardiganed backs. They were going bald anyway, those old biddies. You could see little pink patches where pillows had rubbed a roller curl flat. And that metronome of curlers, it just struck a walking pace, that's all it did. Faster and faster, past the Baby Health Clinic with its starched Sisters and their Pine O Cleen and nipple grease, past the raw foundations of the new Civic Centre to be opened in ten years by some fat old bigwig, stuck right out here because they didn't know where else to put it and because no-one quite knew what they would use it for even when it was built. Past the fake town lake with its perfect flotilla of ducks.

It was a dream, the way these things flashed by. Like pieces of road peeling out from under a car. This town was Limbo, that place where pagan babies trailed empty souls like wrinkled balloons. Or Purgatory, where people were always waiting, in that blank hiccup between God's Everlasting Inferno and God's Inexhaustible Love.

Von always got these two a bit confused. She'd copped it from Sister Bonaventure once because, when asked to draw a picture of Purgatory, instead of drawing angels with harps and clouds like fairy floss and God chucking down butter-coloured thunderbolts of love, she'd drawn

Dr O'Shaunnessy's waiting room of a Saturday afternoon. She had old Mrs McGregor sneezing into a hankie and Uncle Frank with little zigzags to indicate a headache and Aunt Mavis bleeding and bandaged, right down the end of the queue.

Sister Bonaventure smiled when she saw Von's picture. Sister had snowy hair and creamy wrinkles, she looked like the old woman who lived in a shoe. She folded the piece of paper carefully and then she threw it in the bin. She opened her desk drawer. She had a whole bunch of rulers in there with pictures of Auckland on them; either she got a good deal on them or she crossed the Tasman a lot. Thirty canes Von got, because when one ruler broke Sister Bonaventure, with fingers hovering as if over a box of Black Magic, just picked another one from the pile.

Afterwards Von had to stand at the front of the classroom in the hot and dusty sun. All afternoon she stood there till her legs went numb. Right under Sister, whose skin opened and closed like gills. Sister sweated under the weight of God's ring. She gave off serge-smelling BO. She was drawing a diagram explaining the mystery of the Holy Trinity, as if God was something you could cut open like a frog. But if you tried to pin God down, He just wriggled away into something else. And Sister, drawing her yellow arrows and pointing with her Auckland ruler and screeching her fingernails on the blackboard because she never wasted the smallest nub of chalk, just kept adding more threads to God's cloak. In the end He was as impenetrable as algebra or crochet.

Even while Sister went through six different rulers, even while the other girls giggled and smirked and swapped holy cards, arranging them by shape and gender, by colour and size of halo, by their standing in the heirarchy of saints, Von still reckoned she was right. She reckoned Purgatory would be a lot like that waiting room. An eternal queue for a check-up, with nothing to read except *Reader's Digest* jokes from ten years ago. Smelling strongly of disinfectant, with rows and rows of slightly soiled dead people still trapped in their bodies. Like Spanish flu victims. Like parachutists hanging patiently by a strap.

Everyone was waiting for God's door to open. Everyone was relying on Mavis for a decade or two.

It was pies for lunch. Mum was right. But there were three little girls round Frank's playroom table, not two. Mavis had a visitor after church. Three pies, three cakes, three little girls but only two Dragsters, because the visitor had left hers at home.

One little girl was sharp and pointed and had blonde pigtails and sly fingers which pinched and poked under the table where no-one could see. She wasn't that little, she was much older than the other two, in fact she was far too big for Frank's baby chairs. She looked just like a skinny tarantula, legs up under her chin.

The second little girl was fat and rosy and cried in a panic about nothing at all. The last little girl was somewhere in between, not on the top, not on the bottom, a little afraid of what might happen, but with her fingers curled into a fist kept ready between her knees. That was Ruth.

The mothers sat in the kitchen around iced yeast loaf and a pot of tea. They had the door open a crack so they could keep an eye on the progress of the pies. One mother had soft kittenish hair and a tendency to blush. The other mother had long crimson fingernails which went tap, tap, tap on all the glittering surfaces of her kitchen, and silver bangles which tinkled and clinked. She was particularly all bones and angles under her best bouclé that Boxing Day was Mavis; righteousness enlivened her, made her sit up straighter, if that was possible, made her eyes shine a hard and glossy green. Both mothers stuck their fingers out sideways when they drank their tea.

The play table rocked when you leant on it; Uncle Frank had used cast-off fence palings and old bits of rivergum, so some legs were shorter than others, but he'd reckoned by the time you slapped on four coats of red verandah paint and stuffed pickled onion lids under the leg feet, you wouldn't be able to tell. Mona jiggled harder. Libby Lang spilt her milk. Mona sniggered. Libby's lip got a wobble on. Ruth kicked her. If you cried in front of Mona she'd pull you apart slowly, like a fly.

'Oh my giddy aunt.' Aunt Mavis stuck her head round the crack in the door. 'Where on earth did you find that?' Ruth shrugged, under a surfeit of purple poncho, Mona's most treasured dress-up from the bottom of the box. Usually if you grabbed something Mona particularly fancied—one of the hats perhaps, the straw one with the wax fruit or the yellow polka dot boater with the orange ribbons, or a pair of pink high-heeled slippers Mavis discarded when velour 'went out'—Mona would attach herself to the other end and pull. In the end a hat brim would part from its plastic apples or a heel from a fluffy slipper and Mona would yell: 'Auntie Mavis! Ruth Cook broke your shoe!' But this time Ruth had pulled harder. She'd won.

'It wasn't mine of course, Margaret,' Aunt Mavis giggled. She was in a particularly good mood due to the sherry she allowed herself when she'd been to double Christmas Mass. 'Only person who'd wear a get up like that was Gwen. Used to be a bedspread. I ask you.' She cocked her head and her earrings jangled. 'Colour suits Ruth though. Brings out her eyes.'

Mona glared balefully from under a hat-load of plastic fruit.

There was a rule about the way you ate the pies. One of Mona's rules, which made no sense except in Mona's universe but had to observed. Only when every bit of meat was eaten, until the pie case held only a thin smear of brown, could you eat the crisp pastry lid. Ruth reckoned this was the best part, especially when you smothered it in sauce. Mona stuck her little finger out sideways and rubbed sauce delicately through gravy until the whole thing was one big reddish-brown meaty swirl. She snuffled close to it, like she was going to inhale pie through her nose. Finally, picking up her fork, she scooped tiny mouthfuls, a speck at a time.

Libby and Ruth watched Mona take her excruciating bites, hungry for clues. Mona was the kind of child who saved up all her Easter eggs, breaking off tiny bits of chocolate at set times of day. They lasted until the next Lent, when the chocolate had gone white and crackly and Father McNally was ranting about his Compassion Home money boxes and Mavis was stocking up on salmon mornay.

Mona stared sideways at the others through slitted eyes, those green squashed eyes like a cat. Beneath the golden sun shining through glass louvres, inside the bright play-room colours and softness of Mona's stuffed toys, Ruth could feel a mean sort of danger running. Like a dark and purple thread.

. . .

Von slowed down a bit when she got to the last open pub on the bad side of town.

Old Lou was still there on the Imperial corner. Even though the Imperial was closed now, shuttered against dust which had turned windows impenetrably red. But Lou navigated her own universe, as if normal time didn't apply to her and in an hour, a month or a year from now the pub would open again, people would gather once more on the verandah and Lou would scowl and spit and mutter until someone handed over the last two inches of warm beer.

Every afternoon round pub closing the coppers moved Lou on. Every morning there she was again, unavoidable as sin. She dozed in scant shadow outside the boarded-up doors. She wore three kinds of jumpers in any sort of weather, her face was crumpled and seamed like an old brown paper bag. Baked bean tins, half-chewed sandwiches picked out of bins, a Woolies trolley filled with cans you could trade in down the Alco for five cents a pop, everything Lou owned lay around her like a moat. Her three dogs slept across the footpath in a pile of ribs.

When Von was a kid out shopping with Aunt Mavis, they always walked on the other side of the street if they had to go past here. But out of the corner of her eye Von used to watch them, those people lounging in the gloom of the Imperial verandah, in tipsy huddles, like one dark organism with myriad arms and legs. Their slurry voices ran like a brown river under town noise, the car horns and the shoe store spruiker and Marconi going on about his grapes. Now and again it would erupt, that blackness. With a thrown bottle, a broken curse. Jagged as glass.

'Ruddy travesty. Disgraceful. Where decent people have to walk.' Von could hear Mavis muttering it, her catalogue of grievances, her heavy necklace of sin. It was threaded through a hundred Saturday afternoons.

Grey leaves and barbeque chicken foil scuttled along in the verandah corners, wrapping themselves round wrought iron once spun fine as wedding icing, now rusted thin and booted through. Rubbing a circle on the outside of a window didn't help because the dust on the other side was equally thick. But if you looked really hard, with your hands cupped around your face and your forehead pressed against grey-smelling glass, you could still make out the row of Reschs taps strung with spiderweb, the green and yellow tiles like a public toilet, the Brylcreemed tuxedo men and tiny-waisted women with their cheeks blooming like neat roses, smiling so brightly under pancake hats you wanted to go and live there, in that pink and pastel world where all you did was eat Nobby's Nuts.

Von was backing away from the Imperial window, hearing Mavis nag, feeling parched but there was nothing in there, nothing but cobwebs and dust and an old pot plant riddled with thirst, when she tripped over Lou. The bottles in the trolley rattled. Lou cocked one rheumy eye. Von thought she was going to say something. But the working of her mouth wasn't talking. She spat a big globbie on Vonnie's thong.

Von lost a bit of steam then. Her legs were buggered, her throat was dry. So she crossed the road to the last open pub this side of town.

Swing doors puffed dust into the heat. It was dark as the grave in there. The barmaid's bust glowed milkily in gloom. She was the only other woman in sight.

chapter 5

Even in the furry haze of an early opener, Von recognised those men propping up the bar. Like everybody else here they wore checked shirts and wide hats, they bent their elbows at lazy intervals, they nodded and muttered and spat when they lost the race call on the TV. They could have been lorry drivers on a beer break or blue collars from the morning shift out the South. But Von could always pick them, those white collar bosses from the mine office where Frank worked, in his little demountable tacked like an afterthought on to the official bosses' block.

'Got a little friend helping you, eh Frankie?' white collar bosses bellowed when they found Von giving Frank a hand of a Saturday afternoon. When white collar bosses stood in the doorway of Frank's little demountable, they blocked the light. Their hard hats loomed, their bellies filled the room. They made Frank and his old desk and his neat piles of paper look suddenly small.

White collar bosses settled with the sound of escaping air into Frank's visitor chairs. They had big whale stomachs which hung over their belts. They rolled up their sleeves as if they might be about to do some mining. But these men never did. These men wore clean white shirts and lairy ties and opal cufflinks, and when they raised their arms to point at the rolled-up blueprints they brought with them, they gave off little puffs of their wives' Preen.

Von had to ask the bosses how they wanted their tea. 'White, strong and sweet,' they winked. It was such an old joke you didn't need to say the punchline. 'Ta love,' is all they said when she handed over the mug. But they didn't say it to her face. They said it to her tits.

While the bosses pointed at something on their blueprints, Frank nodded and nodded, far too fast and much too agreeable, like one of those dippy birds on the side of a glass.

Von used to think the mine proper must be like the bosses' diagram of tunnels: all blue and crisp and cheerful looking, shiny as a new pin. But when she finally peeked through the big iron gates with the padlock on them, the real mine wasn't like that all. It was dirt and noise and mess. There were drifting piles of slag not yet carted to the heaps and rusty cogs and winch things and chunks of rubble left lying where someone had spilt it off a truck. There were men taking showers in the tin sheds near the shaft. The sheds had pieces of corrugated iron missing, so sometimes you could see the tops of dusty heads, or the white flash of a bare-arse bum. Four times a day when the hooter blew, gangs of these men filed in and out, long grim lines snaking all over the yard. When they came in they wore clean overalls and carried little crib boxes, like they were off to their first day at school. When they came out they had no shirts on, their eyes stared whitely out of dirty faces. Their nipples were black with dust.

Women weren't allowed in the mine proper, except for the pearls and twinset wives who came to drop off a crib. Wives wore lipstick and high heels, even in the middle of an ordinary afternoon. Then there was fat old Mrs Theopolous who ran the tuck truck. It wasn't a man's job that, selling cups of tea and pies. And Mrs Theopolous with her legs like sausages and her hairy wart, well she didn't really count. In any case, Mrs Theopolous was a gyp.

That was just one of the rules, the way some people didn't count. It wasn't written down anywhere that rule but everyone knew it just the same. There were hundreds of them, all invisible, running like a fine set of trip-wires just under the ground. They formed a dense grid of right and wrong and what Frank would call 'grey areas', crissing and crossing until they formed a fragile but irresistible web. If you stumbled over one rule, other rules you didn't even know about got caught around it; they were sticky and fine as gossamer and one rule hung on the other, that's how things worked. It held you there, that mysterious pattern called Doing The Right Thing.

You were like a rabbit frozen in headlights. There was no escape. People shook their heads and tut-tutted but really they were pleased. It gave them something to do. They stood and muttered, they pointed and poked. They worked you round their cheeks like a hard boiled lolly until you got smaller and smaller and what you thought you might have been just disappeared.

One of the rules was that women didn't go into pubs alone. And if they did, they sat in the ladies lounge, not in the front saloon. And they didn't perch on a bar stool, getting six sheets to the wind. And they sat with their knees together. And they always wore a hat.

In the Duke of Gloucester the white collar bosses didn't make jokes or point to blueprints or even look at Von's tits. They just stared at her, grim and hard across the gloom. They leant on the counter supported by square elbows. They were solid as the digger on his granite heels.

As Von drained her glass and got up to leave, she heard them mutter it, one to the other, like a set of beads they were stringing, those smoky words hung dull and certain under the wide brims of hats. Their lips barely moved, like Frank's when he had a mouthful of nails.

'G'arn. Yer bugger! Get out of it! Yer bloody b—'

But Von didn't hear the last bit. The pub door was swinging shut.

'Not as if she wasn't brought up right,' Aunt Mavis leant over the teapot, cupping a hand to her mouth. This meant she had something particularly vital to impart. Her voice deepened to a stage whisper, drowned by a tumult of silver and gold. Ruth could only make out the odd stray phrase. 'Gallivanting.' 'Even at Christmas.' 'Skirts up to here.' 'Couldn't do a thing with her.' 'Nuns at the end of their rope.'

Ruth thought Mavis was talking about those soap things for the shower you could buy at Moores; mostly they were ducks or baby rabbits but some of the ones at the discount shop, the ones under the counter, they were rude. Ruth couldn't imagine why you would want to wash yourself with a nun. 'Cleanliness next to Godliness' circled a bit but she couldn't make it stick.

She could feel the tone of it though, a steely jangle, getting sharper, the thrust rising and rising, like the notes made when you hit the xylophone at school. Right up the top end there was a sound so high and piercing it was shiny, white-sounding. Like a plucked nerve.

Through the crack in the door there was just a slice of face. Mavis as her own quotation: bright pink mouth, some sweaty nose, a dash of green eyeshadow, topped off with one drawn-on caterpillar eyebrow, slightly raised.

'What time's your mum due back, Ruthie? Suppose you'll have to come out the lake with us.' She rolled her eyes at Mrs Lang.

'Ruth? Answer me please.'

'Dunno.'

'I don't know. I don't know, *Auntie Mavis.* Don't slur.'

Mavis did one of those sighs that went with an elaborate folding of elbows. You could almost hear the weight settling on her shoulders. Heavy loads of wet washing hanging off each arm.

Two Malvern Stars with the streamers sticking out in the wind, three little girls. Garden paths curved through small flower-beds, neat and gay as a cartoon. Even the rare flower was fussily spaced. Uncle Frank was out there, a row of nails in his mouth, so that when he had to say something, his lips disappeared. He was sticking small gnomes between painted rocks. He often did this, moved gnomes to different locations. Like he said, everyone needs a change of scene.

Frank gave Ruth a nail-shaped smile. Mona scowled, scuffing along, eyes glinting mineral green.

Round and round, picking up speed, turning the corners at the last minute to miss the vegetable patch and the back shed, then back again, in ever decreasing circles, until you reached the clothesline and started all over again.

Mona was taller, bigger, stronger but not smarter than Ruth. She had a new striped dress and longer legs. Libby Lang was shorter, smaller, weaker, uglier, bikeless, trying hard to join in. She was stuffed into her clothes like a sausage, her body was a burden, it weighed her down. Ruth's burden was she wasn't extraordinary at all.

Round and round. Up and down. For the first time Ruth felt there was something disturbing about the child-like colours, the smallness of the paths.

Once Von was out on the new overpass she felt safer. There was nothing here but the town sewerage, the old North Mine, the RSPCA. The crying of doomed mongrels rose in tune with the whine of car engines negotiating this, one of the town's few hills. Trucks and lorries skimmed right past her, the stink of diesel slammed her sideways like a blow. When a driver leant out of his window and yelled, 'Nice arse, love,' she could almost smell his faggy breath.

The minerals had run out here, right on the edge of town. They'd dug it up, pitted it with tunnels, disem-bowelled it, wrung it dry. Only a few old miners' shanties struggled on, looking like drunks from the Imperial, those old iron humpies, leaning against each other to stay upright but sinking into a treachery of tunnels underneath.

All that was left now were the slag heaps, the guts of earth exposed. From up on top of them, you could see the whole town laid out like a dull game of snakes and ladders: the spidery scaffolds, the blocks of squat houses, flat as pancakes, as if the weight of a hard life had ground them down. Acres and acres of metal roof twinged in the heat.

Like frontier wagons every square faced inward to its perfectly straight street. And on every side, just like the slag you were sitting on, there was more of it. Mountains and mountains of it, towering up. Until you wondered whether they would run out of earth to turn inside out or space to pile it up in or minerals to dig up and spit out.

Now and again there was an aching boom as earth gave another inch. Townspeople flinched a little, then remembered they were used to it. So they just kept on doing whatever they were doing, as if nothing had happened. Shopping. Talking. Doing crosswords. Knitting. Drinking tea.

You weren't supposed to go up on that slag. It was strung with barbed wire, peppered with skulls and cross-bones, reverberating with stories of landslides and kids locked in fridges and girls buried bike and all. But after Von got expelled from St Joseph's she used to go up on the slag all the time. After those nuns came round with their hands snuggled inside their batwings, eyes fixed sorrowfully on their pointy nun shoes, and told Mavis Von had been caught kissing Trevor from the Marist Brothers behind the bike sheds, that she'd been seen wearing shorts on a Sunday, that she wasn't the St Joseph's type, well Von didn't care what happened then. She went and sat under a sign saying 'Danger. No entry. Subsidence and slides.'

She sat there for hours while the sun climbed to its highest point then started to sink. She sat there while Mavis slammed saucepans and did endless Stations of the Cross. Mavis tried to make Von go with her, to the cathedral, to make her confession, but Von just kept sitting there, defying sudden falls of rock. She smoked Stuyvesants she'd nicked out of Uncle Frank's packet. She never took Mavis's, they were like smoking mint-flavoured air. While she sat there, feeling tunnels swoon, the sad hollowness of earth, she thought over and over about how every girl she knew wore shorts on a Sunday. And how God was just a fat old man in fancy dress get-up, like Mr McGregor pretending to be Father Christmas down the shoe store in town.

When Von tried to tell Uncle Frank about it, he just shrugged. He said, 'Don't rock the boat.' 'Don't upset the apple cart.' 'Don't stir the pot.' Von imagined Frank balancing precariously in the prow of his little tin fishing dinghy, two steel toes all that was keeping his big belly from overbalancing, one hand with a wooden spoon in it the only thing keeping Mavis's Dutch oven from spilling sweet and sour all over the clean kitchen floor.

When Trevor first lay on top of her, on top of Von lying on gutted earth, Trevor was light as a feather and his hair ruffled like little birds' wings in the wind. He didn't feel heavy at all. There was no warning of the heaviness to come. He felt like a fluttering leaf which might just blow away.

So Von held onto him and watched the stars moving up and down; it wasn't them moving of course, but it was an old game, that one, like pretending the telegraph posts in a car were moving, not you. If she squeezed down her eyelids, stars multiplied, stretched their incandenscence, exploded with each blink. Stars born in a matter of seconds instead of the millions of years it took and the thousands of years after that before their light could reach your eye. Von thought about infinity in the few minutes it took Trevor to come; the way Frank used to tell her about it, and the way every time your mind tried to latch onto it, it receded like a slippery fish. It was like the kid eating

Cornflakes on the box with a box of Cornflakes beside him, and you thirsted to grasp it. It niggled at you like a tooth hanging by a thread.

When Aunt Mavis found out Von was pregnant, she said a straight row of Hail Marys. Added a couple of Our Fathers, just in case. Then she clapped her hands together like she was shutting an unsuitable book.

'Right. Let's get cracking. You ring the flower shop. I'll do the church. Old McNally's free except for those ruddy Marconis. Must be all that spaghetti. Christening every second bloody week.'

While Mavis planned pink rosettes for pew ends, mushroom vol-au-vents, almond icing, swan-shaped serviettes, while she fluttered and bustled and skittered and swirled, excited as water racing from a bath, Von just went walking, as far as town borders would allow. Walking and walking on straight straight streets until the day she had to go to the cathedral and face Old Father McNally in his best vestments. Waiting like a purple full stop at the end of his aisle.

'Hey, Mona. It's Libby's turn.'

Like a fat Christmas beetle Libby kept lumbering after Mona, who always took a sharp corner at the last minute. The visitor had started to cry, big drops dribbling down her fat red cheeks.

'Mona. Give her a go.'

Mona just kept riding in circles, jeering, her laughter like a bell tinkling but ending in a croak as her adenoids caught up.

'Giv'er'ago, giv'er'ago.' This was Mona's favourite trick, to just keep repeating what you'd last said, no matter what you said next. It was an old one of course, but there was more to it with Mona. It was a dull and eerie fascination with words, like they weren't words at all, just blocks of brightly coloured objects Mona was piling up, then knocking back down.

Mona hit on a new thought. She made it last another four trips. 'Libby Lang's a big fat whale. Libby Lang's a big fat whale.' Round and round she went, liking the rhythm of it, the way it clicked along with the plastic bike clips she got from the Cornflakes, which she lined up on her windowsill, counting them, arranging them in different colours, choosing new ones to put on her wheels.

'Give her a bloody go!'

Mona changed her chant to 'Ruth Cook said bloody, Ruth Cook said bloody', going round and round, Libby trailing behind her with a red-streaked face. Ruth pedalled faster, but Mona's legs were longer and faster, she couldn't catch up.

'Uncle Frank! Make Mona stop!'

But Uncle Frank wasn't listening. The dark hole of his shed had eaten him up. He was fiddling with his paint cans and ice-cream containers, putting his tools back onto their special spray-painted shadows and admiring his jam jars full of bolts and nails all screwed by their lids to the ceiling, as if that was all that mattered, as if there was nothing wrong at all.

'Fight your own battles. Don't be a sook. Don't tell tales.'

'I'll tell my mum, Mona. She'll give you a smack.'

Ruth really believed her mum was coming. She could hear Lily's crying getting louder as she was carried across the road. Ruth had heard her own front screen door bang. She knew it was her door because the spring which should make doors like that snap back, to keep the blowies out, was broken. It had been broken for ages. So instead of the neat efficient slap which everybody's else door made, her door gave a dead-sounding thud. Then it made long sad creaks, hanging off the broken hinge.

Mavis had heard the door go too. The sound of Lily's caterwauling, filling the street, bouncing off bitumen and getting louder all the time, could have been heard in Brisbane, or so she believed. Mavis Kelly's own back door shut with a businesslike smack.

'Frank Kelly! Can you hear that or have you gone conveniently deaf? I'm telling you right now, I'm not putting up with this any more. Not one second more. It's a bloody disgrace, that's what it is. A baby crying with hunger and her mother out gallivanting, God knows where.' Mavis was talking to the black hole inside Frank's shed. 'You know what they're saying, don't you, Frank? You know where she goes when she takes off like this. It's all round town. We may as well put an ad in the bloody newspaper. Vonnie Cook, the town . . .'

'Slut,' Mona suddenly piped up. She threw it over her shoulder like a new rubber ball. 'Von Cook's a slut. Von Cook's a slut.'

Mona had read it just like Ruth had, on the toilet door down the park. Ruth had spent nearly a whole afternoon trying to scrub off the black texta, the words written with big curly swoops over the V and the C, like it was the title of a Golden Book, like it was Dear Someone on a Christmas card. She'd coloured over it, again and again, with one of her school textas, but underneath her patchwork of scribble, like those little black tags they put over tits on dirty magazines, she knew her mother's name was still there.

. . .

Beside the overpass where Von was walking ran some old railway tracks where they used to cart the slag. A few feet before the mine gates they petered, they suddenly went to ground. Right at the end of line, where the tracks ran out like a sad weary thought, there was an old sign, faded and curly: 'Watch out for the trains'. Von thought, I know how that feels.

And right at the end of those old railway tracks there was an old-fashioned pram. It looked disappointed, like it had missed its bus. When she peered over the railing at it, Von's heart gave a sort of lurch. But no, it was just a doll after all. It did look real though, lying there all tucked up with dead leaves. It was beige coloured, tangled, born, a baby thing. Made silent with embroidery. One bald lid lolling. A nervous plastic eye.

Von walked even faster then, past the railway tracks and the dead plastic baby, past the slag heaps and the padlocked mine doors. On and on, up the rise, down the other side. So fast that town and mine and even slag heaps melted to a blur. Maybe Von was crying, maybe she just had dust in her eyes. But she kept walking, until even miners' humpies petered to vacant lots, back fence palings to plain post and rail. Until all signs of town disappeared. Until it was just dust and spinifex and wire fences strung for cattle, twanging in the wind.

'Von Cook's a slut. Von Cook's a slut.' Up and down, up and down, round and round.

Uncle Frank erupted from his shed. Pushing past Mavis like she was a noisy garden gnome on its wonky pedestal, so that she fell and banged her head, Frank started undoing his belt. His face had gone red as a house brick under his old travelling hat.

The purple poncho with the dangling tassles came in handy. Ruth just chucked it under Mona's front wheel. Blood shot out in an impressive kind of spurt.

Then it was just lots of screaming: Mona screaming through snotty blood bubbles, Mavis screaming, Ruth screaming when Mavis smacked her, and into it all walked Trevor, screaming at Mavis to bloody well leave Ruth alone. Lily's thin wail, which hadn't stopped since seven-thirty that morning, threaded through it all, settled now into a weary harmony getting thinner all the time. The noise ringing out of Number 57 Bauxite Street almost drowned out the mine whistle. Mavis would never live it down.

The only person who wasn't screaming was Uncle Frank. He stood there with his leather belt hanging. His pants had slid around his hips. That look on his face, lost, blank-seeming, gaze fixed on something far above the garden, far above the fence palings and Bauxite Street and the squat horizon of town itself, was the same look the digger had. Like he'd lost, not won, the war.

The town road, old-fashioned grey concrete, widened, became blacker and more expensive looking, sprouted official DMR signposts filled with big important place names against miles in three figures. Finally what had been a potholed town thoroughfare resolved itself to sleek and glossy bitumen, pointing like a ruler, always away. The cold language of distance gave early warning: you had better be prepared.

Von had no water with her. She wasn't wearing a hat. And she wasn't carrying a handbag, it would have made her feel weighed down. All she had was a few bob in her pocket, a couple of Kleenex, and a blue ribbon tying up her hair. Her breasts, tight and heavy under summer cotton, were already starting to leak.

chapter 6

Town was buzzing. The feeling ran like electricity up and down the march of telegraph poles. It curdled in milky cups of tea. At first it was just a small eddy, drifting like the dust in the supermarket, circulating like stale air underground. But there were opinions forming in the flurry, hard knobs of allegiance which stuck out in certain places. Like outcroppings of rock.

All the secret bits of gossip people had been stockpiling, saving like money under a mattress, hoarding like brown paper and string, the rumours running sly as septic, they surfaced, little spurts of spite. Two hours after Mavis Kelly had rung the police to say Von had gone missing, there were straight lines of right and wrong on every street.

People had disappeared before of course. In a place like this, rising as it did like an important-looking pimple in the middle of just about nowhere, it was not surprising that certain people just fell right off the edge of the known flat world. Sometimes it was because they were a bit soft in the head. Or because they were too young, like the

Finlay baby who drowned in a bucket. Or they were too old, like Mr Simpson who'd had a heart attack, tripped over his Victa and no-one found him for a week. And who could forget That Wally Thompson, who went on a bender which had lasted, at present count, for over ten years. Drunkenness, ambition, grief, lust, even just plain forgetfulness. Any or all of these could be to blame. It just strengthened your faith in the middle ground.

But this was Vonnie, Frank's Vonnie. There was an irony to it that niggled, like bacon stuck in a tooth. Frank Kelly, the man reknown for his disappearing acts, an irregularity of his that had become so regular it was no longer surprising, was as traditional as Midnight Mass or the woodchop at the Easter Show, well it was Frank's Von who had disappeared. And while Frank always turned up later when you least expected, like a shiny new Coronation bob or a misplaced car key or the St Christopher you'd put through the wash, this was Von Cook you were talking about, the town trollop, last seen strutting up the main street wearing a dress the size of a hankie and far too much lipstick and her hair in dire need of a brush.

'Reap what you sow.' 'One bad apple.' 'The life you deserve.'

Sayings worn as an old rosary or a few useless coppers, leached of any real meaning, having been strung endlessly, one cheap bead on top of the other, over and over, in order to fill the long hot reaches of the everyday, were suddenly true. Life was Trinity-shaped after all. This caused a certain amount of relief.

In the end Frank and Von were just two outlandish bookends between which lay that country called Doing The Right Thing. A flat trajectory which continued to the scaled-down cul de sacs of Sleepy Hollow where neighbours from town, complete with toy letterboxes, fibreglass fish ponds and dwarf strains of shrubbery, holidayed side by side.

'That Ruth always looked like a dog's breakfast,' pronounced Bernie Whelan over tea and leftover Christmas cake in her new annexe. The tone was the same one Father McNally used when he said 'Let us pray'. Brandy fumed powerfully in the overheated air. 'Y'know, I had to bring her in the shop for a bit of tea and toast once. She was picking rubbish out of my bin.'

Bernie was pointing out the rust-proof zips and press-studs on her annexe, exclaiming at the extra space you were allowed in each corner for your fifty dollars more. Made out of the same stuff they might use for the astronauts. Would survive re-entry. Guaranteed not to fade.

The Whelans' caravan had all mod cons alright. It was also directly across from Mavis Kelly's. While Bernie showed how the miniature ironing board folded out from behind her bantam-sized fridge, the women squinted and nodded and craned their necks. But all you could see was the plump female-looking bottom of the policeman near the barbeque, waiting for Frank and Mavis to turn up. An old pair of Cottontails flapped coyly on the line above his head. Everything else was hidden by Bernie Whelan's fold-away Hills Hoist.

'He's been there for ages, that copper. The cheek of Mavis Kelly. To keep him waiting all that time.' Bernie clicked her tongue. Now Mavis had even made her drop a stitch. 'Apparently Trevor has taken the baby and the littlie and hared off in that truck of his. And the copper—no, not that one Vera, the other one, the young long drink of water. Kirkeland boy, married the Reynolds from the bakery, the eldest, who had her First Communion with the Marconi girl, one who married the Finlay. Finlay who played the flute. Well. He's been taking notes.'

'What about?' asked Vera McNally. But Bernie Whelan just tapped her nose.

'You'd reckon they would have found her by now though, wouldn't you?' Vera said. 'Only two directions she could take. East. Or west.' A blowie buzzed among the curtain frills. Someone squashed it with a rolled-up *Truth*.

'Anyone could see That Von Cook was headed off the rails.' Bernie Whelan shook her head so hard her card table rattled. Tea slopped weakly and overflowed.

'You know I saw her this morning, don't you? Right before it happened. Dressed like a hussy. Skirt up to here.' Bernie pointed to her left armpit, where a roll of fat crusted with Rexona hung over her bra. Everyone looked away. 'I was probably the last person to see that girl alive.'

Then everyone remembered when they'd last seen Von Cook. Margaret Lang said she'd heard from the motel manager's sister's husband who cleaned rooms at the Silver Shovel that Von had been seen drinking in the Riverside Pub. A couple of times. With one of 'them'. Mrs Marconi said Mario her husband had seen her hitching on the Airport Road during one of his fruit and veg runs to the Settlement. Margaret Rafferty on her regular pre-Christmas trip to the city had seen Von buying cigarettes at the Shell. Two packets. Nine months gone. Relatively late in the day.

Gwen joined in with something from Psalms. The other women rolled their eyes. Gwen had completely forgotten about Wally Thompson, who'd wandered off one night after drinking his own weight in beer. She'd also forgotten about Mona, whom she was supposed to be meeting up with out here for the holidays but who could have joined a three-ring circus in Venezeula for all the notice Gwen Goddard took.

'That Trevor was never up to much.' Vera drained her tea. The grimace on her face was equal parts disapproval of Trevor Cook's lack of substance and the fact she'd just copped a mouthful of dregs. 'Wouldn't have thought he had it in him. Looked like he wouldn't say boo to a goose.'

'Still waters run deep,' said Bernie Whelan.

Everyone nodded, creating another small whirlpool, another pocket of rancid air. It swirled powerfully in the brandy-sweet heat of the Whelan's Deluxe Vacationer Mark II.

'Shouldn't have done that you know, Mavis.'

Mona knew Uncle Frank was what Aunt Mavis called 'a bit shirty' by the way his fingers clenched so hard on the wheel. Knuckles rose in beetroot-coloured knots.

'What? What are you going on about, Frank?' Mavis was putting on lippie in the rear-view. She'd twisted it haywire to get a better view. From the angle of the mirror and from where she was sitting, Mona could see the brown stained undergrowth at the back of Aunt Mavis's teeth. It reminded her of the toilet bowls at school. She was going to mention it but had second thoughts. Even Mona could sense the hot strained feeling, the ozone smell like a thunderstorm, which enveloped the car.

'Rung the police.'

Mavis clicked her compact shut and broke a nail. 'Bugger it.'

The dead nail fell under her seat, so Mona picked it up. The nail tasted interesting. Sort of sweaty. So she put it away in the pocket where Mona kept things like that.

'Well what did you expect me to do, Frank? Sit around and wait for the cavalry? Someone had to do something, didn't they? And it wasn't going to be you.'

Aunt Mavis went on about starving babies for a while, so Mona tuned out, thinking she was talking about those wog kids on TV. Uncle Frank floored the old truck and the wind whistled up what he called the chassis, the bit where the carpet was missing and there was just bare metal with rusty ridges, like those nonslip things which hurt your bum bone in the bath. There was even a splintery crack there like in the Flintstones; you could see white dashes flashing past on the road. Mona's head jiggled on the window. Her teeth chattered. Mona liked it. So she kept it there.

It was midafternoon on Boxing Day by the time they got out to the lake. But it looked like sunset, light filtered through a sick pinkish haze. It looked like something from the Bible, Mona thought. It looked like the sunset at the end of the world. Everything was enraged: the usual tedium of grey water now florid, earth glowing crimson, even the sky blushing, thready bloodshot picked out by feathery clouds. Frank's face was purplish under the brim of his hat.

The police car was parked beside their letterbox, inside the neatly painted stones. Mavis could see a row of frilly curtains twitching up and down the 'street'. So she got out carefully, swinging both legs to the side with knees glued together, like she was Rita Hayworth arriving at a premiere. As she walked carefully toward the caravan, she imagined she had a very heavy Bible on her head.

'When'd you last see her, Mrs Kelly? Your niece?'

'She's not my niece, thank you very much. She's from Frank's side of things.'

Mavis told the police Frank saw Von outside the shop early, well before Mavis had opened up. Frank was supposed to be cleaning out the meat slicer. You know, before the holidays. Gets a shocking smell. While, she, Mavis, was over the road. Feeding that baby, wasn't she? While its mother swanned all over town. Mavis the Mug.

Von knew the shop didn't open till nine on a Boxing Day holiday and Frank knew that Mavis didn't like to make exceptions; there were rules and regulations and if she started making exceptions, then where would everyone be? But Von was banging on the shutter making a racket and Frank reckoned she looked a bit under the weather, and he always made allowances because she was family and for the sake of that baby, although for the life of her Mavis couldn't understand why everyone thought her shop was the cathedral.

'How's that?' asked the policeman.

Mavis rolled her eyes. 'Open all hours. That girl would try the patience of the Virgin Mother. Always running out of tea or bread or milk.'

Von bought two packets of Camel, Mavis told the constable, who was trying hard to look acute. No Gold Top. Mavis raised an eyebrow. The lad goggled. She sighed. Milko wouldn't deliver to Von and Trevor. Never left out the change.

'Cigarettes would have been for Trevor. Although that was a bit left of field too. He smokes Craven A.'

The thick-headed policeman nodded. He stored this up. He considered writing it down. You never knew what might come in handy a bit further down the track.

'The milk? For the baby? How old?' he said helpfully.

Mavis withered him with a look. 'Just said she didn't get any, didn't I? Five weeks. Just told you that, didn't I, on the phone. So she wouldn't be drinking cow's milk, now, would she? She'd be on the formula. Don't need to be Einstein to work that one out.' Mavis folded her arms. 'In any case, Lil's mostly on the breast.' The plump policeman blushed furiously and looked down at his shoes.

'I was more surprised by something else.' Mavis paused. She waited to see if this little twerp would write it down. But his notebook stayed, like him, pure as the driven snow.

'She didn't get any ham or bread or sandwich things. And the shop was closed on Christmas Day.'

Mavis waited for the penny to drop.

'Trevor already told me they were going to have a picnic lunch by the river. Then come straight on to the vans.'

The policeman looked back, pen still poised.

'There's no barbeque out by the river. To cook sausages or chops.' She said it slowly and painstakingly, the way she did when telling Mona to take a bath. 'And Von knew the kiosk out here wouldn't be open. In fact it's never open until the day after New Year. So you tell me.'

The thick policeman was thinking hard. A vein pulsed in the side of his head.

'Maybe she bought her stuff down at the Foodtown.'

You could almost hear his brain ticking, the cogs turning on a rusty lift. But he was a floor short of a building, in Mavis's opinion. 'They open early. In fact, it's open all day.'

'Maybe she did.' Von going to Foodtown for lunchtime smallgoods was unthinkable. The police had bloody well got it wrong.

'What was she wearing?' asked the other copper.

'Didn't see her, did I? Just finished telling you. Probably the usual. A dress halfway up her . . . I don't know. What's that got to do with the price of fish?'

Frank waited then, in his special silence, waited for them to ask what Vonnie looked like when she went walking down the road. How her face was swollen from crying, how she was black-looking under the eyes. About how thin and frail and faraway she looked in the heated shimmer building even that early in the morning, arms poking like sticks out of her thin summer dress. That dress all crushed and dusty, those thongs which wouldn't last a mile in this heat. Her eyes too bright, walking way too fast to last the distance, like a jerky puppet, like someone who'd had too much Nescafé.

Von had looked at him once, through the front bay window. Her eyes screwed up against the light. Then she'd turned the corner and she was gone.

'What about Mr Cook?'

Frank shifted in his seat and lit a Stuyvesant. He let Mavis take the bit between her teeth.

'Taken off, hasn't he. Typical. As if we don't have enough to worry about. Ranting and raving. Swearing a blue streak.'

'And he's supposed to meet up with you out here?'

'Yes, well, that'd be Trevor Cook all over. Full of good intentions.' Mavis spat on a finger and wiped Vegemite off Mona's chin.

'We heard Mrs Cook was,' the thin one cleared his throat, 'in the habit of this kind of thing.' They looked sideways at each other. The thick one failed to hide a smirk. 'You know. Wandering off.'

'Where exactly did you hear that?' Mavis bristled. 'I'd like to know who's been saying it. I'll take them on it any day of the week.' She stared daggers. They scuffed their snub-nosed shoes, rubbed their fluffy chins.

'Some of 'em are just like that.' The thin one looked at his mate sideways. 'It's sort of . . . in their blood.'

Like he was talking about breeds of livestock. Like it wasn't men who did all the wandering in Mavis Kelly's experience of life.

The police told them if Von wasn't back in a day or so, they'd put some posters up. Milk cartons. Telegraph poles. A notice in the paper. Might get the Adelaide boys to have a sniff around.

This was just to shut the bloody woman up. But the thick one got carried away with it. He puffed his chest and cocked his hat. 'They'll probably take it quite seriously, I reckon. We heard there's been A Spate.'

Mavis knew exactly what A Spate would look like. It was a whole row of posters with Von Cook's head on them, stuck to shop windows all around town. Her name plastered across the front page of the *Daily Truth*, in big black letters, and next to it, in smaller print, Mavis Kelly's own. She suddenly remembered her long-standing admiration for the police.

When Mavis offered them a beer, the coppers looked at each other, and then at the sun, as if to check it was actually headed west. Then they tipped their hats back and sat down on the folding chairs, keeping an eye out for that city detective, who'd probably be a real smart alec, a rule book up his arse. Mavis touched her perm and recrossed her legs. Today they ended in size five sandals of bright metallic green.

. . .

Dad just kept driving and driving, flat-footed, white-knuckled, poker-faced, while the baby screamed blue murder and the miles drawled by. Ruth's stomach grumbled. That pie seemed a long time ago.

Everything was wrong, Ruth felt it. The pattern going haywire, things falling through the holes. Dad hadn't done his shoes up properly and they dangled above the brake. His hands on the wheel fluttered paley, barely making contact. As if what he really wanted was for the car to swerve into the nearest tree. But there was nothing to hit.

Ruth was thirsty as well as hungry. But every time she opened her mouth to say so, the hot air of the car rushed in. And the way Dad had pulled her across Bauxite Street, so fast and hard her feet barely touched the ground, and stuffed her in the back seat and Lil in her bassinette, so roughly, so silently, and the way he did that screeching U-turn in the middle of the street, she knew better than to say a thing. Now he was just driving and driving, straight along the Airport Road.

Ruth tried to shoosh Lil, playing This Little Piggy with her toes. But Lil was too young. Her lips pursed, her mouth opened but there was nothing to put in it, nothing but hot air. Ruth gave her a finger to suck.

'Bloody bastards.' Dad kept muttering under his breath. Ruth thought he was talking about Auntie Mavis and Uncle Frank. But Trevor was fuming at those men in the Duke of Gloucester, those smug check-shirted bastards leaning up against the bar. As if they owned it. As if that pub counter and their fat bellies were joined at the hip.

He'd stopped there on the way out of town. Because he knew Von sometimes went there for a drink.

'Got a bit of a cheek, hasn't she, your missus?' Men watched Trevor carefully through the blue furl of their roll-your-owns. 'Bold as brass. Our Von.'

Like she belonged to them. Those fat bastards leering down at him, adjusting their belt buckles, filling the room with rugby size thighs.

'Needs a good talking-to, that wife of yours.'

Trevor went to school with those men. But while they occupied the centre court for cricket, Trevor lurked in the shadows where two square brick buildings met. He tried to make himself smaller, tried to melt between cracks. Even the Marist Brothers found something sinister in it, the way Trevor Cook skittered and scuttled and crept crabwise round that playground. Like hell itself was after him. Like he'd done something wrong.

'Here, take it easy,' they said when Trevor punched the door. 'Don't bust a tug. Not your fault, is it? Bloody women. When she needs a feed, you can count on it. She'll be back.' Men rocked lazily on the balls of their feet.

One of these men hit Trevor with a cricket bat once. Just for a joke. He was a boy then, that bloke, but a big one and his fingers itched and tightened on that bat handle like he was about to crack a century at Lords. Trevor cannoned off the edge of the metal lockers. He'd needed six stitches above his left eye.

'Gotta know how to handle them.' Men nodded, one to the other, stringing their dreary beads of good sense. 'Gotta let 'em know who's the boss.'

Another time Brother Augustus held Trevor out the top window of the science block. Because he couldn't remember the formula for zinc. Brother's hold on Trevor's wrists was vicelike. But he was letting it slip, inch by inch. Just bare-faced, point-blank cheek, the way the little sniveller wouldn't say anything, the way he cowered under Brother's skirts. It made Brother Augustus spit chips. Seeing red in Brother's case was an actual affliction. He could almost taste the secret throb of blood. His married to Jesus ring bit into Trevor's neck.

'Not wearing a bra either, was she?' Men dug each other in the ribs. 'And in her state.' Men made cupping movements in the air. 'Oughta tell that missus of yours to be careful. She'll get into trouble, mate. Runnin' all over town.'

It was the way they kept saying it, the way their eyes slid sideways, beer froth foaming on blue upper lips. There were images of dark nights and early mornings, of Vonnie rolling away from him to the cold empty reaches of an unmade bed. Her arms wrapped tightly round herself. Hiding her breasts. She hated them, hated the way they'd gone large and milky, the way the veins stood out. If he touched her, she flinched. The pillow over her head to shut out the baby so it was Trevor who always had to get up. The way she stared down at Lily while she fed her, like she'd found a leech attached to her skin.

Von was wearing a bra. Bloody liars. Because Trevor couldn't forget the sharp final snap of the strap this morning, across her freckled back. Her face in the mirror as she fastened her buttons. Done up tight as a zip.

'Dad. Can we stop? I'm thirsty. I need to wee.'

But Dad just floored the car. Just kept driving. Grim. Black-faced. Hopeless. Straight ahead.

. . .

Frank kept sitting in his banana chair while the police drank their beer, while Mavis argued with him about heading back into town, while the sun dipped further over the lake. The colours now were purple-red with streaks of overblown yellow, a rotten light, ominous as a bruise. It caught the flatness. It sliced it into shards. They glittered, those colours, they slashed, they hurt the eye. The sun, swollen and sore-looking, the texture of a blood orange, was furred with a halo. Big weather coming. Frank could tell.

Under her flowered sunhat Mavis was telling the police how she'd seen it coming, how this was just like Frank's family, how many times was this Von had done it, just wandered off, but this time with a newborn baby to care for, you wouldn't credit it, would you, wouldn't read about it in a book.

Frank got up so roughly his chair fell over.

'She's like me, Mavis. Now and then she needs to get off on her own.'

Frank started up his truck with a roar. Mona started to slither after him and Mavis, used to the little Houdini, tried to grab her by the wrist. But Mona was far too quick for her. She scuttled into the back tray like a skinny spider, like a cockroach bumming a ride. Then Frank's truck was just a white speck swallowed by red distance. Against earth the colour of blood.

'You'd better come on back to town with us, Mrs Kelly. Just in case those kids turn up.' The copper stared. But Frank's truck had disappeared behind the hills.

Mavis kicked off her sandals and settled back to finish her cuppa. The cops could bloody well cool their heels. Van curtains twitched like they had a nervous tick. While she was sitting there Mavis couldn't help noticing, out of force of habit entirely, that their garden here needed a good water and that those pickets could do with a good lick of paint.

chapter 7

Von was seventy mile out on the Airport Road by the time the white truck pulled up. It was mid-afternoon by then, the sun had reached its climax but, instead of descending, it just seemed to hang there, an indisputable fact. Those cheap Woolies thongs of hers had almost melted into tar. She'd walked ten of it, hitched a fair swag of it, now here she was walking again. Down a road sleek as black ribbon. Buckled slightly with distance. Curved under the sheer weight of sun.

The next little milepost still said a hundred to go, in cracked and faded black and white. You were meant to see it flash by harmlessly from a speeding car, just a round number holding some dusty boredom, hot seat leather, a thirsty wait for fuel. Not any real fear. And here was Von standing and staring at it, as if it meant something. As if it was a story she could reach the end of if she tried.

She stuck out her thumb. But there was no magic in it. The road stayed empty, as empty as a road could get. Intent only on where it was going. On where it might have been.

Townspeople always took the Weir Road to the lake. Even though it was longer. Even though it was dirt road and full of potholes and wound like tangled wool all round about the river course. Just so's they wouldn't have to go through the Settlement. So as not to spoil the holiday mood.

Von had forgotten how far it was to the Settlement. To someone who didn't drive, miles didn't mean much. And in a place like this, where there was a glut of distance, where miles were spent carelessly, where only great wads of empty flatness qualified as a 'bit of a way', people thought nothing of driving a hundred mile to have a picnic or visit a sickbed or round up a cow. To a good hitchhiker, even a hundred mile could seem a walk in the park. Right now though, with the sun beating down and her skin crinkling and her mouth dry as blazes, Von almost wished she was back there, lying flat out under a sapling in the town reserve. With Lily sucking at her like a little vacuum cleaner and Ruth throwing Tip Top at overfed ducks.

Von was dripping. Milk, not sweat. Breasts swelled regular as clockwork, fat blue veins travelling a vast and foreign skin. No matter where she went, what road she took, how far she walked, that soft white artery fed off her, suckered her, held her fast to a square grid of streets. If she was gone from Lil any longer than a couple of hours, two coin-size circles soaked the front of her dress. By now, in hot sun, through thin cotton, she smelt like a bowl of old sick or a wedge of Mr Marconi's parmesan cheese.

That lech McGregor, when he'd picked her up on the town outskirts, he'd kept staring at them, sniffing at them like a bloodhound, eyes snaking greedily all over the front of her dress. He'd driven extra slowly, pottering at town's twenty mile an hour down a road so straight and empty you couldn't hit something if you tried. Von thought she might as well get out and walk. She nearly did too, what with the stink of him and his creaky old Ford. McGregor kept it wrapped up in string and brown paper inside his garage except for his annual runabout to the lake. So the inside reeked of too much Kitten polish and dusty spider-web and mouse droppings, and McGregor stank too, of so much Old Spice the bloke must have had a bath in it, revelled in it like the Brylcreem, whole bottles of blue pong tipped over his head.

'That Baker girl who hitchhiked. You know what happened to her.'

The tip of his too-red tongue licked toothpaste spit from his lip. The way it flicked in and out, Von wished she had a pair of scissors on her, she would have whipped it off. He kept digging at her with it, at what he thought were her soft bits, the bits he'd like to expose. In the end Von told him to stick it. So he'd pulled over in the middle of nowhere and Von had got out.

Now there was nothing else for it. Down the black dry draught of it, skin turning red but the earth always redder, redder than town dust or gouged-out creekbeds or the ore dirt from the mine. Red bounced off itself and, finding only its own reflection, gathered force. Earth lay low. Air glittered. Red beat you over the head. It drank tears from eyeballs, sweat from armpits, even the spit from your mouth. It burned down as if through a magnifier and Von imagined her skin was curling and blackening, like news-paper through a broken bottle under a childhood sun.

Von was thinking so hard about water while she walked—gallons of it, rivers of it, flat round lakes of it, big tin sinks of it, cold and clear—that she could almost taste the furry staleness of the radiator water Murrie gave her that first time, when he'd picked her up out along this road. She imagined she could hear him now, right there beside her, his old ute idling clunkily, the back tray an uproar of kero tins and dogs.

'You alright, love?' is what he'd kept yelling above the roar. But she'd just kept walking, eyes glued straight ahead. A ute and a strange man driving it and that voice out the window could easily have been one of those that yell, 'Hey love! What about a fuck?' She would have stuck her finger up at him but she hadn't been that keen, not all the way out here. So she'd tried to saunter, like she was just on her way to the dry-cleaners, not heading toward what was a blank dot on any DMR map.

'Hey. Why don't cha have a bit of this.'

When she'd turned to say something smart, tell him what he could do with it, something to do with brains and dicks, she'd realised the man was offering her a drink. So she'd stopped walking. She'd got in. And she'd taken a huge gulp out of that old Caltex tin, cupping her lips round all that oil and rust. Aunt Mavis's warnings, the way she always wiped the lip of a bottle with a tissue or dress hem if she had to share it, and put a folded piece of Sorbent on any toilet seat, saying, 'You don't know where it's been,' had all rung hollow inside the petrol heat of Murrie's ute.

'Where you goin'?' was all Murrie had said the whole time they drove. His words flowed lazily together, no hard and fast ends. 'Enunciate,' Mavis always said crisply. 'You're not a builder's navvy, Evonne.' Mavis was one of those people who said 'filim' because it was fashionable and made her Os so egg-shaped it was like she had a marble in her throat.

'Dunno. What's it to you?'

He'd left it at that. He'd drummed his fingers and whistled and left her alone. Town people were always asking questions, pretending they were worried, like they were good Christians, but really they were just waiting to trip you up. Like McGregor edging her across his bench seat, his gearstick hand creeping up her thigh.

When Murrie took a drink his neck muscles knotted out like rope. Sweat trickled round his Adam's apple. Von wanted to put her mouth on it and suck.

But that wasn't the real reason she did it, got in the front seat beside Murrie and later in the back. It was because he was 'one of them'.

She'd been hoping a town gossip like Mrs Whelan or Mrs McNally or that sly little Marconi fella on his Settlement fruit run might come driving by. In the end it was even better, it was more than she hoped for, it was the express telegraph to town. It was that pair of old penguins, Sister Loyola and Sister Bonaventure, on their way to the airport to pick up a church bigwig for the cathedral on the hill.

Bigwigs were always coming, on feast days or at Lent or on their annual archsomethingorother inspections, which seemed to happen about six times a year. They were fat old men with funny hats on, a bit like the ones you get in Christmas crackers, with three sides and a festive-looking tassel on the top. They reeked of stale pipe tobacco and dusty vestries, of heavy-lidded books dozing in slats of stained-glass sun. Their hands, plump and waxy, stank of pew polish and occasionally of the wine they turned into blood. They had skin like cream parchment and their fingernails were too clean and too long and too pointy, like the false ones shopgirls wore down at Moore's. The visitors ran their hands lightly down your cheek. Their skin felt dead. You had to kneel down and kiss Christ's bleeding feet, then their big ruby rings. Even the rings looked fake, like those plastic ones you can get out of an egg for twenty cents.

After some Mass that went on and on and on, the old bloke gargling away in Latin and saying 'Body of Chrisssst' so wetly his spit kept landing on your stuck-out Communion tongue, the visitor usually inspected a hospital or laid the foundation of something that wouldn't be built for years. Or they'd pull a cord and some velvet curtains would part and the thing you'd been waiting to see, hoping it was worth it, knowing it wouldn't be, sitting there cross-legged and sweltering in the playground, asphalt scorching up through your knickers, was just a piece of cement with someone's name on it, not even someone you knew. Then the visitor would get in his big black presbytery car, be driven to the airport, get in a toy plane like the Flying Doctor one and go home.

When Von got in the ute with Murrie they saw her alright, that stinky bishop in purple vestments and those nuns sweating pink as Fritz inside their wimples and wings. They saw Von Cook sitting up there plain as day beside a black. They would take the news straight to Mavis, like a string and brown paper parcel marked 'Urgent, Handle With Care'. Then Von Cook would be so far beyond the pale there would be no rescue. No airless web of certainty closing over the head.

'Drop us at the river,' is what she told Murrie after they did it, after they'd climbed back in the front. 'If yer goin' that way.'

She'd been careful not to say Settlement, in case it wasn't his name for it. Names they called things in town might seem ordinary, harmless as chair or table, just because people used them all the time. But Von was getting town out of her system. It was a slow but thorough vomit, involuntary as a sphincter, the way flesh was tightening and hardening, expelling bits and pieces she'd swallowed wholesale just a few years before. Now there were whole chunks of what she'd thought were vital organs rising in her craw.

Words you heard and even used, harmless on the surface, were weapons in disguise. Townspeople muttered them at gas stations. White bosses spat them into the gutters of pubs. Nuns dangled them in afternoon classrooms. They hung, barbed and dangerous, in serge-smelly air.

You just couldn't see them or feel them. Not until they were buried in your skin.

'Cockroaches.' That's what Uncle Frank called nuns and priests. He whispered it like a voodoo, like a guilty but delicious sin.

'Bloody cockroaches. Just lift a body and that's where they'll be.'

Uncle Frank was saying it as they stood at the Mother's funeral at the little windy city cemetery above the sea. Black habits flapped in the gale. They looked like crows at a kill. The wind whipped Frank's greying hair too, parting it and revealing bare patches of scalp. He stood twirling his hat in the exact same way he used to when he entered the Mother's dining room all those years ago. He hadn't changed much back then, apart from the hair and the big belly. When the priest finished warbling and shut his Bible,

Frank said Amen, like it had just slipped out of him, like he was putting the last bead on a black necklace the crow priest had been muttering into the grey and gusting wind. Frank's eyes were a bit watery if you'd looked closely. Von was a bit smaller, a fair bit younger, but even at fourteen her eyes were as dry as they were right now.

Frank wouldn't go into the church, despite all Mavis's pleas and threats. He went and sat on some old gravestone out the front. The Mother would have been scandalised that not even then could Frank 'make his peace'. As they sat there smoking stale Stuyvesant, Von knew that the Mother was still watching them, polishing a grail with holy Brasso, cutting a Communion Host into slivers, from some big polished cedar dining room Up There.

Strangers dropped the coffin, all gleaming wood and shiny handles, into a dark and hairy hole. There would be dirt under the Mother's fingernails, and Von thought of fingernails rotting, of grass curling slyly round sharp elbows and papery too-thin skin. Worms would snake through the holes of Mother's broderie anglaise, infest her sprouty shoulders and slither through the hooks and eyes of her too tight too shiny too pointy shoes.

Late the next day, after driving all night over the mountains to flat plains of blackness, so black they were like a single drawn-out note, Frank's truck broke down coming in on the Airport Road. It was probably round about where Von was walking right now. She recognised that funny looking anthill, a bit like a pyramid, or a Sunny Boy turned on its point. Middle of summer it was, and even though the sun was setting, the temperature nudged a hundred in the shade.

Frank swore when the engine sputtered. Just Jesus H or Bugger of a Thing, nothing too bad. Mavis wasn't there to hear it anyway, she'd stayed on in the city to look after Auntie Gwen. Auntie Gwen had gone off the rails completely now the Mother was dead. She'd started accosting people on street corners to tell them things she'd read on the newspaper, not even real newspapers but old ones wrapped around her fish and chips. Once she'd worn a tea-cosy as far as the corner. Mavis couldn't be having that, even if Gwen was seven hundred mile away. She was still a Goddard after all.

Uncle Frank was kicking himself, he said. That he hadn't stopped at the Settlement to top up. But he never stopped at the Settlement if he could help it; he kept two tins of petrol in the boot. You were nearly always in danger of running out. Most of the time you limped into town hovering on empty and you just had to hope that your fuel dial was crook. Because it was a two-hour journey between the Settlement and town, or the Settlement and the next place, there was nothing, not even a picnic shelter or a rain tank, between here, there and home.

But one of the tins had sprung a leak, the boot stank, and the other one, well it was half empty, he'd forgotten to fill it; there wasn't enough to put in your eye. Frank propped up the bonnet and scratched his head. Von wasn't worried. In Von's world, having the bonnet up meant action; when a man looked at car guts and did all that grunting and prodding and stroking, it wasn't long before things kicked back in.

The sun was setting in a blaze. The ground was even redder, taking the blood colour and bouncing it back at you, brighter and harder than before. Dryness glinted everywhere, in the sand which held the seeds of glass-making, in those bits of black cubic mineral, razor-sharp and perfectly cruel.

Once the sun set it would start to get cold. And darker than any night in town. No streetlights. Just cold and endless stars. You could miss the turn-off easily once you got off the highway, in that utter blackness with only a nail-paring moon. There was nothing, not even a dirt track or a signpost, to show you the way.

'Nothing else for it.' Frank reckoned. He set the tent up in a little dry creekbed and it was like a picnic, watching Frank tie the peg ropes with his special knots, the ones he learnt when he was a pearler, then make a fire by rubbing two twigs and burning a newspaper with broken bottle, in the sun's last hurrah. He never carried Redheads, what did you need all that paraphernalia for, all those primuses and eskies and thermoses people humped along like top-heavy snails? There were always a few sticks handy or a bit of glass by the side of a road. There were things to eat too, Frank said, certain leaves and insects, the moist roots of plants. If you looked hard enough. If you kept your eyes peeled, even in darkness. If you listened hard. Not just with ears. You'll miss something. Listen with fingers and eyes and nose.

Frank was happy now, cutting a fork for the billy, feeding his fire, grimly making do. He always kept a tin of Bushells in the car, along with some white flour and a gunny sack of sugar and an old kero tin full of radiator water, which tasted stale, like metal and oil. It was alright when you boiled it, though, and made stiff black cuppas out of it and put in four heaped sugars so that all you could taste was sugar and gum smoke, not bitterness and rust. In the light of the fire dancing on ghost gums, while they drank the sweet black stuff from jam jars, Frank told Von stories, the only stories he knew.

About how this creekbed, cracked with its red furrows, dry as an old boot, used to belong to the river, before they built the weir. How even when it dried up, earth remembered, river remembered, that water memory which earth never forgot. It kept a map of old water in the lines of that water's passing. Water remembered was plain as the lines on your hand. Frank pointed to his deep cracks and crevices, burnt by radiator caps and smashed by hammers, mapped by fence wire and abalone and God knows what else.

Earth recalled water. A steady stream of remembering. As blood remembers a heart.

'Here. Can't you feel it? Can't you smell it? Have a whiff.' Frank picked up a handful of dust, let it blow away in the direction of wind. Then he stuck what was left under Vonnie's nose. All she could smell was dust. But Frank held it for a long time, sniffing like old Tige with a rotten bone.

'Water coming,' he said finally, and let it blow sideways. Von thought he meant rain.

Night was so thorough now, you could taste the blackness. You could finger it like fur. But Frank's stories of water, his little heart of fire, kept them warm. Frank told her that even now, even now that they'd cut the river and the lake with their dams and their pipelines, their roads and their caravans and their tame leaping fish, even now, if it rained hard enough and long enough, the river would come home.

How, Von asked, it's so far away. Because the river and the lake are sad for each other. When sadness is too heavy, then the sky, in the face of it, starts crying too. If it cried long enough and hard enough, it would wash the river home. Even if it wasn't raining here, even if it rained further up, at the river, far away. Because earth was so dry and the river so sad, this heavy old sadness could make them whole. The river remembered. Even these thin dry creekbeds, even these little fingers and sparse legs and tiny veins.

'What would it look like?' They were in the tent then, fire just a glow.

'Wouldn't see it. Not till it was on you. You'd hear it. Like the ocean, roaring. Only, by then it'd be too late.'

'If you could see it, what would it look like?' Von looked side to side, at the blackness in which an angry river might hide.

'Wall of water,' Frank told her. 'Fast and hard. High as a mountain. Angry as sin.'

And later, when Von was nearly asleep and everything was so quiet, so quiet you could hear a bird fold its wings softly or a leaf falling from a tree, could almost imagine that thin moon lapping its ocean, hear the stars twinkle, a sound like ice cracking when you defrost a fridge, Von lay dreaming Frank's water. She thought she heard the roar of trucks on a highway. Maybe it was just the wind. She imagined idly it was the river, howling and crying and roaring, rushing headlong, in brown anger and dry anguish, down all its shrunken limbs, tracing the precise path of what had been lost to it. It made a hollow roar like grief.

So when Frank sprang up and grabbed Von, just picked her up like she was light as a feather, like she weighed nothing at all, and carried her, quick as lightning up and out of the creekbed, leaving the tent and their clothes and even his hat behind, she still thought she was dreaming, lost in Frank's water dream. But the roar was louder and her eyes were open and in the dark she couldn't see it. She could just smell it and hear it, the salty growl and spit. The smell of angry water, kept from itself too long.

It crashed through the creekbed, swept away the tent and the billy and the fire. Von felt that rush of rotten air. Like breath collapsed to black within the lungs. Frank was still holding her, she could hear the steady beat of his heart. He didn't sound frightened. He had breathed life into the river with a story. He had made water with a word.

From then on, Von knew Frank's stories were powerful. Like the silence in between.

Von was thinking hard about that water, about how she wouldn't mind a bit of it now. Heavy rain like fat bullets, a flood rocketing through. All the dryness and the dust and the straight straight road, even that bastard McGregor, everything gone in a blink.

Water is what she dreamed of as she walked on hot and burning earth. Cool deep mud and dusty trees. Out at the Settlement they would be sitting under big shady willows, in languid humps and piles, sitting so still, skin so dark, you couldn't see where shadows ended and where arms and legs began. Flies hummed and settled, no-one brushed them off. The water slow and thick. Dark as the people's skin. Cool reeds grew at its edges. They floated and swayed, strands of black river hair. Mud between your toes was dense and ancient, and when drought hit, it would withdraw from the slow vein of water, shrinking like an old person's gums.

Murrie would be down under there by now, with a big bottle of long neck, not saying much. Big drinking time,

Boxing Day. People still drunk from the night before. His hair would be curling from the river water. He would have his shirt off, little sweat creeks mapping the finer bones of his back. He wouldn't be saying much. Just drinking. She would sit beside him, feel the endlessness where skin stopped and water began. Murrie would put one hand on her thigh.

Old Jacob would be down there too, trailing his gnarled old pegs in the river reeds, yearning for the lake. Old Jacob would be talking and talking, his talk rising and falling in muddy rhythms until it stopped and silence took its place. Then it would flow again, in creaky starts and broken mutters, like it was hitting a rock and going round it, wearing it down. It wasn't the voice of God, those soft hills and valleys where the nuns with their murmured prayers and Latin gobbledygook put you off to sleep. It was a country of sheer cliffs, dark holes, sharp rocks. You had to pay attention or fall between the words.

Von was staring out there, toward the river, thinking about water but feeling heat instead. It made a high hum like a stroked piano string. Like a finger rubbed around the rim of a glass. Then the white truck pulled up.

The motor chugged. Dust hung in puffs behind each wheel. The passenger door swung open. The inside looked dark and cool. The driver held out a bottle of water. So Von got in.

chapter 8

'He won't be back, you know. Not today.'

Aunt Mavis was standing at the back screen door. She had pert ankles above too-small high-heeled shoes. The minute she got back from the lake, in the police car, she'd changed into them, along with her best blouse and second best skirt. So that by the time the police arrived with Ruth, looking bedraggled and clutching one old thong, Mavis looked like she was ready for church. If there was going to be a crisis Mavis would at least be well-dressed,

Through the grey mesh you could only see her bottom half, like she'd been cut in two by a magician: bright pink apron, strangled waist, gold wedding ring on a bony finger, finger ending in a sharp red nail. If those fingers grabbed you round the upper arm and dragged you to the bedroom, the nails left angry half-moons on your skin.

'Uncle Frank's off looking for That Mother Of Yours. As usual, I'm the mug.' Arms akimbo across an aproned stomach. From the pocket a pair of knitting needles stuck out like a murder clue. 'No point just sitting there. Got no idea when he'll be back.'

Ruth knew if she didn't turn around, just kept sitting on the third step of the back verandah, keeping an eye on the horizon, Mavis would go away. And she did, eventually, disappearing behind the dusty mesh, back into the gloom of her too-clean kitchen, which today smelt strongly of floor polish and Mavis's Alpine cigarettes. She always left one burning in a brass ashtray while she cleaned, a tidy red lipstick mouth around the end. In between scrubbing the bathroom with Ajax, vacuuming the long strip of carpet with the red roses, polishing the red and white lino with the big snub-face polisher which looked like a cartoon dolphin, Mavis took rationed, ladylike drags. She shot smoke out in vicious little plumes.

Mavis the mug. She even had to clean the shop, usually Frank's job, scrubbing out the meat slicer and wielding Windex with a vengeance. Frank had been so busy with his ruddy tomatoes, he'd let everything go to pot. Out of pure spite and not inconsiderable frustration, Mavis had made Ruth scrape the gunge out of the big bay window where they kept the bread. The floor was always slippery with detergent and sloped steeply toward the street. But Ruth had kept her head down and kept at it, bracing herself against the cake shelf with one knee. She'd imagined Mavis was the brown muck on the laminex, she'd scraped so hard she'd felt herself sliding toward the bellied glass. She'd seen herself falling, in slow motion, ending up on the footpath as a mess of minced meat. Mavis would be sorry then.

When Mavis had opened the shop refrigerator it smelt of dirty socks. That cheese was supposed to smell though, it was the veiny one Uncle Frank got from Mr Marconi's secret stash. No-one but Frank liked Mr Marconi's slimy pickled vegetables or his spaghetti which came out of a packet, not out of a tin. Uncle Frank loved to eat that vomit-smelling cheese on his crib, with a pickled onion and a thick slice of buttered bread. But Mavis had wrinkled her nose and, carrying it with a pair of sandwich tongs, thrown the whole wedge to the dog. When Aunt Mavis came back from the club this evening, she wanted only her own virtue to greet her at the door.

'I'm much too busy,' Mavis was fond of saying, but to whom and with what, Ruth was never quite sure. She was baking now, creaming out butter and sugar and kneading scone dough with the heel of her hand. The lamingtons were done already, they were cooling on a wire tray. When finished they would be put in the special Coronation tin on top of the cupboard, a place where if Ruth wanted to sneak one she would have drag over one of the kitchen chairs. Mavis would hear that of course, because the chairs were steel and two rubber feet were missing, and even in the middle of the night Mavis never seemed to be asleep. And that, as Uncle Frank was fond of saying, would be about that.

'I've got the washing too, you know, and the baking, God knows there's enough of that.' Mavis was just a dim grey burble from behind the door. 'But it can't be helped, can it? Frank loves his sweets.' As if she was the only one who knew that. As if the knowledge was hers alone.

She would be off to the club when the cooking and washing were done, Ruth could tell. Mavis's hair was set in curlers under a spidery net. Those long red nails were freshly painted under pink rubber gloves. She would go first to her dressing table with its three mirrors—one big oval one in the centre, two smaller ones like the bevilled wings of angels—and get dressed in one of her going-out outfits, the pink suit or the mauvish Angora. Perhaps the pale red twinset; most things she owned were in the vicinity of pink.

Then she would put on her lips. Coral Dawn the lipstick was called, Ruth knew, because she'd stolen a stub from Mavis's drawer. A last look in the mirror—front, back, sides, a lip smack to her own reflection—and she would close the door on the afternoon-smelling house with its crackly plastic on all the furniture, even the patchwork poufs.

Mavis would clacket down the garden path wearing most of her jewellery and her red high heels. All the metal and her energy, those kite-strung elbows, everything would make her snap like a crisp dollar bill. At the club she would play the pokies and drink small shandies through a straw. Clicking, clacking, snapping like the levers, tinkling like the two bobs falling into slots. Like her very bones had come loose, defeated by thinness, and were rolling around beneath her skin.

They had Trevor Cook down the police station the rest of the afternoon. But he'd hardly said a thing. He'd been wandering like a madman up and down out by the weir access, holding tight to one old thong. Wouldn't let it go, even when they took his shoelaces off him, even when they relieved him of his belt. The little girl was out there. Just sitting on a picnic rug. As if she was about to have some sandwiches. But there wasn't any. No food, no drink, no

mate for the lone thong. No sign of the wife. The baby,
she was gone.

'You in the habit of going out there to fish?'

Trevor both nodded and shook his head. You couldn't
tell if this was an answer or part of his general malaise. His
pants hung round his hips, his shoes kept falling off. This
bloke looked like he'd blow over, next strong wind. The
way he just kept sitting there and grizzling, rocking like a
spastic, made the sergeant want to give him a good back-
hand to the head.

'Can't have it every which way, mate. Didn't find any
gear in the back of your truck. What were you planning
to do? Catch fish with your bare hands?'

The others thought this was a good one. They laughed
and rocked back on copper-shaped heels.

'Okay. Let's back up a bit. Your little girl reckoned you
picked your wife up out on the Airport Road. What the
hell was she doing all the way out there?'

Trevor's hands fluttered at his hair, like he was trying
to pull some thoughts out by the roots. But nothing came.

'Wife went for a bit of a walk. That's what you said to
this McGregor fella. Is that what you said?'

The sergeant ruffled through the statement given by
McGregor. He'd helped Cook change a tyre. They'd chatted
a bit, the price of petrol, the cinema fire, the rain in the
offing. But McGregor couldn't see anything in the back of
Cook's truck. There was a tarpaulin over the tray.

'Bit of a walk.' The sergeant rolled each word over and
over, sucking them transparent as travel sweets on the end
of his tongue. 'What was she doing all the way out there?
More than a bit of a walk, that. Don't you reckon, Trevor?
And in this heat.'

Now and again Sergeant Peterson's big head struck the bare light globe on its string. It swung back and forth, a moonish yellow glow.

'Been hitching I reckon. Heard she was a bit too fond of hitching. Our Von.'

There it was again. Our Von. Trevor really thought he was going to spew, mashed-up carrot over those bullet-shaped shoes.

'Anyway why'd you need help? What's the matter? Can't you change a tyre, Trevor?' More chuckles from the chorus. More big belt buckles, more oversize thighs. 'Although the mother-in-law could believe it. Said that sounds just like Trevor Cook.'

Trevor could see the faintly pleased look on Mavis's skinny lips.

'And you were headed in the wrong direction, mate. Toward town, not the weir. Where was the wife and kids?'

'Went to get Lil's bottle. Left it at home.'

It was the first time Cook had said anything resembling a sentence. And each word seemed to weigh a ton. And they knew everything already, or so it seemed, these fat bastards standing legs wide to give the hefty hang of things a bit of space. They kept pushing useless words to the top of the same mountain and rolling them off onto Trevor's head. Heavy details, in different orders, mixing them up, until Trevor didn't know whether he was coming or going, for hours it seemed, in a peeling paint police station with one flyspecked seasick globe.

'Why'd you need the bottle, Trevor?'

Why'd he keep asking about bottles and fag brands and whether Trevor had defrosted chops or sausages or taken a picnic lunch? Trevor shook his head. Nothing got any clearer though. Nothing made any sense.

'Mother-in-law said that baby was on the breast.'

Again. That cupping movement in air.

'Wouldn't need a bottle, would you? If the baby was on the breast. See where I'm headed, Trevor? We on the same train?'

Cook had started to snivel. The sergeant fluttered his man-sized square. Trevor used it. He tried to hand it back. The sergeant threw it away in disgust.

'What time'd you get back?'

'Where? When? What now?'

'To the weir, you bloody moron!' That voice detonated inside the little police station. The sergeant leant forward until Trevor thought he'd choke on the stink of aftershave, on the blue-shaved jut of that chin. 'Where do you think I mean, you bloody waste of space?'

Those fingers were like sausages. One wore a thick gold ring. Trevor saw the fist those hands could make, the imprint that ring would leave on flesh. The fight went out of him like someone had stuck him with a pin.

Trevor started a fit of sobbing then that no number of glasses of water could stop.

'Ruth! Don't you dare forget to bring that washing in.'

Washing wouldn't dry today anyway, Ruth knew it. Well it might dry a bit but it would get filthy again, and have to be washed all over, by Mavis, in a very bad mood. There was going to be a storm. The sky had that bruised greenish-black look which in other places, in other seasons, might herald thunder, but not now. You could tell by the red in it, by the sore rawness in the sky. And there were no real clouds, although the sky was not blue either, just a thick red haze which blocked the light and sent it back in a dull yellow clot. If this light had a taste it would be like fur. If it had a sound, it would be a thud, like a fist on flesh. No echo, just the thump of airlessness escaping. A dead light, like the underwater eyes of fish.

The red paint on this verandah licked halfway to the laundry, then stopped, like a mystery, like that saying 'paint yourself into a corner'. When Ruth heard Uncle Frank say that, this is what she thought of, this verandah with its sad little patch of grey concrete, where Frank must have stood one day, paintbrush dripping, wondering what on earth to do next. But he was wrong because if you really stretched out your legs and pushed out from that corner, you could jump over the red paint entirely, past the back step, past the red concrete footprints, onto the back lawn. If you touched the paint or the step or the first footprint, you were dead.

It wasn't really lawn of course. No-one here had lawn to speak off, because the ground was too dusty and refused to stay in one place. 'Everyone's equal in the dust,' Uncle Frank always said. People thought Frank was a communist because he said things like that. But even Frank's lawn, with all his watering, was just as scabby and faded as everyone else's. It straggled like strands of hair over an old person's skull. By the third footprint gave up entirely, defeated by dirt.

Fruit trees were about the only things that did well here, according to Frank. They liked the heat and all the minerals in the soil. The fruit Frank's trees gave was better than anything you could buy, apricots big as a fist and bright orange, a taste more apricot than apricot. Juice running from chin to elbow to knee.

Right down the back, past the lemon tree and Uncle Frank's shed, along the old paling fence which was weathered and grey and nearly falling over but not quite, running like a tunnelled wave held up by some trick of flat earth, were Uncle Frank's trucks. There were three of them: the old A-Model, the white Ford, the red Holden with the exploding seat. Cars traced the history of his travels, like lines on a map which continued over the page. Something had happened to the Holden's transmission, the Ford was minus two tyres and its engine had been sold to the McGregors next door. There was one missing of course, the new Ford, which usually sat in the space where the fence had fallen down entirely and which Frank used as an impromptu driveway when he came up the back lane. The missing truck was the one Uncle Frank was driving now.

The A-Model was Ruth's favourite, with its flat shelf and funny rounded hood. It had an old-fashioned steering wheel and cracked dials with curlicued numbers and even a special holder for your cup of tea. Ruth and her mum used to sit here on dull afternoons, on that seat losing its stuffing, changing gears. Ruth pretended to work the old gear shift with half a yoyo stuck to it, the real knob having fallen off long ago.

Ruth steered with her eyes shut, blocking out the grey fence, the back lane with its unpicked seams of houses, the birdshit on the windshield, the storm pushing down like a glassy bowl. Where she was the ground was red, the sky was blue, the horizon flat. The road pointed like Sister Loyola's ruler. Straight ahead.

. . .

'There's a point here where you can see the curvature of the earth.'

Mum was standing near the cave paintings when she said that, her head crooked up under the lip of rock. Her finger ran slowly over faint red-grey markings, feeling the shape and feel and passage of a story, but all the time she had her eyes shut, like she was telling a rosary, like she was reading a page of stone braille. Uncle Frank nodded and winked and pointed, folding his map back into his pocket, he didn't need it, the knowledge was there in his palm. He stood facing a sunset. Elbows perpendicular to hips. Earth. Water. Sky. The crisp horizon of a hat.

Ruth squinted, following an eyeline, trying hard to believe. She didn't know what curvature meant but she liked the sound of it, and from the sound came the meaning. The idea of roundness. From flat earth, flat water, flat sky.

The paintings too were round and curved, swooping in dull red forms like a language unbroken by letters or ordinary sounds. Mum traced the shape of no sound with one finger, learning silence, seeing rust colours spark and glow. But when Ruth tried it, the rock was smooth and silent, like one of Uncle Frank's scars.

He could tell the story of his life through those scars.

'This was from when I roped a bullock, out Mudgee way.' Frank took off his hat and laid it carefully on the ground. With one hand on the paintings, those ancient scars, he pointed to his own, to his own temple, like the mark there, a gash where flesh had gone missing, was the opening paragraph of a story he was in the middle of, though you'd never heard him start.

'Did a sudden turn, the bugger. I was off that horse before I knew what was what. Barbed-wire fence. Mongrel stuff.'

Then he indicated his left foot.

'Coral.' Frank had his shoes on and Ruth had never seen coral but she imagined a watery pinkish growth.

'Diving. Got infected. Nearly died.'

Ruth was used to his hieroglyphics but this time there were too many of them and Frank was fixed on some horizon nowhere to be seen. Her mum could see it though. With one hand raised, Mum was looking out there. They were trying to tell her something, but at such an unflinching angle that words glanced uselessly, falling fractured to the ground. Sentences were too short and stunted, too full of verbs and nouns but no adjectives, like scars could carry those stories, like scars had a thread of flesh. But they were closed over. White. Already in the past.

Watching Frank watching Mum watching the horizon, Ruth could see all those barb-wire sentences, stranded in flat red space around their skulls.

'This here, bugger shot me. In the DTs. Bullet went in here,' Frank pointed to his shoulder just below the collarbone, 'and came out here.'

He was indicating somewhere in the area of his heart. The scar there was moon-shaped, with a lunar surface. Carrying no blood.

The light now, even through Ruth's closed lids, was a faint seasick green. And even with eyes open, she could barely see the gearstick, the back fence, the steering wheel. 'Storm's coming,' Uncle Frank would be saying if he was here. The hair on his hands would be standing to attention, nostrils quivering in tune with the brim of his hat. He liked storms, liked the waiting, the rise in pressure on internal organs, expectation pricking like tears behind the eyes. He would rub his palms together, that old skin fairly crackling with glee.

In backyards down the hill housewives were dashing for washing, pricking up ears under poodle perms. They scurried out of back doors like bull ants from a nest. Sheets billowed and folded in the rising wind, white against the red, and the women looked ghostly, washing weaving and wrapping and trailing a warning, T-shirts blown horizontal like little stripy flags. The tension built and built, like a thunderstorm really, but when it came, it wouldn't be rain.

It would be dust, a sheer bank of it, inexorable as mountains or tidal waves or fear. It would make another world, one with its own rules and properties, where earth behaves like water, where mountains and borders move. It would coat fruit trees in a fine powder, sift under doorways and windows, insinuate itself into old engines, pit the polished duco of cars. Disturb the carefully marked boundaries between fake lawn and slag heap, town and desert, front door and back. Days later, people would find it in the carpet, under the toilet seat, on all the windowsills. Sprinkled in a fine mist on cakes and tarts.

It would creep into Mavis's underwear and sit like worry between her too-tight girdle and her crepey, too-thin skin.

Uncle Frank had once returned from a long trip in a dust storm. From then on Ruth connected his arrival with such cataclysms, with a thrill of grit and a foreboding heaviness of sky. As if storms could pick Uncle Frank up inside their raw stomach and spit him out reconstituted. Himself now made of dust. Ruth peered but she couldn't see him, couldn't see anything, not even the fruit trees or the Hills Hoist or the shed. Just dust, the colour and texture of rage.

She waited and waited and in her longing for it, she imagined she saw him, just a faint black outline against the red. Feet first, then legs, then shoulders, finally a broad-brimmed hat. The storm would find his syllables, the dust speak his limbs. He would come walking as if earth, red and powerful, could give him birth.

Frank would be coated head to foot, his grey hair red, his fingers as if sunburnt. He would be carrying Mum in his arms, as if she'd just been out walking again, just too far this time, and she was just tired, as if everything was alright. As if Mum weighed nothing at all.

Frank would be smiling. Breathing dust through his very pores.

chapter 9

Mona was hiding inside the secret rock. She was almost small enough to fit herself inside the hollow, although the roof scraped her backbone and her feet stuck out. But if she curled up real tight, knees tucked like a diver, hands furled like tiny rose buds, she could do it. Be a soft sly snail. Hair stuck to eyelids. Flies buzzed in each ear. Her neck ached, her leg cramped. But Mona stayed there. The inside was cool and dry.

The sun had risen to its highest point, descended, it was headed straight for the edge of the known flat world. But that was the only familiar thing about it. A trajectory from east to west.

By true sunset it was a monstrous dust-red ball. As if light itself had fractured, broken to dull molecules, and been ambered, sore and furious, inside earth's empty husk. You could stare straight at it, at sun wearing dust like a pelt. Sun spiked off flatness: red earth, flat boredom, water like blood.

Mona closed her eyes. The sun was still there, like an inside eye. Then and only then did she look through the hole. That was the magic. Outside it there might be toy caravans, tiny policemen, Aunt Mavis perhaps, an angry pink dot. But in the hole there was nothing but water. And in the centre of the water was Frank.

He'd been there for ages, until Mona thought his feet must have grown duck webs and his toes gone all pruney like an old grape. Except he still had his boots on, which was pretty stupid. And the bottoms of his trousers were getting all wet. He just kept standing there, like he was planted, feet disappearing into smooth water, and with those skinny legs above a big stomach, he looked like a tree swelling fatly, like something gone rotten but still standing, like bones holding a dead bloat of skin.

Mona had seen a drowned dog like that once, floating stiffly along the river. It was upright, gliding not walking, like Jesus in a miracle, like swollen and fly-ridden fruit. Of course Mona had to poke a stick at it. It popped like a balloon.

Mona knew if you stood too long in that water the sand moved like a lazy muscle, sucking, shifting, sliding and curdling, until before you realised you'd sunk down in it up to your knees.

Further in, if you weren't careful, you could fall down and down and never come up.

Frank was remembering the day of the trucks. The sound of them, the stink of them, the roar of wheels and the angry belch of dust. Like the church God was coming down from the clouds in Maudie's book.

Standing knee deep, skin whitening, river whispering, deep underground, Frank was remembering everything,

everything flowing back. All the spurts and threads and byways of it, from dry extremity to wide brown river, to secret lake and stagnant pools.

It was the day of the scars. It was washing day. Mission women had told Maudie she must stop using the rain tank, that she had to get water from the river, that water must be boiled. So Maudie had all Frank's clothes and two of her three dresses in the big copper pot on the fire, that round hole in the Board house floor. She kept rushing forward and backward with saucepans and kettles and kero tins, trying to fill it. God was white. She'd seen him in the Mission book. White clothes, white skin, white cloud. Cleanliness next to Godliness. A soul washed clean of sin. The pot boiled and bubbled. Then Maudie went to Mass.

Frank was down at the river, and the motorbike crow fella, that white man dressed like a crow, he'd come down to the swimming place and sat there, shoeless and sockless, smiling, calling boys over with one long thin birdy hand. Black flap clothes, patch of white collar, twig ankles snapping from black trouser cuffs.

There was the sly brown water, the gloss of it on others, the murky hum of reeds. Frank swam down and down. His skin was whiter and he had a different nose to the others and the boys laughed at his paleness, poking at his belly as he rested on the rocks. Once he'd tried rubbing ash from the fire on his arms and legs. But it was the colour of dead smoke, not brown skin. And when he got out of the water, he was as white as before. Only under brown water, legs flicking and twining, face flattened by pressure, could Frank look the same.

Maudie was pale like Frank, a copper colour, with long thin green eyes. Maudie didn't come from the river country, which is why she looked different, why she was afraid of water, why she drank too much. Maudie and Old Tommy came from the place of red clay. Old Tommy told Frank that when he was little, a baby at the Mission camp, Maudie had carried him on her back with reed nets round his bottom so he wouldn't fall in the river and drown. Like all those other babies, drowned in brown water, dark blood, red earth. Tommy said where he and Maudie came from there wasn't much water but here they had to sleep near it, and they were sick from it, from the smell of it always in their noses, like an old and salty fear. The red clay was far from her but still in her, she had to carry it around. It was heavy, stronger than the smell of water or the love of God or the stink of Maudie's wine. Her earth was a long dry string sucking her. It was dark and rotten mud.

The crow fella called, in his slow powerful paddle, bringing Frank to account. As if the priest was God fishing and Frank a pale minnow reeled clean from the river mouth. All the boys stood in a circle, water running in glossy streams. The crow fella put his fingers to his lips. The old men didn't like Mission people being in the special place where earth takes water deep underground. The crow man shooshed and twittered, his breath made a birdy whistle through crooked yellow teeth.

He said if they didn't tell the old men he'd been there, he'd let God's love come down from heaven. He said it was stronger than any other magic they knew, stronger than Old Tommy with his fire and feathers, more powerful than Jacob's message sticks or the snake spirit in the cave.

He made them all hold hands. One of the crow man's hands was on Tommy's and the other stroked the round hump of the bike. Those fingers quivered like an animal caught in a trap. Frank being smallest was right on the end. But even there, being the last bead at the end of God's necklace, dangling hopeful on the string of words the crow man was muttering into hot and gusty air, the magic was still strong. Like a little shock of understanding: is that what they meant by God's love?

Maudie believed in God. She wore a gold cross between the breast folds of her yellow dress. She crossed herself and knelt up and down with the others. She muttered those long words like a necklace which linked all the kneeling bodies, making them go up and down. They made a necklace on their faces and shoulders too, up and down and round and round. Maudie rocked and prayed for her dead ones, those white pale babies at the end of broken cords. She wore the cross and made the sign to save her, from the snake, from the Holy Devil, from the snake spirit in the secret caves and the Holy Devil who Maudie thought were one and the same. The Holy Snake sat on the rock where the Holy Mother stood. God, Holy Mother, Holy Snake, flesh from rock, man from clay, Holy Devil, water and a clean white soul, Maudie got it all mixed up. She even spent all her money one month on a silver tea set ordered from what the Mission women called the cat a log; she poured her drink in it just like the priest did when he raised his cup in the church. But Maudie's cups had no magic in them; when she poured her rum in there, God's blood didn't make her safe. When Maudie woke dry mouthed and bleary, she smelt the salty stink of water, she was not in the place of red clay.

Even the Mission women couldn't make Maudie sleep in the Board houses, where poison from river bones seeps like an evil spring. At night she returned to dry ground and slept next to Old Tommy, who understood.

The silver bells tinkled and tinkled and Maudie nodded and nodded, lulled in the stained-glass dream of God's window. But all the while the Holy Snake was sliding through a crack in God's door.

After the crow fella left, shooshing and whistling, the boys tried to hold Frank down in the water. To make his colour run off. But he'd run and run, out past the river and the Mission houses and the church and the windmills, across the gibbers and the bore sink and up through rock hills into bush. He knew where he was going. His feet found the winding snake paths and they led him through the place of the bones. They curled and beckoned and wrapped around him, until his toes traced rock coils where snake spirits live. He hid there, his heart thumping; they passed right over, the other boys, he could hear quiet dry soles on the rock above his head. He made his breath fit the rhythm, all those sighs and hollows. He made blood beat in time with wind.

Old Tommy had taught him that. Jacob the river man had told him about the snake spirits, all about water, about the message sticks which could come floating up the river, carrying warnings from lost river people, those sticks covered in red paint. You couldn't tell anyone about them, not the Mission women or the red clay people or the crow. Jacob had shown him too the trick with the wiry water plant, how you buried it deep in the ground with the saltbush and how you could eat it if you were hungry enough or spin it into bags of rope. Even Maudie, as if caught in some car headlights, as if it had floated to her surface like a shiny fish, remembered how her brothers danced round the fire, how they painted their faces white. Her mother used to sing the songs. But when Frank asked Maudie to sing them, she couldn't remember them, and she slapped out with the heavy pain of it, sinking back into the drink. As if those lost songs were drowning her, as if the sound of lost singing was a roar across dry earth. And Maudie, she was just a heavy piece of clay.

No-one but Frank made the rope from the water plants any more, they got hessian sacks from the Mission store. And Frank had never seen a message stick come floating up the river; he'd tried to make one but the red paint washed off and, turning and tumbling, it sank like a stone. Jacob reckoned those message sticks were coming, one day, but when Jacob looked at that lake and then far away at the river, Frank knew what he was thinking—how could water sticks travel over dry land?

Once Frank told Jacob, not knowing what he was saying, just making it up, but wanting to do something, stop those tears weeping from Jacob's sore sticky eyes, that one day the river would cry for the lake too, like Jacob, and the sky might cry with it, and when they both cried too much there would be a big flood, like the one Tommy remembered when Frank was born. Tommy reckoned that a long time ago the river and the lake rushed to meet each other across all that dry hot earth.

Jacob just got angry when Frank said that. He pushed him away, said it was bad to make things up.

'None of you listen. Don't know the country stories, you. Just money, that's all it is.' But Jacob was still crying inside, Frank knew.

Frank remembered, he stored it up. He carried it inside him. It meant he could lose himself, despite his paleness.

Inside a rock, beside a bush. In the thin black attitude of trees.

After a long while he crept out from his cave. And he ran and ran, back down to the water, thinking he'd run back to Maudie's and the boys'd give it up. But as he was walking across the shallow part of the lake, a spine where river and lake might once have been together, where water dives deep underground, he was suddenly exposed, in water so clear and thin he could see toes shifting in sand. Sky was big here, in the middle. It sucked breath from you, wide and blank. You were a tiny ant under God's hand. So big that hand, you couldn't tell where fingers ended and God's palm began. God pressed him down, Frank fought water's sly suck and pucker, felt water clutch at bad pale skin.

If God held him down, all his colour would run off. Like ash from an incinerator, like paint from a message stick. Frank would be like the crow man. Thin and pale and lost-looking, always in pain because of God.

When the boiling water fell onto Frank's back, that was God's love.

Maudie rolled him in blankets and ran with him to Jimmy; they rubbed the special red clay into Frank's skin. The whole night Maudie talked to him, about where she came from, about how the bravest men had the pain marks on their back. But Frank, swimming up through dark and pain, he didn't listen, couldn't hear her, didn't remember, not until too late. He only knew that when the pain was gone, all that was left was this whiteness, smooth and terrible and dead. White pain, whiter than Mission people's skin.

. . .

On the day of the trucks it was the white pain that singled Frank out. He and Tommy and Jacob sat with the rest of the people, some of them river people, some from the water tank and some, not many, from the place of red clay. The trucks seemed taller than anything Frank had ever seen; there were no mountains in that place to measure them by. Behind the dark glass windows it seemed there were no men, that these trucks had driven themselves up the road. To swallow the people in bright steel bellies. To make them disappear.

The crow man came walking down the path beside the river, long feet stuck sideways like a wading bird. He was smiling but his eyes were afraid. They flickered side to side. Tommy waved his arms back at the people by the roadside, asking, 'Where we going, what about the trucks?' Sometimes trucks were for cattle but there was no cattle, no sheep, no horses, not out here.

Jacob waved his hands at the Board houses, at the streets, at the houses he hated, at the straight streets the houses sat on, then to the meeting places and the lake where the river people swam. Jacob's eyes were weeping, water streaming down his face.

Cars drove up and Mission people in wide hats and white flowing dresses got out, more and more of them, and walked around, looking inside people's houses, getting down on their hands and knees to poke about with their white gloves in the wurleys, and the crow man directed them, his long black dress flapping, his thin fingers flicking, scratching spiky words in his special book. He made Frank and the other kids line up in front of the trucks. Mission people touched their hair and faces, poked fingers into the corners of their eyes. Then they pulled open their mouths,

and tapped busily at their teeth. While they were doing
this the crow man hid behind his paper collar and clip-
board, he ticked and whistled and clicked. He put his claw
hand on Frank's head but Frank shrank back, afraid that
God's love would be much stronger this close up. It would
strike him down dead.

When the white dress women pulled Frank's shirt up,
they saw the white pain on his back. They shook their heads.
Frank was suddenly frightened; he pulled away from the pale
cold fingers of the women and the hard hairy hands of the
men. He ran and ran, to where Maudie slept in her wurley,
far away from the water smell. She'd crept out of the Board
house in the middle of the night like she always did and
gone back to her own place, where the Mission women who
were fat and had long hooky noses couldn't fit their white
soft bodies through the door. It was dark as pitch in there
and Frank was trying to wake her, shaking her, calling,
'Maudie, Maudie,' over and over, and in the dark crunch of
leaves and the huddle of the blanket he sniffed the bottle
smell like a rich sour tent over his head.

The crow man pulled him out by his ankles. He held
him round the shoulders, as if to deliver a kiss. One of the
women was pushing Frank toward one of the big black
cars. Frank kicked her in the shins; she fell over, top-heavy
with her wide hat and fluttering whiteness. She fell softly
in the dust. Like a cloud billowing, like a white soft cloud
falling out of sky.

Men dragged Maudie out between them. Her torn
yellow dress showed her breasts, the gold cross dangling
between. Maudie's feet dragged in the dirt. Frank screamed
and screamed but Maudie couldn't hear him. She was deep
in the silence of her earth.

They loaded her in the truck with the others and then the crow man got in beside the white cloud woman and drove the car Frank was in far away.

Frank never saw Maudie again. Nearly twenty years on, when he finally found where they took her, she was one of the few Mission people still left living in that place. It was far from the river, far from the lake, far from red clay. Most of the people had taken one look at the new Board houses which looked just like the old ones and at the straight black streets which ran into strange sea country and at the square brick church which squatted like a toad in the centre of it, and they went away. In the middle of the night they walked off, taking only some sticks of furniture. Headed in the direction of the river, the water, the lake.

No-one walked to the place of the red clay. Tommy was too old, he just got too heavy. The earth in him pulled, he lay down and died. They buried him in soil that smelt like the sea.

Maudie was too lost in the drink, it was the water that killed her. Full of old earth, she sank like a stone. In the room above the pub Frank found her yellow dress, her flowered housecoat, her gold cross. Everything stank of piss. In an old black handbag given to Maudie at the Mission, Frank found a picture of the crow fella sitting on his magic bike. He put it in his wallet. Later he buried that crow fella, deep and dark, under the lemon tree.

He stood there for an hour looking at the thin grey bed where Maudie must have lain for all those days. He could see her lying there, in the hot afternoon, with the flies buzzing and the sun burning her through the window, and her not feeling anything, just watching light pouring through broken glass and sparkling on the bottles, so many bottles, lined up on every shelf and sill.

The light in the bottles was green, blue and brown, the colours of water, in all its shapes and forms. Maudie would have thought they were pretty with the light coming through them, and she mustn't have heard the roar of water death in their open mouths. And as she lay there Frank could see that crow fella on top of her, grunting and pushing and hammering, driving the heavy earth in her further down. Delivering God's love.

Maudie was gone. Maudie's body was already in the coffin, on the altar at the church.

Frank wouldn't go in there, not even then. He waited outside until they were finished singing and kneeling and getting up and kneeling down again. Through stained-glass windows Frank could see the crow fella standing at the altar, dressed now all in shining white. When he was at the Home of Compassion they'd made Frank go to Mass. He'd worn a white dress too and rung a little bell; its tiny tinkle could make the white people move, up and down, sitting and kneeling, forward and back to the cross and the rail. Frank had helped deliver God's broken body to the waiting fringe of tongues. As he'd carried the silver cup and plate to the priest and the open gape of mouths, he'd thought of Maudie's gold cross and her silver tea set. He'd thought of where she was and maybe that she was in the church too, but he hadn't been able to see her, only feel her crossing herself, humming to the Holy Snake.

After Maudie was dead, Frank never went inside a church again.

They buried her in the same bad earth as Tommy. Frank put on his hat afterwards and walked over to the house the white copper had told him about. He walked in the door, through the broken flyscreen, up every hall he could ever remember, carpetless and littered with kero tins. Everything was familiar, enough to make him sick. He saw the lounge room of every Board house, with its bareness and missing floorboards and rusty cooking pots. The burnt round holes in the floor.

Four little boys peered up at him from the kitchen table. But they were too dark, it was none of them. Maudie's friend held out the baby; the woman's arms were dark but the baby was the light brown of the river, the gold in her light like sand.

'What's this one of Maudie's?' asked Frank.

The woman told him Maudie's secret name. But Frank didn't call her that. He kept it safe, like a coin to be fingered, that name which sounded like the sea.

He called that one of Maudie's Von.

Mona saw Frank sit down in the water. First he took off his boots and his socks. Mona thought that made sense. But then she saw him stand up, pants dripping, undo his belt and drop his trousers; she could see the pale tops of his hairy legs. Her face burnt as if the sun was burning her through the magic hole. Then Frank did something she had never seen him do before, not even when he went swimming or when it was very hot. Frank took off his shirt.

Frank felt Mona see his scars. They flowed from neck to waistline and down into the water, where they belonged. He could hear them, those bloodless syllables travelling a

river of dead white skin. It was the sound of his not
screaming. It was the speechless language of Frank's guilt.

Uncle Frank dived under the water. The dust storm hit.
Then everything disappeared.

earth

chapter 10

They're coming now, the city people, down the long straight highway, Ruth hating these white-bread towns which seem to make J so nervous but just make her feel bored. To travel for hours against the sternness of it—flat as a tack, dry earth, bushes thin as veins against the sky—then to come to these shopping mall places. It's a great disappointment. There's a dullness in the stomach as though the lawn-mowers and TV antennas and Saturday football voices have won.

They left the city at dawn. No-one about except a dero waiting for news under his Heralds and the Lebanese guy manning the Food Plus. And the drunk Koori woman outside the early-opener pub.

'Is this it?' J is asking. 'Does it look like this? Are we nearly there?'

No, no and no. This isn't her place. This isn't her home.

Her street is not black and flat and straightforward but snarled, potholed, awry with sudden elbows, what some would call scum. Her street is grey and littered and sneering, the only bright spots the colourful posters, the eccentric hair. It is a place of make-do and make-believe, of patching up and tearing down, a vein of graffiti where people walk in a special rolling lope, centred by the gravity of heavy boots. All along the main drag they walk, riding in the swell of it, pitching in its sway. They surge that languid rhythm, pump its lazy heart; in and out of pawn shops and cafes and pubs it beats, taken up by one then the other. Flaring out suddenly with the smash of a bottle. A jagged voice.

'Fuck off, yer cunt!'

The Koori woman had teetered in her impossible red shoes. Right in the middle of it, swaying in the tide, flotsam or was she jetsam, but not to be avoided, not to be ignored. Early morning motorists turned their heads and looked away. They were stuck; the lights hadn't changed, there was nowhere to go, like being caught by a mad person on a train at peak hour, with your hand clasped sweatily around the pole. They hoped, they prayed that she would quieten down. For their sake, not for hers. But the rhythm of the street was there, not of their making. Just for that moment it belonged to her.

'Yer a fucking cunt, I hate you, fuck off!' She'd leant into it, dangerously close to it, awash in the wake of a passing car. Her boyfriend loitered on the footpath in his home-boy tracksuit and reflective sunglasses, looking innocent, looking bored. She'd swayed some more, another lull. She'd tried to hail a taxi but the driver had locked his doors. It seemed like it was finished; her hands hung loose, she looked exhausted, she was nearly gone. Still the yuppies on their way to early morning power breakfasts straightened their suit collars, found their pantyhose interesting, walked fast the other way. She was dangerous, not because she might attack them but because she'd dredged up what was under the polite rhythm of the street. She'd spewed it out. Like raw meat on a white plate. She'd made them feel sane.

And just when everyone thought it was over, as these things always happen, in slow motion, in several stages, so it seemed that the ordinary had returned, had never left at all, the swell rushed in and she'd lunged across the flow of it, argued with the tide. Narrowly missing cars and buses and a truck delivering to the Italian deli, she'd sprung on the boyfriend, kicking and punching, those bright red shoes flailing up and down.

'Yer cunt, yer fuckin' cunt!'

For a while he'd pretended to cower, like an innocent bystander, like a member of the street. But then he'd entered their private drama, he couldn't resist, and he'd hit out, fast, too fast to see, and he was on top, he was in power, not just because he was bigger and stronger, but because that's the way it really was, all the time, underneath. Her head had gone down, her dark hair parted, the pink of her scalp revealed. And because she'd revealed herself, put herself beyond the pale, no-one helped.

She'd sprawled in the gutter, nose bleeding, red shoes askew. She'd hit bottom. She'd gone under. She was panting but calm. It was over, the same thing enacted time and again. It was what she wanted, people felt. What she deserved. They'd left her alone.

It wasn't over, not by a long shot. The traffic lights had changed. Ruth and J had moved on.

As they'd made their way through the city centre, following the money vein on some million-dollar bypass, across raw-looking flyovers, with the sun coming up, heading west, Ruth had kept thinking about that woman. About how she would have to drown, again and again. About casinos and retail developments and peach-faced bankers swelling plump in a carapace of suit. About being digested through intestines worn thin on the surface of a skin. As if by exposing its ligature, its bloodless sinew, the city thought it was closed over from people like her. Home might be different now, at least to here, to what she thought she knew was there.

And J had been singing out loud to the radio, and lighting cigarettes and sticking his hand up under her dress. She'd stuck her feet out the window to let him and stuck her own fingers up at the city as they left it squatting under all that smog.

They stop at a milk bar for lunch, the sort of place which has coloured strips of plastic hanging across the doorway. It has RSL carpet and wood-panel walls. Outside the heat is atomic but in here it is musty and cool. Nothing happening, in that particular way nothing can happen when you visit old aunties and sit in their living rooms, surrounded by lace doilies, pictures of a married daughter drowning in meringue puffs of white. The plastic clock ticking. Carpet swirling precisely between your toes.

'Afternoon.' This is categorical not a greeting, and the woman behind the counter is not looking at them but beyond them, to the bright square of life outside the door. She is fat but nubile and wears pink slacks with ridges up the middle and hair in wings either side of her head. 'What can I get you?'

Ruth looks and looks but there seems to be nothing to eat. There are Coke signs in every conceivable place. There are pies and vanilla slices and finger buns and everything else is fried. J sneers in his polite English way but that gets you nowhere out here.

They settle for salad sandwiches—white bread of course—and get lettuce, beetroot which turns the bread pink, and a blob of that carrot and cheese mixture they keep encountering in these towns. J thinks it's a code, like a Mason's handshake. If you look surprised, You're Not From Here.

'You from Sydney then?' the woman asks, laying out another two slices of bread.

The woman has her niece or daughter helping her; it's school holidays and there'd be nothing much else to do in a place like this. Three pubs, forty houses, an RSL and a Rotary park. The baths are closed for cleaning, there's been a water scare; it's still the middle of summer, but the council is a stickler for Health Department rules and regulations, even though it's still stinking, it's ninety in the shade. It's too hot to go bike-riding and there's not much on telly and the local cinema burnt down. Ruth knows all these things without anyone opening their mouth.

'Yes,' J is telling the woman politely.

'Which part?'

'Newtown.' J eyes a fly crawling over donuts and into the cheese.

The shopgirl is dressed head to toe in lime green. Even her earrings are big green plastic daisies, the type you clip on. The lime green is also familiar; two summers ago city beaches turned citrus in swarms. But it's more than that, more than such outdated stylishness this far from the water, something about how country girls always get it vaguely wrong. Ruth remembers Mona, her white jeans accessorised with a red velour jumper in an agonising sort of way.

'Is that near Penrith? My sister lives at Penrith. I've been there twice. At Christmas, in the usual run of things. Not bothering this year.'

Ruth hates her; look at my clothes, look at my fucking haircut, what planet are you from? Here it's just city or country, nothing in between.

'It's a hell of a long way.'

Making sandwiches seems to unleash a flood in the woman; her fingers flash between lettuce and beetroot, she revels in the mayonnaise, that big lipsticked mouth just runs on and on.

'Are you doing it all in one go? It's a bugger of a trip. We usually stop at Dubbo, stay at the motel. The Sundowner. Do you know it? Next to the RSL. It's the best if you're just passing through.'

J nods and nods, watching the woman fondle his sandwich, leaving pink beetroot prints on white bread. Her gold wedding band is biting hard into her finger, the skin rising above it in a plump married lump.

They get drinks from the fridge, pay their money, and the fat woman's story peters down. The city people take their brown paper bags and push through the plastic strips, pulling down dark glasses and rolling up the sleeves of hot black clothes. They climb into their brand-new rented Commodore and its doors close behind them with a smugsounding click. J throws his sandwich straight in the glovebox but Ruth starts eating hers, to make a point.

She looks back when they stop at the highway corner. The fat woman is holding the lime green girl by her T-shirt and yelling, pointing to the perpetual motion sign on the footpath. The kids who knocked it over are already halfway up the street. Then the lights change, and Ruth and J move on.

The last Ruth sees is two figures, one big, one smaller. One pink, one green. Swallowed by a dull gape of door.

'Is this the desert yet?'

Ruth sits up with a jolt. The road is getting straighter but not quite straight enough. And they are still passing the odd landmark—a church, a pub, a tractor, a cow. Then the road rolls out, these things cease to exist.

'How far to go?'

How far now, whines a childish voice, propped on the back seat with its pillows and its barley sugars and an unshakeable sense of self. Seven bridges in all, she used to count them; the big grey steel ones where the water still flowed, the last three in grey wood with black and white signs, like metaphors for old danger. Out there, water is mostly an abstract idea.

All the same, light is glowing and spreading, turning red in a long low rush. And between towns, trees thin and flatten, leaves furl green to grey. But the soil in the paddocks is still dun-coloured and coastal; if you picked it up, it would still stick together in your hands.

'No, it's not the desert. Long way yet.'

Now you're in the dead time of long sun, when you've just had lunch and there's a whole stretch of nothing to get through before tea. Road rolls out before you, unrelieved by a single tree. Wives sleep in the flash of a car passing, guillotined by sun visors. Heads loll bonelessly, a spiderweb of spit between the teeth. Men drive with hands clenched grimly, fingers calloused like old dinosaur hide. Split with cold mornings and hammers, this skin is uncharted landscape. It crackles as they jockey the wheel. Men hunch forward and breathe noisily through grey hair nostrils, as if sheer force of will propels a car, nothing else.

Ruth used to think that a man's job of looking after his family was so difficult it required the utmost in concentration; now she knows it was the same joyless virtue Frank, in the absence of Vonnie, applied to most things he did.

J's hands are different; they are both strong and delicate, with veins standing out from playing guitar. They lie loose as an athlete's, gripping the wheel. If some idiot came up the wrong side of the road he'd react.

When she looks at J's hands she wants to sleep with him. They are strong and sly and she knows exactly where they've been.

chapter 11

The sun rises, the kettle boils, the grandfather chimes.
These are the new heartbeats of Mavis Kelly's days.

Long after Frank had stopped working at the mine,
long after he had trouble waking up, he would put a Big
Ben in a steel bucket by the bed. Even after Von disappeared, when they lived in the caravan at the lake and there
was nothing to wake up for and Frank had trouble sleeping
anyway, his eyes clicking open the moment the sun hit the
roof, he continued the practice, like a man drowning at
intervals, like someone chaining himself to a rock. Even
now, with Frank's garden buckets gone all rusty and the
Big Ben sprouting sprockets at the tip, Mavis can hear that
shrill racket when she first wakes up. It filled the house on
Bauxite Street, then the little tin van. Now its absence fills
the flat above Marconi's. It eats up all the air.

But the sun shines. The grandfather chimes. The kettle
boils. These at least are still regular as clockwork. Regular
as some things which have just ceased to be. Trams in the
city. Children's bathtime. Fish on a Friday. Curfew, Mass

bells, genuflection. Other events, dimly remembered as messy and dangerous. Holding secret rhythms of their own.

Fence stringing. Sheep shearing. The rhythm of Frank looking from old fob watch to sun rising, light breaking in black ribbons across a yard. Frank never needed a clock. And the watch was broken. But he still checked it, sun to watch and back again, as if verifying a pulse.

'Time for school,' he'd say and when Mavis checked against the grandfather clock in Mother's hallway, Frank was only ever a few minutes wrong. Frank was never surprised. He'd just go calmly on with what he was doing. Fence stringing. Sheep shearing. The steady tumble of fleece and forearm, brown against the white. Frank's brown fingers, now boneless on white linen, then etched with sheep burrs, wire and weather, turning sheep to blubber with methodical ease. Frank could flip a sheep with one flick of the wrist. And it would just lie there, feet lolling to the ceiling, as if eager to be made into chops.

'Oi, Mavis. Give us a hand with this fence,' was the first thing Mavis remembered Frank ever saying to her. If she'd known this would be the pattern of most of their adult conversations—Mavis being expected to do something while Frank half did something else—she would have turned on her heel then and there.

'Here. Hold it a bit tighter. Pull it out a bit. Like that.'

Frank's hands on hers, her finger on the knot, like you do with a shoelace, and Frank winding the wire down the length of the post. Twist, wind, pull, twist. She could smell him, and it was a curious mixture rising out of hot sun, the sharp rhythm of the stringing: faint sweat of course, which Mavis forgave him—how could he help it, shearing all day then, because he was on staff, not an itinerant as

Mother called them, also feeding cattle, fixing tractors, mending chicken houses, stringing the fence. Underneath the sweat was something else altogether, sour and fresh all at once: Sunlight soap, flannelette, tobacco. Something remembered from kissing an uncle's cheek.

Mavis used to be able smell Frank on her fingers, even after she'd had a bath. Now he doesn't seem to smell at all. He is airless and closed over as a snail.

'Ready, love?'

Gwen is wearing her blue. She blunders into Mavis's flat without knocking and collapses with a sigh in Frank's favourite chair. Immediately the place feels messy although nothing in particular has moved. Mavis fusses with the detail but can't remove the unmistakeable presence of Gwen. Gwen seems to spill—hat askew, flesh budding in too-tight nylon, even her varicose veins plotting escape.

'Bus was early today, Mavis. Nearly missed it. Had to run halfway down the Adelaide Road.' Gwen's fanning her fat face with a dainty hankie. Trickles of sweat leave damp patches on Frank's chair. 'Cripes I'm hot. Of course we don't get the humidity here, do we, not like in the city. Don't know how lucky we are.'

Mavis nods. She lets it go. She concentrates on holding things together, on making elements stay where they should. In any given space Gwen is like a vortex, like a hole punched in an aeroplane, and Mavis's little efforts—the antimacassars, the dried flowers, the row of china ornaments on the mantlepiece—are sucked of weight and colour, set hopelessly adrift.

Gwen has always been an unstoppable force. Before her bouts of 'resting', she had a special rhythm all her own. When she made her way across a dance floor, she made men hungry. They were fascinated by her ampleness, at something contained only by girdles and Mother's iron-hard will. Gwen's big bosom moved through shoals of men like a prow. They gathered and fell, propelled and repulsed. Helpless before a greater force.

Mavis hid behind potted palms, storing everything up. The bright colours, the rouged cheeks, the morse code of high heels on a polished wooden floor. The gossamer words of women as they sank like flowers on the broad shoulders of men. Gwen's lips moved but making no sound, as if a luscious membrane lay between her and the rest of the world.

'Read about that new shopping centre coming in on the bus. You heard about it, Mavis? Sounds real go-ahead. It'll have a pitcher theatre and a place to drink, whatchacallit, cappacheeno. Space for over four hundred cars.'

That's one good thing about Gwen coming on these hospital visits. With the multitude of useless facts she has absorbed in her lifetime, she relieves Mavis of the necessity to talk. Mavis used to talk, quite a lot in fact, about news items and washing powders, recipes and stain removal, films she has now forgotten the names of and the potholes in the highway out south. She has talked less and less since Frank got sick. Unlike Frank's silence, hers is not powerful but a hole which others rush to fill. Like a sponge, she attracts the talkers, the prattlers, the people who use words like stitches, looping on and on. For Mavis there is less to get attached to. One plate, one cup, the occasional funeral out of town.

'Got any bickies, Mavis? I might have some left over from the bus.' Rustle, rustle, crackle, crackle. Bits of tin foil and old lolly wrappers and tobacco shreds erupt like volcano ash, all over Mavis's freshly vacuumed floor.

Mavis stands drinking tea, at the bay window of her second-floor flat above the Marconis, nodding now and then to keep up Gwen's flow. From up here the Rotary park clock looks far too big. In fact it looks like it's about to cross the road and move in with her. Mavis can't get used to living this far off the ground.

They should really be making a move. That Matron is a real Tartar for visiting hours, you'd think she did heart surgery on the side. But even with the big hand notching to vertical, Mavis can't seem to stir herself. She feels becalmed. The town park looks parched and surly, freckled with sad-looking shrubs. She remembers Frank and his watering. His cactus requiring no water, the bald patches in the backyard grass. The grass in the park isn't much better. It has that grey-green indifference peculiar to public spaces before midday, before teatime and footy games and the kids get out of school. It is a cheerless sensation. Like a table set for a dinner to which no-one has come.

Except of course for the old people. There are always a few of them. They form arthritic knots on park benches, immobilised by heat and bad joints. They bristle with A-frames and walking sticks, on lawn inconclusive as a bad toupee. Sprinklers string a web; when they arc too close no-one moves.

Mavis can never understand why senior citizens feel compelled to inhabit public spaces, as if they are gazebos or gas barbeques, as if they too have been donated for the common good. Mavis's irritation stems mainly from the fact that if she and Gwen went out and sat there, they would look just like them: two greying women in Osti dresses. One fat, one thin. One vacantly cheerful, one inexplicably grim. Navigating a long dry day.

When exactly did she get old? Mavis wants to protest about it. Wants to object officially: 'I used to wear pink lipstick, I have tiny feet and autumn russet hair.' But she's not quite sure where to lodge the complaint.

'Better make tracks.'

Mavis waits until her sister has hoisted herself from the armchair, collected the fraying threads of her personality, and descended the stairwell, leaving a fat chug chug of words in her wake. Then Mavis tidies the folds in the rug caused by Gwen's shoes, moves the chair Gwen was sitting in an inch to the right, rinses her teacup and upturns it to dry. Gwen's steps are still shaking the staircase though, rattling the pots in the kitchen, making pictures nervous on the wall. Gwen may have got all the men at church dances but Mavis was the one who was light on her feet. She could move so quietly that people didn't hear her coming. Not until she was right on top of them. Seeing something she shouldn't have seen.

A faint rhythm this one, faint and faraway. Mavis picking dainty steps one in front of the other, wearing the new shoes Frank had bought her, hopscotching over river stones, heels clicking and clacking, following a path beneath a bridge. Dappled light, then dark, the lilt of red dust, dark mud, brown water, as tree shadows shifted in the wind.

Then nothing. Blue veins mapping a journey. To an alien world. The rise and fall of large white breasts, keeping urgent time. With a heartbeat not their own.

Mavis casts a final eye. Making sure no-one has been there. That there are no signs of life. This isn't Mavis Kelly's real home and she won't pretend it is.

chapter 12

It's Back-To Week in the next place. A Tidy Town this, last stop before the big stretch. There are signs everywhere, rosettes and ribbons, a big plastic banner across the town hall: 'Welcome Back.' Not a soul to be seen.

It's neat though, you'd give it that, gutters all spotless, footpaths as if vacuumed, cars all freshly washed. The houses, in rows and rows of equidistance, are low to the ground and exhausted looking, like flat-out dogs. What's going on beyond those curtains and lawn squares, so freshly manicured they seem to have been cut and pasted from a book?

J drives up the main drag, passing the first of three wide verandah pubs on the right. Two are named after green English villages, this in a place where rain rarely falls. Ruth hasn't been here for over fifteen years but would be willing to bet that if she walked into that ladies lounge and peeked into the saloon, she'd still see the same three blokes sitting round a table. Wagering how many times e occurs on a matchbox and maybe about a fly crawling up the wall.

'Happening place.' J's trying to be casual but Ruth knows he's nervous because his knuckles are whitening slightly on the wheel. He watched *Wake in Fright* before they left as a sort of travel briefing and he keeps his eyes down if he has to pass a group of men in the street. Inside the car, he assumes an anthropological disinterest. Like he's David Attenborough on a trip to the zoo.

The park is on the right, the one and only service station on the left. 'Garridges' J calls them, like he calls doonas 'duvets' and says vitamins and yoghurt all wrong. This was the ice-cream place, a Drumstick from the servo then a thermos break on a bench. If it was dinnertime, you might get fish and chips; if it was lunch, a pie and a cream bun. Mostly though it was that wilderness between lunch and dinner, when time just stretched on and on.

You could fire a cannon, as Uncle Frank used to say. Ruth always thought it was the old cannon she was sitting on, ice-cream turning to milk in the sun. Mavis told you not to bite the end off it, she warned you sternly, but you did it anyway and ice-cream dripped all over bare legs. Your bum was gluey with it on the swing seat, it slowed you down on the slippery dip, your hand stuck to the old wooden merry-go-round, one of those that you have to run with round and round to get it going, then jump on fast, heart in mouth.

Thongs lingered stickily on the seesaw when Frank showed you how to walk the plank. But every time you got to the middle of things, where fate hangs in balance, you couldn't do it, you had to retrace your steps.

Frank pointed out the list of dead men on the memorial; you counted them and as he promised there were exactly one hundred and thirty-four. Ruth can't remember what else he told her about the relevance of the cannon, except she had the vague idea Hitler must have got further than she thought. Back in the car legs stuck to vinyl and made a zippery noise when peeled on and off.

'Don't they get bored?' says J, watching a young woman pushing a pram, head down, thongs slapping doggedly, intent on the shopping strip.

Too right, things were fucking boring, one hundred degrees, sometimes a hundred and twenty, sometimes you just stopped counting and the mercury hung, a listless fleck. The TV came on at three and then it was just the test pattern with Frank Sinatra or the Ray Conniff Singers or an instrumental version of a pop song, played over and over to a picture of two gum trees and three cows. At four it was 'Play School', pumped in like foreign water from a place you'd never visited, somewhere where mothers always had pipe-cleaners and the black and white people just kept smiling, on and on.

You lay under the evaporative cooler in a dim grey lounge room, listening to water and ideas percolate. To someone humming tunelessly, to an older cousin perhaps. Bob Dylan, 'Tambourine Man', 'Blowin' in the Wind'.

You watched Mavis watching you watching the test pattern. Paralysed by washing. Flick, crease, fold. Heat made no sound but grew, thick and silent. Like a second skin.

At the Sunrise Motel Ruth remembers country courtesies.

'Back-To Week, eh? Been busy?'

The receptionist pulls her cardigan around her bosom in a way that says Churchgoer. CWA Member. Baker of Sponge Cakes and Coconut Rough.

'Been rushed off our feet.'

Ruth crunches across the empty car park to their room.

'You didn't have to come, you know. I could have done it by myself.'

They are lying in a chenille and seascape room after peas in plum sauce. The Chinese was in a fibro shed tacked onto the back of the pub. It was still light on the street, early for dinner but people always eat early here and anyway, inside the pub it was dark and furry as an armpit, frying smells mixed with old ashtray fug, beer carpet, petrol from the highway, the stink of wet dog. J questioned the waitress on the exact type of bean curd in the stir-fry, the presence of meat stock in the corn soup. Through the archway Ruth could see men lined up at the counter, flannelette elbows, hard eyes under wide hats. They stared back at her, a blank and unflinching gaze.

It was an early opener this place. Uncle Frank used to go in there on trips back from the city; if he'd been driving all night, if there was nothing else open, if he wanted some Stuyvesants and a copy of the *Truth*. It was named after a famous English poet, not that anyone there would know. The frail old man with a face like a child sitting next the jukebox, he wouldn't have known a poet if he fell over one. And the barmaid with her blonde hair in a scaffolding arrangement and eyebrows drawn above where nature intended, she was reading Danielle Steel. And the beer-bellied men around the pool table wouldn't have read books at all, poetry'd be a rhyming joke with a punch line, they knew the name of their National Party member and they didn't want any sacred sites in their backyards.

'It's not as full-on as I thought.' J has his hands folded tragically across his chest. Waiting for the MSG to hit. 'I mean it's not really desert, is it? More like tacky scrub.'

Ruth ponders this for a while, the fastidious way an Englishman can say 'tacky'. How they can make consonants snap to attention, like press-studs. How they can make you feel personally responsible for a lack of camels and hundred degree heat.

'We're not there yet, I told you. After this there's hundreds of miles with nothing in between.'

'Kilometres.'

'They still have miles on those little posts.'

J's complaining about how cold it is in here. The air conditioner's missing a vital knob. So they lie there shivering, listening for city noise in country heat. But there's only the odd slow car in a wide wide street.

'What did you order for the morning?'

'Continental.' That's the nicest, the motel woman told Ruth, nodding her steel-coloured perm. Ruth thought she was right, considering the alternatives, all that grease and dead meat. J's thinking espresso, English marmalade, fresh croissants. But it'll be cold toast, UHD milk and Vegemite if Ruth knows what's what.

'You know this motel thing's for wimps. When we used to drive to the city, we left at four a.m. We drove all night.'

'What on earth for?'

'Don't know. But that's what Uncle Frank always did.'

'No wonder he had a heart attack.'

'A stroke. This time it's a stroke.'

They have sex and it wakes J up, it always does. He's pacing, humming, drumming, eyes fanatical under fluorescent light.

'Why don't we do it then?'

'What?'

'Drive all night.'

'But we've already ordered breakfast and messed up the bed.' Ruth knows country towns, fears their elephantine memories. The way they can look at you sideways when you walk down the street. When you turn to stare back at them, they are already looking the other way.

'Fuck it. They're all in bed watching the tractor ads. Let's do it. Let's go.'

He's excited by the arduousness of it, by Ruth's stories of Uncle Frank at four a.m. How they used to roll out of bed and dress in ragbag layers like Resistance spies. There was clean formica in Mavis's kitchen, curried egg and mock chicken sandwiches in plastic, the comfort of toast burning, the smell of kerosene. Dark pressed in at the windows, porridge steamed. Uncle Frank listened to news by the hour, on the hour, waiting for floods, hurricanes, harbingers of doom. In those years after Mum, you could show him some kids playing on a swingset and he thought about the one who was going to crack its head. Give him a view of the sea and he worried about the lack of a fence. The car was always ailing, the kettle about to fuse, the blackout candle might topple and burn them all to death.

'What about the petrol? There'll be nothing open, remember. Did you bring the oil?'

She nods and nods. Like Frank, she packed the car the night before: spanners, water, oil, maps, a blanket for the cold. In her head she could hear him say, in a way he never talked to her as an adult: 'No, not this one, take that. Don't forget the other.' Out of habit she made up the back seat as a bed, cleverly disguising suitcases with pillows and rugs.

She did this in the same way daughters of certain mothers roll socks and clean baths identically. As if hypnotised by something in the blood.

'We've been up for fifteen hours now, you know. That's almost a whole day.' The enormity of this place excites J. He keeps talking about 'the desert' in inverted commas. He's pulled his baseball cap down low and grim. He looks like a skinny John Wayne.

'How long are we going to stay?'

'Don't know.'

She hasn't told him about that other thing; she keeps meaning to but that little remnant floating up in the water, it's the tip of an iceberg, and she'd have to keep explaining and explaining it, going down and down to the frozen blue roots of it, so far under she would be drowning in things she didn't know. It's a bit like those four blind men with the elephant. All you can hold at any one time is an ear, a trunk, a tail.

They pack the car and do a runner, rolling over motel gravel with headlights on and engine off.

Lying down on the back seat, Ruth has the same feeling that she did coming through the mountains this morning: this is all wrong, it's all back to front, they should have been on the long straight highway when the sun was rising, and if it's night-time now they should be on the winding mountain highway, they should be going the other way. They should be going to the city, for a Christmas holiday at the ex-convent by the sea. It should be dark except for the yellow glare of the odd streetlight, and Mona should be in the back seat, with the boundary between them the groove in the middle where the old bench seat divides, no more, no less. If Ruth's feet crept over, Mona pushed them back with exaggerated malice, digging fingernails in just to show that she was older, her legs were longer, she always ended up with three quarters of the space. If Ruth yelled out and Mavis turned around, Mona smiled sweetly and asked for another lolly, because Ruth was feeling a bit sick.

Ruth hated barley sugars because every time she sucked one it reminded her of the taste of vomiting, the sweetness identical with the nausea, as if they caused it not cured it, those lollies wrapped in gold. At some point after Mavis made her eat one, they'd come up again, in helpless retches, in brown and sugary streams. There was the tang of bitumen and wet grass near the side of the road. Keep your eyes on the road, Mavis used to snap, but that's difficult in the dark. Mona could read in the car but Ruth never could; Mona had a bunch of Archie and Superman comics and she was gobbling them up, they'd never last. Ruth was saving her books for the long straight road, on the homeward journey. *Biggles* was one of them and *Anne of Green Gables* and one of Uncle Frank's called *Reach for the Sky*. She read the war ones to please him but drew the line at his toilet books with the red and gold covers called things like *The Last Gun At Sunset* and *The First Stagecoach West*.

There was one book she always kept hidden under her pillow so Mona wouldn't get it covered in sauce. It was *Jane Eyre* and it belonged to her mother. 'Vonnie Cook' it said on the flypaper with a little smiling face. She stuck her hand down now and again beneath the blanket covering the suitcases on which they were lying and fingered the spine, making out a gold word here or there. It felt substantial and serious, not a paperback but a bound one like a library book. It was a talisman against boredom and the never-endingness of Mona and a long journey to come.

Mona dropped off. Mavis snored. But Ruth kept pinching herself when her eyes started to droop. She imagined she had a matchstick propping each lid. Uncle Frank used to joke about that, about how it was the only thing that kept him awake. Sometimes he used to stick a couple there with his eyes wide and clownish and mouth open in mock horror, trying to keep them up. She didn't know he was joking, she thought he really did stick matches in his eyes. Because the idea was no stranger than some of the other things Uncle Frank did. Like suddenly popping his dentures out, pink and glistening and looking like those fake electric ones that chatter, at the dinner table, right onto his plate. Or making a coin go in his mouth, through his brain and come out his ear. Or wrapping a cigarette in a hankie and tying it in a knot and stamping on it, then with a flourish unwrapping and smoking it, the Stuyvesant a bit wrinkled but miraculously whole.

On those long trips Uncle Frank kept a match permanently in the corner of his mouth, chewing on it, the end waving, up and down. You could judge his mood by the angle of that match. It stuck straight up when he grinned, lay slack when he frowned, fell out of his mouth in spitty splinters when there was a roo or a pothole or floodwater blocking the road. But after Mum disappeared he just let it hang there, a habit he couldn't break but couldn't be bothered to observe. The match stuck out grimly. Pointing straight ahead.

At the top of the mountains, your ears popped and blocked and you had to keep yawning to keep them clear. Frank leant forward, his profile grim and lipless, shoulders hunched over the wheel. There might be black ice, there might be fog, there could be hailstones, a semi might career brakeless down the hill. In the faint glow of a dashboard, Frank looked lonely, trapped in his green hemisphere, that prison of flickering bars. Full or Empty, Slow or Fast, Hot or Cold. A sickly radiance infected him, turned his face pea green. He was drowning in phosphorescence. A planet where only he could breathe.

Even now, with J driving, Ruth pinches herself to stay awake. Through tired bloodshot she sees a sky and distant constellations, and she's confused about direction, old miles and new kilometres, journeys multiplying like stars. She is thinking, then and now, about infinity, about how Uncle Frank once explained it and about that big empty mirror feeling which, like thirst after running, seems to have no end. She imagines they are going home, that they are going the wrong way. That moon and stars and telegraph poles are moving, not her. All this arrogance is delicious, like a strange-tasting drug she has invented, and the feeling keeps getting bigger and gathering form. The telegraph poles on a mission to their horizon, sky wheeling on a pivot of stars. The car rocks and turns on a lazy spiral and death if it came would be incidental, swirling and languid, a soft descent through fog and night.

'There's the lights of Lithgow,' said her mum once, on a trip her and Uncle Frank and Ruth took to the city, and they craned as the car came up the hill, on their way to Sydney and ice-creams and the old convent by the sea. Ruth saw the lights, laid out like a twinkling carpet, 'like jewels on a black carpet' Mum said softly, tossing to Ruth another of those images which she gave like rare and precious stones. To embed in memory and shine painfully on.

Then the car swerved, the lights were gone. In the dark, Ruth could only see Frank, crouched over the steering wheel in the glow of his terrible instruments. A symmetry of hand and foot the only thing between him and the sheer spin of space.

J keeps asking and asking, into unswerving blackness, until she wants to shoot him, 'How far to go?'

chapter 13

'Had to move him, Mrs Kelly, Had a rush on those east wing beds.'

Piles epidemic was it. The way Matron is sticking those overstarched bosoms out, she's in danger of taking out someone's eye. 'West wing'll be nicer in the winter, you know, Mrs Kelly. Gets a bit more sun.'

As if it wasn't the height of summer. As if Frank hadn't had enough sun to last him a lifetime. As if he will still be here next winter. As if there's an east wing anyway, like this was a ruddy metropolis and not an old shack of a hospital, with Frank stuck out on a weatherboard verandah in a makeshift bed. In Mavis's day it would have been used as a sleepout for shearers. In Mavis's opinion it was somewhere you wouldn't put a dog.

Gwen and Mavis walk slowly up corridors of dull antiseptic gleam, bottlenecked behind old Mrs Finlay with her stale Morning Coffees and her endless cups of tea. All day the old timber building has been stoking its hothouse smells of boiled cabbage, old sweat, dry rot. By now, at evening visiting, the smell is enough to make you sick. Mavis used to volunteer here before she got married, arranging flowers and delivering tea and biscuits, and everything, the busy squeak of Grosbys, the reheated steak and kidney, the way venetians scourge sun in stripes from dawn to dusk, leaving pale scars on the lino floor, it all takes her back. Mavis used to be Chairwoman for The Committee To Save Our Hospital. They saved it alright but then the government refused to do it up.

On either side, men like Frank are tucked into even rows of whiteness. Raw-hipped nurses squeak and bustle, sheets crack like whips in capable hands. But despite the show of cleanliness, Mavis knows the lino here is older than Mona. She can't help but think of the infections breeding and multiplying. In the grouted cracks of bathrooms. In sour nests of dirty sheets.

'He's looking brighter,' Gwen pronounces. 'Tad more colour in the cheeks.'

Mavis knows better but can't be bothered to disagree. Can't be bothered to explain what Gwen, if she wasn't a sandwich short of a picnic, should have been able to see. How the texture of a day, even a day just over, is already tipping and draining through all these mistakes and spaces, through the old glass louvres and fibro walls. The scent of well-wisher flowers, cut grass, clean sheets, brown skin. All that will remain tomorrow are some neat flowerbeds, an orderly silence of paths.

With much crackling of paper and heavy breathing, Gwen unwraps the grapes she bought at the Marconis. They are brown and squishy from the heat of her big body and how on earth Frank is supposed to eat them Mavis can only guess. Fossicking around in her carry-all, Gwen then unearths that everlasting knitting and a book. The breasts on the cover are swollen with embossment, bursting joyfully up and out.

'This should perk him up.' Gwen remains staunch in her conviction that illness is a state of mind, that there is nothing that a little 'perking up' won't fix. Of course it never worked in her case but it is in Gwen's nature to keep hoping while the last horse bolts home. Every visit for the past two weeks she's read to Frank. Thrillers, romances, jungle epics, sagas of love, death and pestilence, lavatory westerns—anything to stir the blood.

Mavis thinks Gwen may as well read Frank the instructions for lighting the stove.

For days now Frank has been more absence than presence, beating with the clean green rhythm of machines. His face is unmarked by calamity. The muscles even now look ready to give that lipless smile. His hands, neat and passionless, lie priestlike on the sheet.

Frank is like an urgent telegram left unopened on Mavis's occasional table. He flutters slightly in the breeze from her open door. From being the text which ran through the heart of things he has become the space in which nothing much can breathe.

This space is familiar, it has always been hers. Vegetables chopped, meals cooked, towels hung; the boredom counted, folded, put away. But Frank was there, running through everything like a jugular she never knew she had. Now it is as if she had woken up and found that someone, hours, days, maybe years ago, had opened one of her veins. It welled and welled, filling forty years' worth of Frank's garden buckets, overflowing from the laundry sink, bubbling out the Whirlpool. Pooling in a turgid river right out her front door.

It started after Von disappeared. Frank withdrew and took all the air with him. When he came in late in the evening, instead of kissing Mavis, swinging Mona to his shoulders and retrieving his dried-up dinner from an upturned plate, he just walked straight through them like they weren't even there. Like Mavis and Mona and Ruth were a series of mop water puddles on the floor.

Ruth he ignored more thoroughly than anyone else. She followed Frank around that garden like a little afterthought, placing her body in an eyeline which would admit nothing except the absence of Von. Once she even stowed away under the tarpaulin in his truck. Frank just picked her up and set her down on the path. Like Ruth was a load of rubbish he'd decided not to take to the tip.

He took early retirement. He wouldn't work in the shop. Of course Mavis had to do everything by herself. But she couldn't get angry. In any case the target had moved. Where Frank's big belly and bad food habits and what her mother used to call 'lack of provenance' had been, there was just a hat-shaped shadow on the ground.

When Mavis tried to argue with Frank about all the long-service leave and pension pay he was missing—'They were things you fought for. Now you're just going to leave it? Let everyone else reap the rewards?'—Frank said nothing. He brought home thirty years of work history in a cardboard box. He spent all day out driving in his truck. He traced the town roads as if they were new to him, driving north–south, then east–west, then north–south again. Like a man trying to find a compass point unknown

to any map. As if Von had just been walking and walking
all this time and he would come across her somewhere in
a place or direction now forgot.

Sometimes Frank didn't come home at all. And the trips
were no longer confined to Christmas; he took off on
weekends, at midnight, even on Sundays when she had the
baked dinner ready; it just sat there, her without the heart
to eat it and the girls melting away from the hard edges
of the table, becoming part of what was gone. It swirled
and roared and imploded, that silence. It sucked at the
space between four walls. Mavis sat pinned by a hole at
her centre. She watched countless hot dinners relax to
brown grease.

One day Frank came home from a trip which had lasted
three days, during which time Mavis considered calling the
police. But her hand hovered over the phone for what
seemed a lifetime; it looked so white and nerveless, bones
and veins so shockingly real. She was mortal, objects
were precarious, things could rot. Even the hard under-
pinnings of her now gone so friable she couldn't make the
fingers work.

Then the front door banged. Frank threw his hat at
the hook in the hallway—she hated that, he always missed,
the vase of flowers on the hallstand trembling and jiggling,
nearly, not quite, falling over—and yelled, before locking
himself in the bedroom: 'We're selling the house.'

Through the keyhole Mavis learnt that Frank wanted
to go and live in the caravan. Now whoever heard of
someone doing that? No-one decent *lived* in a caravan,
except for at Christmas holidays, as a sort of cubby-house
away from home. Then, you made do with all the little
inconveniences; the tiny sinks and miniscule fridges and

the plastic tea-cups and the lack of proper serviettes. But no-one proper *lived* in a caravan. Caravans were for ratbags like Wally Thompson who was probably holed up in one with a prostitute this minute, or wasters like Trevor who'd gone bush in his old Viscount, living off beer and bully beef out of a tin. Caravans were for Settlement no-hopers. For people who didn't know the difference between a fireplace and a lounge room floor.

Mavis saying all this only made Frank more adamant. So they packed up everything and Mavis cleaned and scrubbed and hiccuped, and a young couple with a husband in electrics moved into the house on Bauxite Street. Frank sold all his concrete swans and garden ornaments at a garage sale on the front lawn. Mavis was mortified. She watched from behind the venetians while friends, neighbours, acquaintances carried off the Waltzing Matilda garden setting, the stone kookaburras, the terracotta marsupials, even Frank's new steel-tipped spade. They kept a solicitous front but Mavis knew what they would be saying later over coffee down the new 'beestro'. 'We always knew that Frank Kelly was a bit queer.'

The girls had left by then. Mavis had sent Mona to a tarted-up funny farm on the town outskirts—she'd set fire to one thing too many. The school canteen was one thing, Mr McGregor's shed while he was still in it, that was the final straw. And after many sleepless nights and sharp letters to That Trevor to remember his responsibilities, to face up and be a man, Mavis had taken the bit between her teeth. She'd sent Ruthie to live at the old Goddard place in the city. Mother's ex-convent was now, by the expiry date set in stone in Mother's will, a boarding school run by Mother's favourite nuns. Typical, that, when Mavis could have done with the money. As usual, Mavis was the mug.

Truth was, she'd thought Frank might get better if Ruth wasn't there. Ruth reminded him of Von. She even looked like her as she got older. Same hair, same eyes, same snarl. Ruth had slammed the City Express window down on Mavis's fingers when she'd tried to say goodbye from the train.

In a last-ditch effort Mavis tried to talk Frank into taking his birdbaths with him.

'Remember, Frank? You made these. The sparrows came down in the mornings. You used to give them the day-old Tip Top from the shop. Remember how you found those old forty gallon drums out in the lane? We filled them up with hose water. One of them leaked. You welded it with Mr McGregor's blowtorch. Ruthie sat on a nail. Vonnie helped you paint them and that can of paint spilt on the path. See? Stain's still there.'

'Won't be any room.'

Well that was one thing they did have out there. Too much of it, the wind howling in emptiness, making it seem even more hollow if that was possible, water and dust stretching on like a funereal dirge. Sleepy Hollow during the winter was deserted, the vans all locked, the gas and water connections bolted by the council against thieves. Wind off water was like a knife. Mavis had no car to go visiting. Even if she had a car, she'd never learnt how to drive.

Mavis squeezed a lifetime of crockery into a kitchen the size of a cupboard. She tried to fit all her ornaments on two plyboard shelves. Things which had seemed prosperous for a caravan, well-made, solid as a temporary thing can be, sagged under the weight of everyday life.

The rest of their things Frank stored in the new shed he built on the other side of the lake. Mavis wasn't allowed to go up there, according to Frank. He'd taken all his stuff out of the old shed in the middle of the night and driven it up there, in secret. He spent all day there, from dawn till dusk. If she was lucky he came back for the evening meal. Mavis stayed in the caravan. There was nowhere else to go. Sometimes she cried. Sometimes she just sat, not moving, with her hands in her lap. After the tiny kitchen was cleaned and the toy garden weeded, there was nothing else to do. In the fold-out bed at night she breathed out as Frank breathed in, waiting for clocks to chime and suns to rise. In his dreams she watched him thrash and mutter, arms and fists arguing with air. By sunrise fists unclenched, muscles uncoiled, dreams collapsed once more inside his head. By morning Frank was closed over and rigid as a plaster saint.

He had his heart attack out in that shed. It was pure luck that Mavis found him; used to his absences by then, there was no reason she should have gone down there at all. But the gas in the cylinder, which Frank was usually so meticulous about, had run totally dry. She'd waited and waited with potatoes peeled and sausages turning to sweat on the sideboard; she couldn't even boil the kettle for a cup of tea. She waited for hours, until she couldn't stand it any more. All those years of anger rose up in her and, pushing her feet into the old pair of Frank's mine boots she'd taken to wearing—no-one would have believed it had they seen her, Mavis Kelly of the shiny pumps and black patent leather, wearing steel toes like a builder's navvy—she clumped off down the path beside the lake.

She knew something was wrong as soon as she heard the shed door swinging in the wind. In the old days, back at home, Frank always kept the door locked from the inside, even when the temperature cracked the century and his face turned beetroot and the sweat ran off him in streams. The door clanged like a bell tolling. It echoed through hollows. It bounced tinnily off dry earth.

Mavis pushed the door a little, afraid of Frank's newly vicious anger, that it would explode at her out of the gloom. But in the end it was her fault not Frank's. It was as if her own anger had risen electrically from the sharp click and clatter of the old Mavis and been allowed to travel, sheeting through thin dry air. Homing on the metal of Frank's shed.

Frank was slumped over his workbench with his shirt off; he'd grown so thin by then. At that angle, the knots on his backbone poked out, like fingers turned on their sides. All pointing at her. The scars, the pointing fingers, Frank's sideways listing hat. Everything put Mavis in the wrong.

'Time, ladies.'

This is the third time Matron has put her head round the verandah door. In and out, in and out she pops, like the kerchiefed half of a Fine Weather/Foul Weather pair. Gwen's still droning, with no regard to commas or chapters or full stops; words just piled up one on top of the other with dead weight and dull inflection, like primary school blocks. She finished her bodice ripper a while ago and embarked on the Kon-Tiki expedition. For the last hour Mavis has been marooned with her in the South Seas. Even if Frank hadn't had his heart attack and then a stroke, he'd be well out to it by now.

'Ladies! Most definitely time.'

Sister cocks one eyebrow and wiggles it up and down. Mavis believes these appendages could have rivalled Mr McGregor's before Mona singed them off.

Mavis tells Matron, 'We'll see you tomorrow then.' As if Matron didn't know that already, as if they won't be there tomorrow and the day after and the day after too. Frank shows no signs of recovery or imminent departure, just keeps hanging on by electrical threads. But Matron says, 'Very well then, Mrs Kelly. See you soon.'

This time though Mavis thought she sensed something. Just a small curve of the lip, half a raised eyebrow, that's all. But it meant Matron, like every other gossip in town, had read that little item on page fifteen of the *Daily Truth*.

On their way back to the flat they have to walk past the police station. Mavis even stops, with one hand on the glass door, below the sign warning you to take off your motorbike helmet before approaching front desk. Gwen's still rattling on about grapes and shopping centres and how much that nurse, third daughter of the second Finlay boy, has grown. Rita Finlay has three grandchildren and is about to get her long-service leave, but to Gwen she is still that little slip of a thing behind the counter at Moore's.

Mavis tries to lift a foot to go forward. But she can't make herself go in.

Only now, after years of mild curiosity, she realises she didn't even stop to look what was in Frank's shed. But if she had, she would have been none the wiser. There were only the dismembered parts of Frank's inventions, cogs and wheels and bits of wire he was slowly pulling to pieces and re-ordering in old ice-cream containers, first by this criteria then another, like a man rendering life into its constituent parts.

But all Frank had was the old black handbag of Maudie's. The picture of the crow man. The little gold cross. And it wasn't enough.

chapter 14

The road is black and straight. It collapses to the pinpoint from which a long journey recedes. The earth isn't red though, not yet, it's too early. That colour comes from an equal resistance between earth and sky and sun. Then light starts to twinge.

Through the rear window Ruth can see it, breaking in a bloody glow. A straight line describing a straight horizon, straighter than anywhere else in the world. It arrives with surgical precision, north, south, east, west. The flush seems to come from inside the earth itself. Rising pale yellow, then pink, then orange-gold, then brighter, until the ground is a saucy vermillion, threaded with cold blue scrub.

Even sunrise here is a spaghetti Western: big and overblown.

'Well this is the desert. Or as good as it gets.'

But J isn't listening. He's busy calculating miles to minutes, kilometres to litres, litres to gallons, kilometres back to miles.

'We've come exactly nine hundred and twenty-six K since yesterday. We've averaged a hundred K an hour. That means there's only ninety K to go.'

What would have seemed a huge journey to J back in the city is now just around the corner. He thinks he's Burke and Wills. He doesn't know what happened to them; he's only got to chapter three in *The History of Explorers—Men Who Stood Apart*.

'You said it was seven hundred miles give or take. That's over a thousand K. In a day and a half. That's pretty cool.'

All night old-fashioned mileposts have flashed by fast in headlights. They are still there, looking smaller and more overgrown in daylight, only a few letters and obsolete distances peeking above the scrub. Frank used to play a game with these, to keep him awake. Ruth leant on his shoulder, trying to guess. How many countries start with those letters, how many roos will we see before the next one, how many telegraph poles between the twenty-mile marks. But J ignores them. He's on the lookout for big metric ones in glow in the dark green. These only measure modern distances between major cities, big chunks of Australia ticked off in a blink. As if the act of travelling doesn't signify. As if the bush is an aside bracketed by beaches. J's state of the art speedo spits out old miles like pips.

'Jesus! What the hell is that?'

He's spotted an emu. Ruth feels redeemed. Yesterday he thought it was really funny that they had roadside signs with camels on them. The only signs he knows are the ones in the city which show the forking of freeways, the meeting of roads with other roads. There's only one road out here. Only two directions you can take. Of course, they had to stop at every single one. Their roll of holiday film will be mostly of J standing in the shadow of a yellow sign with a black camel on it. Both in solemn silhouette. Below him, red earth. Above, blue sky. J grinning widely, as if all this was a theme park built especially for him.

He pulls up far too suddenly on the verge. Gravel spatters like dangerous rain. Ruth presses the heel of her hand against the windshield. It's just reflex. She's not even sure what it's supposed to achieve.

'Back in a sec. Get the camera. Don't forget to wind it on.'

He's off and out, sprinting over scrub.

She should have told him it's no big deal. They grow them out here like wheat. They use some for feather dusters or cushion stuffing, and sell the rest to the sort of city person who wears a microfibre suit. Country people are beef and lamb people, they wouldn't eat emu in a pink fit. But if city people are silly enough to chew on it and drip exotic sounding sauces over it and pay through the nose for it, well more fool them.

Dawn has reached a crescendo now, a cartoon of Crayola colours, variations on a florid theme. J recedes against this, looking a bit like what he's chasing, all skinny legs and gangling joints. Of course the emu runs the other way. It rocks along the horizon like its on a carousel. Battery-fed, it seems less authentic, almost obscene. Like breeding dinosaurs for dinner. Like archaeological steak.

'Did you see it? Did you? What a bizarre looking thing.' He's panting and flushed and bright eyed and enthusiastic. 'Look. I nearly touched it. See? A feather fell off.' He turns it this way and that, like he's found the kneebone of the Missing Link. Then he files it away with the rest of his collection: jam jars of sand from Australian beaches, flotsam from Australian roadsides, a tea towel with a pumpkin scone recipe on it, an Australiana spoon. He's even got an Opera House which upturns to an ashtray and a coat-hanger cleverly disguised as the Sydney Harbour Bridge.

As they come in on the south road, dawn colours dying back to red, J is still laughing. This time it's at the street names which are starting to pop up. He's laughing at the sheer literal-mindedness of it, at the plodding doggedness which results in a street called Zinc. Ruth tells him that out here having no imagination is a blessing in disguise.

Besides, the street names are a comfort. They mean shopping trips into town, a pie and cake for after. Lime spiders, bike rides with thorns sticking out your tyre. Chlorine and hot concrete, a bob's worth of cobbers at the baths. She opens her mouth to tell him about it. But these things might lose gravity falling into bright modern air.

'And what may I ask is *that*?' J sounds enraged in a very English sort of way.

It is fairly impressive, Ruth has to admit. She thought she'd be used to it, that it would have got smaller as she got taller, that it would become a manageable disaster, just a big pile of dirt. But there is no hope of putting this into perspective at all.

The slag doesn't just appear. It looms incontrovertibly out of flatness, an alternate horizon the colour of blood. When you drive along the road which runs beside it, the sun is extinguished like a wick. This new sense of scale is shocking. Like putting your thumbnail next to an ant.

'This is it?' J is incredulous, peering under the sun visor at the shadow growing along the bonnet. He stares so long he nearly collects the car in front. 'This is what you brought me to see?'

J doesn't believe in such ugliness. Not somewhere called The Country. Where he comes from The Country means brooks not creeks and meadows not paddocks and people in smocks chewing straw.

Ruth says she doesn't know why it's been left there, now nearly all the mines are closed, why it doesn't crumble, why someone doesn't do something, why a green paper hasn't been written, an environmental subcommittee formed. Maybe because it's both ugly and spectacular, and because it reminds the people at the church fetes and the club dinner dances and the bowls comp of a Tuesday that there is a seam of real life somewhere. Running just beneath the skin.

The slag is sheer scope and zero gravity. It is black bans and McCarthy, it is asbestos and mine cave-ins and BHP. Those heavy brows frown over these neat certainties. They make a nonsense of this obsessive geometry, this foursquare logic of streets.

'Hey, get a load of this. I held off on those tea towels. I didn't buy that didgeri thing. But we have just *got* to take this home.'

J's holding up a dead flower arrangement he found in the bathroom. This one has Little Bo Peep amid a glade of tortured wattle, all tied up with a pink velvet bow. Someone has actually knitted all the rosebuds. Individually. By hand.

'Imagine.' He's collapsed on the lounge as if winded, turning the thing side to side. 'Imagine someone thinking, right. Now I'll sit down and crochet a sheep.'

The flat they booked down the tourist centre has a lot of these dead flower things. Taking perfectly reasonable flora and embalming it is a hobby reaching epidemic proportions. Or maybe it's just another of those secret handshakes. You're Not From Here.

While J disembowels the thing, trying to find out what makes this place tick, Ruth wanders aimlessly, picking up ornaments, setting them down. On the coffee table are lots of pamphlets exorting you to 'get out and about'. Which is not such a bad idea. It's like every house Ruth's ever rented, the fake wood veneer and swirly carpets, murder to a hangover, and that stale wet wool smell that greets you as you wrestle with an out of plumb door. It is the smell of people merely passing through, leaving an archaeology of coffee stains and dead silverfish and telephone bills that someone should have paid. Everything says: this is not your home.

She turns on the TV; there are only two channels, a cooking show using exotic vegetables you probably can't buy here and 'Play School', with people wearing ice-cream container hats. Why do they think all mothers have egg cartons? Why do they think all fathers smoke a pipe? The picture dies to a pinpoint then disappears. After she's read all the pamphlets and examined the bookcase—an ancient *Cleo*, the *Yates Gardening Guide*, a history of BHP, 1974— and flushed the toilet and tried the taps and tasted the water—mineral taste, almost salty, gives you ulcers, have to take Berocca and eat lots of Vegemite toast—there's nothing else to do.

J's gone to sleep suddenly, falling sideways, like someone turning out a light. He'll be asleep for hours now. Nothing wakes him, not even a cold washer down the neck.

It's quiet. Too quiet. Just the faint hum of a car, approaching, passing, backfiring. Then taking a long while to disappear.

That afternoon feeling is gathering. It must be avoided at all costs. It's a culmination of sun slatting redly through venetians, dust rising to hang suspended, the wet-jumper whiff of shampooed carpet and the zing of Pine O Cleen threading everything like a nagging voice. It's that old lady feeling of sitting inside on a bright day with all the blinds down so the sun won't fade the carpet. Listening to a radio burble cricket scores in a bedroom down the hall.

Maybe she could go for a walk. Isn't that what you do here, on suddenly empty afternoons? Then she remembers the heat. It's cool in here but it's stinking outside; you can feel it when you put your face up against the wall. At this time of year it's thirty degrees even in the early morning, and when it cracks the old-fashioned century, children drag themselves slowly home from school. They weave like tiny brown fish through heat haze, through sprinklers stringing a buffalo grass park. The rest of the day stretches ahead like a burning footpath to be travelled in bare feet.

Until you are lost in your own dream of it. Heat disconnecting one thing from another. Sweat sliding words from their sentences. Until there is just one thick silence and nothing to say.

From the flat's front verandah, leaning out over the railing, Ruth can see the intimate pink bits on the top of people's heads. Nobody wears a hat now, not any more. They look vulnerable and silly, those little fontanelles. She imagines it, carefully, spit stringing down to arrive slyly on the jiggly hair partings between pigtails, on the freckled bald patches of the men.

She doesn't do it of course. It's just something to tease yourself with, like imagining what would happen if you took off all your clothes and ran down the aisle in the middle of Mass. When Mavis packed her off to that boarding school in Sydney, Ruth used to spend all the Feast Days and Palm Sundays and those endless trips to Confession imagining it. In detail. Jaws sagging open, hair curling clockwise, tongues lolling slack. It was the quietness, the reverence, that did it. All those church ladies with lace triangles perched like doilies on freshly rollered curls. She used to have to hook her feet under the pew rail, just in case it all got too much.

She's got a headache now. After the gloom of the flat, the noonday light out here is like a blow to the head. Floorboards, the outdoor table, even the broom handle, everything faded back to bone. But the verandah has nice old wrought-iron railings and floor to ceiling windows you can walk through, which someone might throw elegantly open to an evening breeze. But they wouldn't. Not here. Too much dust.

This was probably the top storey of one of the town's endless array of pubs. They were all called Duke of this or Admiral that, or something geological, and there was one on every third corner, regular as a hiccups attack. This town had a pub for every hundred and fifty people, a useless fact she's stored up for no good reason at all. There were a stream of them, these odd-shaped little statistics. Least annual rainfall, most iron ore tonnes, first place to have the basic wage. All trying to define this place from peculiar angles. Chipping away at it with spirit levels and speed-ometers and rule of thumb.

You can see the whole length of the main street from up here. It runs straight, as straight and uninterrupted as it would appear on any map. To the north there's the old Moore's building, now an art gallery, and the row of shops where the shoe store used to be. But instead of a milkbar and a newsagent and a fish and chip place, there's a Ye Olde cafe and a 7-11 and the head office of Timbuktu Tours. To the south there's what used to be Simpsons, now a museum for famous rocks. The fake bullnose awning is a meticulous copy of the real one that used to be there before.

On the strip of street which used to house the Girl Guides, the Masonic Temple and that weird religious shop which sold glow in the dark saints, they've built a Red Rooster. This is a first. When Ruth lived here there was Giuseppe's run by that inexhaustible reservoir of Marconis, and there was the Chinese out south. That was it. When J asked the woman at the tourist centre about vegetarian restaurants, she smiled broadly and handed him two vouchers for free chicken and chips.

It smells different too. Instead of the usual heat and dust and truck exhaust which defined the main street, all she can smell now is bread.

The flat sits right above the bakery on the corner where J stopped to buy rolls on the way in. This is new too, part of a big chain from the city. They've taken over all the old corner bread shops which were all known as The Baker, no matter which one you went to; Ruth used to think that man really got around. They don't call them that any more of course; they say in a proud sort of way, 'I'm off to the

Hot Bread Shop' just like city people do. The women promise each other 'cappacheenos' with a little thrill in their voices, as if that in itself is something to do.

The girls behind the counter in the bakery wear little red hats. They have name tags on bright yellow coats. One is called Jasmine, the other two both Danielles. When Ruth grew up here everyone was named after a saint. Unless you were 'foreign' and then you were called Giuseppe or Magdalena or Mario, of course, if you were a Marconi from the fruit or veg. Danielle and Danielle and Jasmine have bright round faces and matching blue eyeshadow and big gaps between their two front teeth. They say, over and over 'Can I help yew?' in their flat country vowels. Every time the door opens they say it, like the buzzer is hard-wired to their brains. Ruth wanted to say, 'No, not really', to see if they'd spring a sprocket, blow a memory bank, wave their arms about like the robot in 'Lost in Space'.

For some undefined reason, she dearly wanted to slap those girlish faces, with their nasal twangs and blue mascara and mushroom cloud perms. All topped off with so much hair hardware, it must be a joke. Scrunchies which could pick up radio emissions, slides with dead flowers and glitter on them, babies' breath going feral on the bridesmaids who emerge at intervals from the hairdresser next to the bakery, giggling and girdled. Followed closely by mothers brainachingly curled.

Under the scent of bread, she can smell it even now, even from up here. Heady bursts of Taft, wafting up from Hair We Go. It reminds Ruth of Mavis. That's why she'd like to set fire to a few perms.

There are only two things which haven't changed. The flatness. Not much they can do about that. And the light.

So clean and big and fat. As if in the city you are looking at everything through a faint grey fog, then you come out here and someone turns the contrast up. In memories it is the light which articulates, which gives the ordinary that supernatural glow. It can render objects both stark and substantial. Make them heavy and solid as certain facts.

The universe is infinite. The sky is blue. The earth is round. But this earth is flat.

The grand opening of the Red Rooster is the lead story in the *Daily Truth*. The headline says RED ROOSTER STORE OPEN. There's a picture of the mayor cutting the ribbon. He's eating a drumstick. They are still having problems with typesetting; the foundations were 'pored' some time in early November and the Mayor was immensely 'ploud'.

They've stuck the article on page fifteen, way back near the crossword and the netball results and the column for the overseas news. This is where they put earthquakes in Chile and new US presidents, next to pictures of octogenarians hanging on grimly for their letter from the Queen. And it's tiny. Just a little box at the bottom of the page.

LAKE FIND STILL A MYSTERY says the headline. There's a picture of a policeman but he looks too up-to-date. All the policemen here used to look like extras from 'Division Four'.

'Investigations are still continuing,' intones Detective Constable Someone Or Other. Mrs Someone Else relates how her husband snagged the thing with his boat. Some mention of the old rigmarole about the lake, how no-one knows where it goes to or comes from, theories by some professor from the CSIRO. 'In 1952 a prehistoric fish was found, perfectly preserved.' Secret underground caverns and irrigating the desert and the possibility of vast underwater seas. They used to trot that out when Ruth was a kid. You can almost see the dust rising off the professor, from his grainy tweed-pattern coat. From a creaky distance of twenty years, he explains the mummifying effects of thick subterranean mud.

And that's it. No sly mutterings about Von and Frank, no invisible taint to it, that touch of the tar. No sly rumours threaded like fishing hooks between the lines. Maybe they've wrung all the juice out of it. Maybe it's not 'done' any more. After all they've got one whole wall down the tourist centre devoted to bark paintings and desert artists and digging implements. Now they're moving into manchester: you can even eat your dinner off the Dreaming now.

The tourist centre is now the Centre for Regional Tourism. With a design 'based on the entrance to the Louvre. In Paris. France.' The main exhibition there, towering over the dot art tea towels, is called The Line of Lode. On modern display panels there are lifesize shots of miners looking grim and heroic, trudging from 1890 to 1980 and back again around the walls. When J saw it he got really excited. He's 'into' miners, he says. He's never actually met one. The closest he's come is a BHP documentary on TV. He strode around with his legs a little wider apart than necessary, thumbs hooked through his belt. Ruth followed, skimming at will. First this. Last that. Tallest, deepest, biggest, widest. Least lives lost.

'They must be quite groovy really. I mean, all the strikes and stuff. Did you know this was the first place to have a basic wage?'

Bassick. That's how you say it. Bassick, but only in front of wage.

J looked so excited she didn't have the heart to tell him. This shiny even flow of history, it's just new bitumen over old slag. It was true, it was real, it was even admirable, but it was just the tip of things. Beneath the smooth tide which made events pull cleanly in one direction, there was a dank wilderness called Doing The Right Thing. Below those hard-faced miners were the people no-one mentioned. Except when they tripped over them in the street.

J's still asleep, still with his boots on and still wearing his hat. Like he doesn't quite trust this place and might have to do a runner at any time. Ruth draws the blinds. The light dies to a nylon-orange glow. She goes to find the White Pages and some shrapnel for the phone.

She's going to start at the bottom. First Dad, then Mavis. Maybe Mona, if she can find the number for the town funny farm. At least Mona might blurt everthing out, just for a lark. The main thing will be to start with the foot soldiers, work up to the tanks. Only after she's pulled all this into something unforgiving will she tackle Uncle Frank.

chapter 15

Dip, drip, roll. Mavis is making lamingtons. Sun slants yellow as buttercake through the kitchen window, as if Mavis is a mother in a Golden Book, a Virgin in a grotto, a haloed saint in a Station of the Cross. As if she is still, after all these years, sitting demurely under fake stained glass in her wedding photo and O'Donnell the photographer is painting in his meticulous, too-buttery rays.

Mavis always bakes of a Saturday, has done for many years. She still does it, even now, even when there is no-one to eat the things, even now the girls are gone and no-one in their right mind does their own baking and Mavis Kelly is no longer instrumental in the CWA. Even when Frank's mouth is taped shut with surgical plastic and he eats through a tube in his nose.

Three times, swirl, swirl, swirl, then turn the pot thrice and wait for three minutes exactly. Three Hail Marys for a misdemeanour, three decades for a grey-coloured sin. Mavis has lived a Trinity-shaped life. But where on earth do you put the tea leaves when you have no garden? Mavis hovers with a wet clump of them in newspaper, in the second floor flat above Marconi's. Everything here smells like slowly rotting fruit.

Gwen has already hoovered up four of them. She eats them nearly as fast as Mavis can make them, she oohs and ahs and she gobbles, brown icing smeared like crooked lipstick on her big pink mouth. Coconut drifts and hovers. It's all over the carpet, it freckles the arms of Frank's favourite chair.

'What did you have for *your* Christmas dinner, Mavis? We get a turkey with all the trimmings out at the home. And sixpence in the pudding. Remember how Frank used to make 'em go in and out his ear?'

It takes all Mavis's restraint not to rush over and slap Gwen across the face. Sitting there like a lump of porridge in Frank's Jason recliner, which when he first bought it didn't have a worn patch where Frank's head should be or that criss-cross of electrician's tape bandaging cracks in the vinyl arms. Back at Bauxite Street it was polished and shiny and had pride of place in front of the TV. He used to demonstrate it proudly to any visitor, the way the back tipped skyward from a cunningly hidden lever and the way the little footrest popped out.

After Frank had his heart attack, and she made arrangements to rent this flat—Frank had taken the money from the house sale and hidden it, no amount of tears and shouting would make him tell her where it was—Frank just sat slumped in that chair by the window, looking past her to the TV. He sat all day, every day, oblivious to everything that used to make him jump up and dig for stray coins down the side: Mr Whippy's creaky 'Greensleeves', the hooter shrieking shift end and pub opening, the milkman giving his 'hey ho' down below. Frank, a man who was always doing, planning, digging and sowing, his hand rarely without a hammer or a shovel or a saw, put all his hats away. He let his hands drop empty. Let coppers collect like dust down beside the lounge.

When Frank had his stroke, the same day they found that thing in the lake, at first she didn't realise. It seemed the stiff body, the head slumped, the hand cradling a heavy forehead, was the way he'd been sitting for days, weeks, maybe years.

Perhaps Mavis will give the rest of the lamingtons to the church fete committee for the Save Our Cathedral Roof stall. Perhaps Ruth and that boyfriend will eat some when they come to visit, if they are polite enough, if Ruth returns the phone call which Mavis has been polite enough to make. If not, Mavis will store them carefully in a Coronation tin between interleaved layers of greaseproof and then forget they are there. She'll find them months from now, when she needs the tin for something else. Hard as rocks. Bearing little resemblance to the soft bits of sweetness she used to lay at Frank's feet, always on a special gilt and pink roses plate. Then she'll throw them out.

It doesn't matter. It's the rhythms which comfort, as do the neat bowls of icing and coconut, the wire tray set ready on its tea towel, the smell of fresh cake. Dip, drip, roll. Mavis keeps to a remembered cadence, to a rhythm written somewhere in her blood.

Mother used to hold a piece of cake above that icing bowl for what seemed like hours, turning it this way and that in the sunlight, looking for missing corners, crumbling edges, unacceptable mistakes. The cake barely touched those elegant fingers, as if it was not the food Mother was interested in but the art of manufacture, that secret affinity between colour and size and shape. Cooking was an abstract pleasure, quite unrelated to things you put in your mouth.

Only the most perfect pieces of plain cake graduated as far as icing and coconut and Mother's Coronation tin. Mother's infallibility could rival the Pope's. While she could cook anything, roasts and stews and pasties golden with perfection, her gift lay in coaxing scones to lightness, in making from dry ingredients and ordinary eggs and lumps of butter a risen miracle that seemed to float above the plate. When Mother cooked, things browned where they should brown, rose where they should rise, and pulled themselves together smartly when required to set. It was not something she could teach you. It was imprinted in the fine lines of her palms.

The Madeira was flipped out on a wire tray to cool. It never broke in half. Things like that only happened to lesser mortals, to ordinary, earthbound cooks. The cocoa, dark as sin, exotic as Africa, was always in the same silver bowl. Coconut rose in a Kilimanjaro drift. Mavis was fascinated with Mother's delicate syncopation, that mysterious dance between left hand and right. Even while one hand was picking up a square of plain cake and dipping it in the icing, leaving it to hover, the other hand was already busy, rolling another through the coconut, over and over, with not a smidgeon of cake crumb left behind. Coconut drifted like talcum powder. It settled, it obediently stuck.

Mavis wanted those hands, patting and rolling and stroking, to be touching her instead. But Mother was always too busy, creating the sublime from the ordinary, bringing grace where chaos had been before. Before the one on the right was put down on the wire tray to set, Mother had another in her left.

Dip, drip, roll, in a steady flow, until all were done.

Mother had a piece of plain cake in one hand and a finished lamington in the other the morning the presbytery car drove through the property gate and up the front drive. The priest was driving very slowly, so as not to run over the goat escaped from the orchard and the chooks pecking about in the yard. Mother stood there, backlit by sun streaming through her kitchen window. Poised between the miraculous and the everyday.

It was Saturday, baking was done on a Saturday, just like Mass was on Sunday and on Friday you ate fish. But Saturday wasn't the right day for Father McNally, that was why Mavis took notice of it, why Mother paused and everything hung there, like Mother was Justice balancing out someone's fate. Parish visits were Thursdays, Mother did the church on Tuesday and it was always Sunday afternoon when Father McNally came to tea.

This was Plain Father McNally as opposed to the Father McNally from Melbourne or the Father McNally who came from Out of Town. All the Fathers McNally were Mother's brothers. It got rather confusing if they all came to visit, so there was Young Father McNally, Old Father McNally and Plain Father McNally, who was neither young nor old nor very handsome and who gave the longest and most droney sermons so everyone avoided his Mass like the plague.

Mavis could never quite connect Father McNally to the idea of Mother having a brother. Both concepts seemed absurd. Firstly it seemed odd that priests should have brothers and sisters and mothers and fathers like ordinary people. They should just descend from heaven, like black snowflakes or immaculate conceptions, floating down via horn-handled umbrellas, air ballooning under a welter of skirts. It seemed equally odd that Mother would have parents like an ordinary person, that she was once a little girl. So it seemed fitting that if Mother did have to have brothers they should be otherworldly. That they should spring to earth fully formed.

Plain Father McNally looked like a stork. A big black and fairly clumsy stork. His nose was a beak, he had a chin like a chisel, his body was a too-thin pencil lost inside a pocket of serge. He gathered his skirts and assorted limbs and got out of the presbytery car. He picked his way gingerly between cow pats and chooks, heading for the front verandah where visitors were received. But he must have stepped in something because he stood on one leg, storklike, inspecting the bottom of his shoe. Mavis snickered. Mother silenced her with a look.

'Hurry up with those bowls, Missy. I have to go out for a while.' Mother took off her apron and rinsed her hands, scrubbing meticulously between the webs of every single finger with Sunlight soap.

'You are allowed one. As a reward for helping. But *only* the one.' Mother gathered up the skirts of her white dress, holding them in elegant drapery over one fine wrist, black ankle boots picking steps neat as stitches through the chooks. With the other hand she headed Father McNally off at the pass. She grasped Father firmly by the meatiest part of his arm. Mavis knew what that would feel like; Mother's nails were sharp, her fingers were strong. She could leave red dents that stayed there all day. Mother hustled Father back to his Ford. Then they drove away.

This was a test. All morning Mavis's mouth had been watering as she watched Mother tipping and patting and measuring and sifting, lining tins with brown paper, making dry ingredients rise to perfectly even piles. Before you even started on the lamingtons, you had to wash up. You weren't allowed to lick the bowls beforehand because Mother believed that was Vulgar and Vulgarity was a venal, as opposed to a mortal, sin. Depending of course on where it led you. Lewdness. Lasciviousness. Lustfulness. Gluttony and Greed. Something as simple as icing could end in the irrevocable. It was a short straight highway to hell.

Mavis never licked the bowls. Even if there was no-one to see it, even though it could have been her little secret, a small and delicious sin. God could see you, Mother said. Mavis, feeling God frowning down at her from heaven, where you were probably allowed to eat all the icing you wanted but you had to get there first, washed all that lovely chocolate down the kitchen sink. She Did The Right Thing.

Afterwards she sat at the kitchen table and looked backwards and forwards between the piles of finished lamingtons and the pieces of Madeira deemed too imperfect to progress. As she sat there she imagined God looking over her shoulder, floating somewhere between the kitchen window and the ceiling fan. He looked a lot like Mother in her flannelette nightie. Except he had overgrown eye-brows and a long grey beard.

Despite the perils posed by icing, the choice was not clear. It was always a delicate matter, Doing The Right Thing. It was a dark and mysterious wilderness, filled with sudden traps and sinkholes, strangling vines and vicious

cliffs. A fine web of forces pulled you this way and the
other, waiting to trip you up. Mother held them all, those
fine unbreakable strings.

One string was called Waste Not Want Not, or Thriftiness Next To Godliness, or Being Frugal In Hard Times.
It was people starving in Africa. The price of sugar, the
scarcity of eggs. The way most of the layers had been eaten
as Sunday roasts. They ate old boilers at dinnertime now,
ancient biddies tough as cooked twine. Waste Not Want
Not was the way Mother ironed brown paper and stock-
piled stray bits of Christmas wrapping, let down hems so
many times there were three rows of stitch marks, and
soaked the labels off every jam and pickle jar, collecting
them in little 'could be useful' nests under the sink.

Thriftiness Next To Godliness was the way Gwen and
Mavis's shoes were always just that bit too small, partly due
to Mother's belief that 'all Goddard women have small feet',
mostly because they couldn't afford new ones until the old
ones wore out. It was alright for Gwen; the minute she got
out the front gate she took them off and swung them, laces
tied together, above her head. Gwen never seemed to feel
the thorns and stones and the blue-looking frost. But
Mavis, Mother's warnings ringing in her ears, hobbled the
five miles to school and waited until she got near the stove
in the classroom to undo the buckles. In winter her toes
were pinched into strange skinny wedges, purple with cold.

The last string was called Being Grateful For What We
Have Received. This was the way sometimes, after all the
vegetables from the garden had been eaten, all you had for
dinner was plain scones and cake. You said Grace over them
all the same. But you could almost forget what you were
eating and how lonely two little scones looked on Doulton

dinner plates because the plates had pink roses twined around the edges and those plates sat on Mother's best damask tablecloth and there were big bunches of flowers in the middle of the table and three forks and three knives lined up beside them, as if confident of a three-course feast. Mother never let her standards slip. Which is why she insisted on fresh cut flowers from a garden which drank up all the rainwater, real Irish linen on the guest beds and most of all the Importance Of Art.

In the end Mavis Did The Right Thing. As usual there was no-one to watch. She sat up at the table eating a piece of plain cake with a corner missing and half the brown skin peeled off. She cut it into little squares with a proper knife and fork. Taking microscopic mouthfuls, each chewed the requisite number of times, she truly believed this plain cake was more delicious than caviar might be.

She was just putting the finished lamingtons away in the best cake tin, carefully lining each layer with greaseproof so they wouldn't stick together, when she heard the presbytery car come back up the drive. Mother and Father McNally just seemed to be sitting there, staring down at the space between them looking grim. At first Mavis didn't realise there was someone else in the car. The boy between Mother and the priest was so small that Mavis thought he was a little curly haired dog.

Father McNally and Mother were talking, right across the top of the little boy, like he wasn't really there at all. Well Mother was doing the talking, waggling her finger in a way that made Mavis glad she wasn't the one in the car. Father McNally was nodding and nodding, so hard it looked like his head might fall off. Even when Mother opened the door a crack and stuck one elegant leg out in preparation for alighting, her white dress foaming around one fine ankle, she didn't stop talking and waggling that finger, stabbing and poking at Father McNally through the shimmering heated air. The priest was shrinking slowly, cowering like the gardener did when Mother found he'd over-pruned the roses or spread too much blood and bone.

Mavis noted that Mother's best lawn dress, usually so snowy, so white she looked like a cloud falling, had red dust all over it, all over the hem.

It was just as Mother opened the car door further and swung both legs out, knees perfectly together and ankle boots at exactly ten to one, that the little boy went wild. He erupted into a whirlwind of hands and elbows and knees. His curly head swished backwards and forwards, dust flew out, his legs and arms thrashed like a windmill, and his mouth opened and shut like a stranded fish. Mavis couldn't hear what he was saying through the closed kitchen window. And all the car windows were shut. But she could imagine that his screaming was very loud. The boy was trying to climb over Mother and get out the door, and when Father tried to stop him those little brown hands bit at Father's face. Father cowered down while the boy clawed at his cardboard collar, at his thinning scalp and stalky neck. The little boy kicked Mother hard in the stomach and the bosom and even the face. Mavis started to feel dizzy, then realised that she'd been holding her breath.

In the end Mother just gave that boy a sharp slap across the head. He crashed sideways, hit his head on the steering wheel and fell down on the floor.

Father McNally fell out of the Ford too. Down in the dust, down among the chooks. Black limbs at indulgent angles, like something in his spine had given way.

Mother wasn't having any of that. She picked Father McNally up by the scruff of the neck. Like he was a puppy who'd made a mess on the floor. Father was bleeding, there was red all over his white collar. It had come loose in the kerfuffle and was fluttering, like a torn paper halo, somewhere over his head.

'Mavis! Bring me the iodine. Hurry, Father McNally's hurt.'

Mavis still doesn't know quite why she did it. She could hear Mother calling, her legs wanted to move obediently to the bathroom cupboard, to find a clean washer, to Do The Right Thing. But she just kept standing there, rooted to the spot. She could see them, through the tunnel of the polished front hall, Father McNally prostrate on what everyone else called the big cane chair but what Mother called the 'chaze lunge'. Mother dabbing with her white hankie at his face.

Waste Not Want Not, Thriftiness Next To Godliness, but then there was Being Civilised, Having Good Manners, Putting Visitors First. Being Grateful For What We Have Received. And the little boy had looked very hungry, those big eyes staring out of his thin brown face.

In the end Mavis took one, just the one. She rearranged the piles carefully, so there weren't any gaps.

The boy was lying wedged between the front floor hump and the bench seat of the Ford. He was curled up in a little ball. He had his hands cupped over his head, as if to shelter himself from a blow. So Mavis couldn't see his face, just his mop of dusty curly black hair. His fingernails were all broken, and there were smears of blood and even stray bits of skin in them, from where he'd gouged at Father McNally's face. But Mavis wasn't looking at that. Mavis,

peering through the dusty window of the big black presbytery car, standing on tiptoe with her chin on the door
because it was an old-fashioned Ford with high curvy
windows and she couldn't quite reach, was staring at the
little boy's back. And the sight was burning her. It sizzled
into memory like hot summer chrome.

The damage ran from an invisible source below the
waistband of the boy's trousers, as if from a hidden spring.
A thin and winding path at first, widening to streams and
rivers, with bubbled flows and knots of it and broken
furrows where skin had burnt to bone. It was hostile as the
moon. Here and there you could see what it used to look
like, faint blotches of ordinary brown. The rest was a white
and bloodless shell. This boy had to carry it around with
him. Like a little white snail.

In the end Mavis just left the lamington sitting on the
bonnet. Like an offering to the dead. But he never ate it,
because when Mavis got back to the kitchen she saw Father
McNally drive off in the direction of the Presbytery and
the Home of Compassion.

The lamington stuck as far as the front gate. Then the
chooks got it in a flurry of beaks and wings.

And when Mavis got back to the kitchen, in a rush to
pack things away before icing melted and blowflies got
stuck to icing and Mother found everything gone to pot,
Gwen had got there first.

'These look good!' Gwen bellowed, picking up two
lamingtons in her greedy cradle fingers. She stuffed them
into her mouth whole. Her big lips were snowy with
coconut and smeared with brown-black icing, she made
little cakey grunts of pleasure, crumbs spraying out the side
of her mouth.

Later Mavis got six hard smacks with the bedroom slipper. Two for each missing lamington. Two each for Lustfulness, Gluttony and Greed.

ch*a*pter 16

There's a shadow of a black man on the corner of the Dew Drop Inn. He's in jagged silhouette, like one of those cardboard cut-outs you shine a torch through to make a pattern on the wall. So it is a black man in the simplest sense of the word. There's no red and yellow, no stake of claim. But there's the fuzzy hair, the long lean limbs, one hand holding a spear.

He looks like the victim of an atomic blast. Except the outline's positive not negative, black not white. And he strikes no attitude of agony. He wasn't taken by surprise.

It's the only piece of graffiti Ruth has seen here. This is another relentlessly Tidy Town. Everything else has had the heritage treatment, where they take something genuinely old and turn it into a glossy approximation, with none of the dirt, none of the squalor, none of the holes. The people too are all well-scrubbed and uniform, if a bit past their use-by; even the young seem middle-aged, the middle-aged preternaturally worn. Must be all that sun.

As Ruth Cook walks down the main street and passes

yet another curlered woman with her gaggle of toddlers, people are staring. Behind her she can hear it, that Mavis-like teeth and tongue clacket, tsk, tsk, tsk. You can always feel it, in a place so vast and yet so stubbornly small. Eyelines form a vector. They arrive smack bang between your shoulder blades. Where they think your heart should be.

They used to do it to Ruth and Dad when they went shopping, after Mum had disappeared. Never to your face of course. Always just round the next corner or at the table behind you at Simpsons, or in the next supermarket aisle over. Voices whispering, tongues tsk tsk tsking, eyes snaking between the Milo and the frozen peas. And Dad never did anything about it, didn't tell them to bugger off. He just slunk along in his too-big shorts and T-shirt, huddling into shadows where two brick buildings met. He was buried alive under it, under those sour milky tea mutters swirling behind wedding-ringed hands.

Catching sight of herself in a shop window she realises, almost with disappointment, people aren't staring now because they recognise Ruth Cook. How could they, it was years ago, she left when she was twelve. Besides, she looks like someone else entirely now, someone who's Not From Here. Jeans Mavis would have given to the Smith Family, not without misgivings, a torn T-shirt Mavis would have used to polish the sideboard, and her hair growing out in tough little bristles, like Mavis's old banister brush. The nose ring, well even Frank would have scratched his head at that. He would have asked Ruth if she wanted to be led around like a cow.

Her head in the window of Crazee Bargains stares back at her in dark and vicious silhouette. This used to be Moore's, she realises, but now it sells five things for a dollar, china lids for your coffee cups, fluffy covers for tissue boxes, knitted coat-hangers, macramé holders for serviettes. Hovering like doom between all this cheerful rubbish, Ruth looks like a Changi victim, like the creature from the Black Lagoon. Her eyes have sunk back inside a suddenly shocking head.

How to explain this is fashionable, not remarkable at all. It wasn't terminal, she hadn't survived a three car pile-up; it would not respond to a few Hail Marys or a stiff course of antibiotics, it didn't merit a lamington drive. It's just something you play with, shave or dye or put holes in, like one of those dolls you pull long blonde hair out of, then push a button in its stomach to shrink it back in.

After a while though Ruth gets sick of being stared at so she turns left at random, off the main street. Back here is the old spiderweb of red dust back alleys, tracing the underbelly of the official foursquare grid. There's no-one around, no-one to stare. These are the only roads which curve and wind like the streets she's used to, and the Tidy Town police haven't got this far yet. The lanes are still full of old forty-four gallon drums and household rubbish: bottles left but not collected, rusting car parts, an old store dummy, a broken-headed lamp leaning like a tipsy queen. A three-wheeled and sideways listing pram.

J would have a field day here. At home he was always retrieving the offcuts of other people's lives. He could have found an entire new lounge room in these town laneways: broken radiators, chairs with no seats, those two little tables, one big, one small, which sit snugly in what Mavis would call a 'nest'. J would root eagerly through everything, hat tipped jauntily, strong calves straining above big bovver boots. He would rescue that mirror black with decay, file that steel boot under 'Useful', one day find it a mate. Stick that brimless hat on his head and sing, doffing it like a film star, all the way home. Holes and ragged edges can be reinvented. If things disintegrate they evolve into something else. Finally, when objects are more hole than substance, they form part of the rich humus of J's bedroom floor.

When Ruth puts her hand in her pocket to get a Kleenex, she pulls out a piece of his hair. When J shaved her head she did his side bits in return. The clippers slipped. She stuffed the dreadlock in her jeans pocket, hoping he wouldn't notice. The pale blonde hair smells of stale cigarettes and of slightly rancid boy. Faint sweat, not so clean sheets, T-shirts left wet too long before being hung on the line. It is the soft private scent of a familiar scalp.

The smell makes her homesick for her own bed. This is not her place any more, with its hard bright sunshine, its little knots of people dwarfed by space. People here don't have scrounged and unreliable lives. Their days aren't patched together by vague meetings on a corner, by the unpicked rhythm of a threadbare street.

Not even the time of day is the same. In her street now it's later in the afternoon, half an hour later, they wound their clocks back on the way in. And while it's still stinking hot here, the southerly might have arrived in the city by now, and the air would have cooled a bit, not much, still sweaty, still sticky with a humidity you don't ever feel in a place like this. But enough that people would have taken their shoes off, be sitting bare-chested and hatless on door-steps, nodding and calling to passersby. She would have come home from her job at the cafe, J would be finished at the pub, they would be lying on the bed, fucking maybe, listening to life pouring through the door. Those on the

dole would have finally got up, ventured out in torn
T-shirts and bare feet for a loaf of bread and a carton of
milk. They'd put kitchen chairs out on their balconies, open
their bedroom doors, tie back faded curtains and turn
music up loud. They'd swig on a beer and feel the air
moving, just slightly, that breeze from the rich people's
coast. And smell food cooking, a thick spicy soup of it,
Lebanese from the falafel, Italian from the deli, Chinese
from the takeway, fried chicken from the Greek guy, curry
from the Indian corner store. All laced with petrol and the
far-off sting of salt. And they'd watch the punks skateboard-
ing, rolling expertly round craters in roads the council never
fixes because nobody is official enough, nobody pays
enough taxes, hardly anybody owns a car.

On her main street corner, punks skid and swerve
elaborate parabola, like surfers beaching, twisting and curving through tar tubes and bitumen tunnels, balanced lithely
on the road's dip and crest. Then they flip their boards
backward into the flat of hands. Only to begin again.

At the overpass, where you can go either south or north,
she realises it's only just gone two. Can't go to Dad's yet,
have to go when it's too late for lunch, too early for tea.
People here always invite you to eat with them if you turn
up at mealtimes, even if they hardly know you, even if they
don't really like you, even if they haven't seen you for years.
Like the way Mavis has been writing Ruth letters, one every
two to three months ever since Ruth left. Because Mavis
wants to Do The Right Thing.

The letters are a catalogue of the dead and the dying.
Cancer, emphysema, heart attacks, old people bowled over

by flu. Never city things like AIDS or car crashes or being hit by a government bus. People who used to be neighbours on Bauxite Street, people related to people who once lived on Bauxite Street, girls Ruth used to go to school with, girls Ruth never went to school with but who she might have made her First Communion with, women who married someone or other, people who never married, other people Ruth didn't know at all but Mavis was convinced she did—'. . . you must remember the Whelan girl, Ruthie, married the Thompkins boy, the one who got into trouble with that Lebanese lass, those Lebanese people who gave us their Eytie bread over the back fence.' And then Mavis would be off on another one of her intricate family-tree tangents and Ruth would let her letter fall, like over-complicated knitting, to a cross-legged lap.

When Frank had the stroke Mavis just sent a four-word telegram. 'Frank. Stroke. Come home.' As if Frank's illness had given her laryngitis. As if adjectives were suddenly sinful. Or brevity could shrink this calamity to manageable size. Or maybe Mavis was just penny-pinching, that's probably what it was. Ruth sent an equally terse one back: 'Arriving January 25th. Call you. Ruth.' Mavis was inordinately pleased. Her next letter recovered its old garrulousness, pointing out local interest spots like Ruth was a tourist in a gumnut jumper. Mavis listed all the people Ruth should visit and the times they were likely to be at home. But even if she knew some of these people or could remember them, the Mrs Whelans and the Mr McGregors and that old McNally priest who'd turned a hundred and five and got a letter from the PM, she wouldn't visit them, couldn't stand it. All the dead and the dying, sitting in their lino kitchens, much smaller than you remembered, among dusty pot plants and china milkmaids, telling their tangled skeins of cancer and heart attack and thrombosis, fingering their dull rosary of pain. Offering you endless rounds of tea and scones and sherry and quondong pie. It would be tasteless and over-sugared as always, the fruit tastes of nothing in particular, like boiled rhubarb, but you have to be polite. And biting into a piece of it you would know as you smiled and sympathised that ordinary dying will leave these people with the expectation of more. They would have been waiting for something hard and sharp and definite, as befits a frontier. Like what happened to Von.

No matter which side of town they lived on, these people would be able to see those slag heaps. In its epic violence, the slag would have seemed to have promised something more.

'Gnomes. Snow White, the Jolly Swagman, Sleepy and Grumpy, all the dwarves. Strange curling cactuses in weird shapes, tortured to grow through trellis and driftwood and up through butterflies nailed to a wall. Three ducks flying. Three butterflies crucified. Everything in threes. Little jokes in gardens: kangaroos fishing, platypus in cork-fly, black fellas standing on one leg. Mostly though it's gnomes.'

This is what she's written in the brand-new diary she bought in Sydney before she left. It has a beautiful hard blue cover and inside the pages are blindingly white. Every time she picks up a pen ready to spew it out, things dry up. So the biro she nicked off the bingo woman droops, falls silent, dangles by its broken string. She's been walking for over an hour in the hot sun, and she came in here for a breather, thinking she'd buy herself a drink.

It's a new club this one, a monolith of an RSL. Its glitzy, new, suburban looking, with fizzing Christmas lights and a gelato colour scheme, pink and green and blue. They've even toned down the vomitous carpet. But everything else is the same. It's still schnitzel three ways, chips and orange slices with everything, pineapple rings on lettuce if you order salad, moselle if you want white wine. The loudspeaker is still calling the bingo numbers, though its a modern address system not some bowls champion on a crackly PA. And there are the same little clumps of people with their eyes fixed on the numbers flashing on overhead projectors, on the Sky Channel satellite TVs. Big ones now, the size of a house. But they still have the races on them and the caller still sounds like Humphrey Bogart on amphetamines and the men are still clustered round the horses flashing, but the jockeys are in colour now, dust red, grass green, sky blue. Schooners hover at the finish line, at the grating climax of the call.

This place is huge, acres and acres of it. Who will fill this alien mother ship, who will come? Who will sit in this plastic coliseum, play that armada of pokies against the walls? It looks ready for an RSL-led recovery, an invasion of Americans saying 'Melborne' and whingeing about the beer. It's eerie, all this space with nobody in it. Just these old people, sitting silently with drinks on neat coasters. Staring into nursery coloured space.

The blank page glares back, blue-white in flourescent light. There's more to write down, but it's been deadened by a surfeit of terylene.

One thing's for sure. If she did write something, it would have to mention the heat.

. . .

Out past the shelter of the main street verandahs and the town park plane trees, it had hit her. Like she knew it would. Magnificently, ferociously dull. Gravel winking, cracks skipping, in that acid mineral sun shimmer. Heat giving its inward turning hum to things. Releasing hard edges. A singularity of sun.

She'd walked all the way over the old overpass on the new footpath provided, past the old mine, now a museum or an art gallery, past a brand-new car yard, past what was once the RSPCA. Traffic whizzed, dust settled, silence returned. A red bus. A green car. A black truck lumbering beetlelike on the brow of the hill.

The old miners' shanties that used to be there, under the overpass, they've gone now. Now they build replicas of these for the tourists, poverty tarted up as nostalgia, right down the malnourished miner-size front doors. Where the shanties used to be they've built a bulky goods centre. People were lugging mattresses and lounge suites out to the car park. Everything hummed with heat.

Everything had changed. The streets were the same, still the litany of minerals, but everything on them had been transformed. Why do they want most of the country to look like the worst parts of the city and the rest like some theme park of what was there before? She'd walked faster and faster, despite the heat and her tiredness and how thirsty she was getting, afraid that if she didn't get there in the next twenty minutes they'd have turned Bauxite Street into a Way We Were museum. Uncle Frank's garden gnomes and Aunt Mavis's pergola and Mum's can opener, all perfectly preserved.

But when she did get to Bauxite Street, nothing much had changed at all. Well some things had—the rubbish piled up in the front yard of Number 57, Aunt Mavis would never let it get like that. And they'd finally finished Uncle Frank's never-ending paint job on the front verandah which took so long that by the time he finished one end he needed to start on the other, all over again. But it wasn't enough. It was all too familiar, made her want to cry. Because the old shop awning, still bearing its Vincent's Powder ad, faded but indelible, and the bellied bay windows and the Grecian pillars, impossibly grand looking, like the entrance to the Acropolis stuck to the front of an ordinary house, they were all still there. The comforting geometry of home.

Uncle Frank letting her dig in the garden. Filling up half an old forty-four gallon drum as a make-do paddle pool. The water turning rust red, a nail sticking in her bum. She didn't care, it was hot, the hose water was cool. Mavis showing her how to dip a lamington and roll it without losing half the cake. Uncle Frank teaching her to ride a two-wheeler on that footpath, and her falling over and Frank kissing it better and smacking the bike. A wheel-spinning insect whirrs on the footpath. Energy cast off and grating. Mum, on those few rare occasions when she returned from that strange sad world she inhabited, reading stories, *Black Beauty*, *Anne of Green Gables*, the snow and porridge and scarlet fever world of *Jane Eyre*. Sitting, for a few precious hours, all too short and all too precarious, on Mum's bony knee.

It wasn't until she was turning the corner out of Bauxite Street, on her way back to the overpass, that she realised she hadn't even looked at Mum and Dad's house. Because it never felt like home. Home was where Uncle Frank was, and now he's everywhere and nowhere, drowning in thin hospital air.

As she turned the corner she did glance back. But she couldn't see it. It was too small. That clinker brick and stone lion monstrosity they'd built next door must have been blocking it. Or else they'd torn it down.

The barman's been giving her hard looks for half an hour because she's just been sitting there without buying a drink. But when she does go to order one, he just keeps staring at her, as if he's never heard of a middy of VB. So it wasn't just that. She's been ignoring it but on either side and behind her she can feel it. People staring. Men mostly, leaning on the counter as if they own it, square elbows and jutting bellies saying this, all this, it belongs to us. So it's still not done. A woman. Drinking by herself. It's just asking for it; that's what they used to tell her mum.

Mum used to do it all the time, go drinking at the pubs round town. For a while they reopened the Imperial, so she went there, which shocked people even more; it was full of blacks. Ruth saw her once, on her way to the baths, saw her mum through the door of that gloomy, beer-smelling, blue smoke curling place. The whiff of that air, furry and evil, was like a physical blow. Ruth rode her bike fast along the footpath. She turned her head like she didn't know that woman. She turned away.

When they closed the Imperial, it didn't stop Mum. She just went to any of the other fifty million pubs round town. She probably did it to shit people, Aunt Mavis mostly, to thumb her nose at all the old biddies down at the club, sitting placidly by the beer bellies they'd married.

That was the only place where women ever drank. And then it was only shandies or sherry, sipped fussily from a straw. After each sip the women would take out a white lace hankie and wipe stray lipstick off the glass.

Mum and Dad used to argue about it, about Mum going to pubs all the time, terrible screamers alive with thumping tables and clattering cutlery and broken plates. But Ruth's mum, she wasn't afraid. Not of anything, it seemed. Mum would just chuck an extra big saucepan which already had a hundred dents in it and slam out the front door. It gave its sad-sounding creak.

Sometimes Ruth followed her, as far as the end of Bauxite Street. Then Mum would round a corner and she'd disappear.

But not really. She couldn't get out. Just walking and walking, like a wind-up clockwork mother, like the Energizer bunny, on the symmetrical game board of town. Until she couldn't walk any more, until her batteries ran out. And then she'd go to a pub. Just to get out of the sun.

Until the time she chose the wrong pub at the wrong time, on a Thursday arvo, mine payday, when everyone's tanked to the gills. Ruth doesn't know where it happened, maybe a back alley or even out on the footpath, those respectable beer-bellied big-fisted men. Whose job it was to make the rules, wear the hats, prop up the bars. All she knows is that her Mum came home spitting up eye teeth and blood. You could smell the beer, she had dust all over her, in her cut lip and above her purple-looking eyes. Dad threw plates, thumped cupboards, swore he'd buy a gun. Ruth wasn't sure who he wanted to use it on, those men at the Gloucester or her mum.

But after the first flush of it, like always, Dad's anger

dried up like sour milk. It was Uncle Frank who went to see them, silent and red-faced under his hat. He knew those men, the ones who drank in the Gladstone and the Duke of Gloucester. They'd worked with him, down the mine. They reckoned Von had been causing trouble, getting drunk, abusing people, bad-mouthing decent men's wives. She'd fallen over in the gutter. She was drunk. That's what happened to her face.

Dad sulked. Uncle Frank was silent. Mum just shrugged. Said they could stick it in their eye. She put a bandaid on her lip and banged out the front screen door.

Uncle Frank cried. Sitting there, at their kitchen table, with his head in his hands. Tears like a corrosive element, like the Tin Man leaking battery acid. Powerful moisture on the dry country of a face.

Mum didn't cry. She just stuck her chin out and went walking. Further and further, past town borders, on one of those four roads leading out.

Dad's new wife would never be caught drinking, not alone, not in an old digger pub. Ruth can tell from the photos and letters Dad has sent her, that his new wife would be happy to sit at home on her modular lounge suite, knitting or sewing, getting fluff off cushions with her Brush O Matic, drinking milky too-weak tea. On Tuesdays she'd do tuck-shop, on Thursdays she'd play tennis, at school fetes she'd make cupcakes and man the white elephant stall. Or something like that. Ruth doesn't really know anything about that sort of life. Dad and Gloria and their three kids called Danielle and Hannah and Rebecca or Ruby or something, they could be living on Mars.

Glor. That's what Dad calls her, even in letters. 'Glor did this, Glor did that, Glor doesn't like the other.' Makes her sound like a brand of denture glue. Like something Dad hacked up and sucked back down. Dad met Glor at a stationery conference. This is equally bizarre. Like Dad had entered a parallel universe while Ruth wasn't watching. Like now he's a Thunderbirds dummy, jerked around by strings. Her dad, who used to wear overalls and a hard hat that was always too big for him and whose fingernails were always dirty and who had beer and cigarettes for breakfast when Mum forgot to buy the milk and who lived in a caravan forgetting to eat or wash when she disappeared and who was never really there anyway, just kept going to work and coming home again, getting drunk, shouting, sleeping, getting up again, well now he sells photocopy paper. He wears a blue suit and drives a company car.

Where Dad lives used to be no-man's-land, the wrong side of the tracks. Now it's a new housing estate; Dad's house is on a street called Second Avenue. Which comes just after First. They must have run out of minerals or something. The roads are not straight either, running north–south, east–west. They are neat cul-de-sacs, curving and looping so that the same street appears twice in places, with a signpost at either end. But the ironclad logic of the old grid still rules, there are no real surprises, everything sticks to the plan. Each street describes the same arc. Each house meets the gutter at the same angle of curve. And grass still struggles. Trees, planted only recently, still grasp desperately at earth.

These houses are a far cry from the originals, the corrugated iron with bull-nosed verandahs plonked in the middle of a red dirt front yard. They have freshly painted letterboxes, they have wrought-iron garden settings. Patios are mandatory. Garden gnomes are big.

'Hi. I was after Trevor. Trevor Cook? Is he home?'

At first Ruth can't see Dad's new wife properly in the front hall gloom. Everyone here keeps their curtains and blinds shut, to keep out the heat. Gloria just seems to be hovering there, a flash of pink apron and blonde perm. Maybe she thinks Ruth is a really polite burglar. But Dad must have shown her photos. Then Ruth remembers that even if Dad had showed his new wife photos, they would have been old ones, because he hasn't seen in her ages, and all he has is those little girl black and white ones taken by Frank and Mavis, her wearing Mavis's collection of home-knitted jumpers in swollen layers, so many she looked like a walking Smith Family bag.

The most recent photos Dad had were from 1968. And she didn't tell Dad she was coming. Because she couldn't be bothered. Because she wanted to take him by surprise.

'I'm sorry?'

'I'm after Trevor Cook. Is he home?'

'Um. I'm afraid he's out at present. Can I say who's called?'

Ruth feels both relieved and disappointed. She shifts from one foot to the other on Gloria's pristine patio, scuffing red dust off her boots.

'He's only out at the hardware though. He should be back soon.' Gloria is rushing to fill the gap. 'He's putting up a pool.'

What she's talking about? Dad putting up a pool? Dad doesn't do stuff like that. If he did, he'd hit the sewerage. He'd bust a thumb.

But Gloria doesn't think it's funny. She isn't worried

Dad will rupture the town water. What she's really worried about is Ruth. Gloria's nervous as a cockroach, skittering sideways on her shag-pile carpet, mushroom curls a-quiver, as if Ruth's an IRA terrorist and Gloria might just have to counterattack.

'Perhaps you can call back later. Or come in and wait. Why don't you do that? I've got the kettle on. What was your name?'

Ruth loiters, partly to check out what she can see of Dad's new life, partly to make Gloria squirm. She can just see the lounge room past Gloria's amply-flowered hips. Dad's new kids' heights aren't marked on a door-jamb with a pencil. Gloria wouldn't like marks on her off-white walls. They are measured by a plastic giraffe. On top of the TV there's a cluster of photos, plotting Dad's new children's path from pre-school to confirmation and everything in between. The only photos Mum and Dad used to have of Ruth were a couple of family picnic snapshots, grainy black and white ones with everyone about a mile away from the lens. They weren't framed, weren't even kept in an album, but slithered, tattered and unmanageable, all out of sequence, shots of World War II uncles next to newborn babies and people with sideburns driving MGs. Of course there weren't any of Lil.

Ruth imagines going in there, sitting down to tea with Gloria, and feels exhausted, seeing all the questions she'll have to get through before dinnertime, lined up like brussel sprouts, those polite enquiries, formless old sock-tasting lumps. What are you doing now, how's the city, what happened to your hair? The minutes of that visit are predictable as a shiny teapot in a knitted cosy and some Chocolate Wheatens on a pink roses plate. Then there'd be

Dad's boring fucking rugby practice and his three girls and their respective netball finals, followed closely by chops and three veg. Everything in threes.

And all the time, edging closer and closer, lumbering evilly across all that hot red landscape, all the way from the lake, it's coming. While Dad and Gloria rabbit on about interest rates and who was out for what in the test, it will be dragging itself across the overpass. It will be hauling itself down Dad's cul-de-sac and up his brand-new concrete drive. It will sit, patient and dripping, on Gloria's wheat-coloured rug.

Even in the heat of the sun and over a distance of twenty years, it won't have got any smaller. It will still leak its blue and inexhaustible water. Still take up all the air.

'Nope. Don't bother. I'll give him a call. See you later on.'

As Ruth walks back up Second Avenue, she sees Gloria's three girls going in at Dad's gate. They are wearing little pink leotards and have huge hair in curlers under old lady scarves, like those kids who went to ballet of a Saturday morning, always called Marcia or Felicity or Jennifer or something, those blonde girls with real flowered-apron mothers and dads in proper suits. Ruth never went to ballet, she didn't wear a leotard. She didn't walk with her feet sticking out. It was an affliction to be proud of, that tortured splay of toes. And as she follows the cul-de-sac to where she thinks the overpass is she gets lost of course and finds herself going full circle on the rigid logic of it, right back to where she started, back to Dad's miniature snow chalet letterbox sitting on his blue and pink front gate.

Down the back alley she feels safer though, down with the rubbish and the junk. But through the fence she can see them, Dad's three little girls riding their bikes, round

and round, in a red earth backyard. The yard itself is like
a minefield, littered with Dad's pool holes. He obviously
can't decide where to put the thing. Or else Glor keeps
changing her mind. The girls are wearing play clothes now
but still with the scarves on, hair too big for their bodies,
like the intellectual chicken in the Foghorn Leghorn cartoon. They are a bit grubby and barefoot but it's just
ordinary kid dirt, their clothes are just play clothes, they're
not unwashed or scabbed from the Salvos or knocked up
from an old bedspread on Mavis's sewing machine.

Everything else is familiar. Three little girls, two riding
in large and swooping circles. The small one plumper and
bikeless, the jeering laughter, the sudden screams. Up and
down, round and round. Keeping a weather eye.

Ruth watches them, eye-spy through a knot hole. The
little one, a blonde child with red tongue and spindle legs,
grips, steers, comforts, negotiates pram and doll like a real
mother, through pool holes and jam tins on a string which
her dad has made her, like those ones Uncle Frank used to
make but Dad never did. The ones you can walk on like
Frankenstein or talk to someone on the other end. Except
there's no-one to play that game with her and the strings
get caught in the pram wheels and the tins rattle along
there, trailing like an old wedding voyage, snagged now
and then in flaccid loops of hose.

'Girls! Time for a bath!'

Dad's new kids are swallowed by the gloom. But their
mother stops and stands there, in afternoon shadow. Arms
akimbo over a flowered stomach. Body dissected by a back
screen door.

Privacy pokes its knitting needle through the knot hole
so Ruth moves on.

chapter 17

Wrap, fold, thump. Mavis is throwing away lamingtons.
Carefully, one by one. Wrapping them first in newspaper,
folding them to tidy squares. Then dropping them in the
flip top. The tea cups have been washed and the table
scoured with Ajax but sticky coconut still freckles the tan
leather of Frank's favourite chair.

In the end Mavis realised they were all quite imperfect.
Cake crumbling here, a corner missing there. It makes her
feel lighter, this particular rhythm. Gives the silence less
heft and pull. Wrap, fold, thump. Until all are done.

From the kitchen window Mavis can see her sister
ambling down the main street. The smell of slimy veg and
overripe grapefruit, the hump and clatter of fruit boxes, the
swearing of Marconi boys, thankfully in Eytie, all this drifts
up. Everything says to Mavis, 'This Is Not Your Home'.

Gwen stops every few paces to excavate in her carry-all,
as if a vital clue to normal life might be hiding in there.
Mavis wonders what on earth she can be looking for now.
It can't be another lamington. She scoffed six while she

consulted her bus timetable, she must be full to the brim. And it can't be money. Mavis just lent her a fiver for the taxi out north.

Gwen finally unearths some woolly thing from the bottom of her bag. She takes off her visiting hat, which was a relatively respectable straw one, and stows it carefully away. Then she dons her usual headwear for everyday travelling. She continues down the street, smiling pontifically at total strangers, nodding and waving with that little vertical hand flutter she has affected ever since she saw the Pope on TV. People stop and turn, hovering uncertainly, wondering if they know that woman in the football beanie. Then they shrug and scratch at their receding hairlines and move on.

Even now, after years of accumulated pavlova, with a body like a badly sprung sofa, Mavis can still see the young Gwen lurking underneath. She carries the weight of the new Gwen, now old, with a certain lively spring to her step. As if any minute what has turned into too much upholstery will once again be an abundance, not an embarrassment of flesh. Mavis almost expects the young Gwen to stop and suddenly shed the old Gwen. Like someone unzipping a deep-sea diving suit.

As for Mavis, she expects no such resurrections. Always thin and pointed, never luxurious at all, her flitteriness has dried into something overvarnished, attenuated. Newly fragile. Like one of those cavemen they dig out of bogs.

She stands at the fireplace drinking tea so she doesn't have to look at Gwen. But she can't look at herself in the mirror above the mantelpiece. Whenever she looks in that speckled glass she has a feeling of vertigo, as if she is being sucked bodily into dry blue air.

There's a picture of Frank on that mantlepiece, one from the old days. Mavis doesn't appear. Because she was the one behind the camera. But she's preserved there anyway, she can still see herself seeing Frank and Gwen through the viewfinder: youngish prettyish but always average Mavis, rosier then, less angled, but from that precise moment starting to get that thin-lipped look to her face.

Gwen is grinning into an ever friendly lens. She strives to look serious—it's Sunday, she's wearing that bouclé Mother bought her in the city, and she's under strict instructions not to undo it, not one single button, not even the top hook and eye. But she ruins everything with that ridiculous hat. Her eyes shine with indiscriminate goodwill.

Frank isn't looking at the camera but off into middle distance. No matter where Mavis stands in relation to the photo, he always seems to be looking over her shoulder. At something or someone else.

Click, click, tap, tap. The click and clatter of new boot heels hopscotching over river stones. Frank gave her those shoes, in a proper white shoe box with an old Christmas ribbon tied around it to hide the 'Discount' sticker on the side. Then he asked her to marry him. She looked at the box as though Frank had handed her a bomb. Time ticked by. Frank leant easily on the doorjamb, gazing out at empty paddocks; he looked like he didn't care one way or the other, that he had nothing to do all day but lean around and think thoughts.

Mavis took them in the end of course, but not until she had made close examination of the cattle dogs, the vegetable patch, the precise angle of the sun. They were cunning little ankle boots with real hook and eye laces and punch holes on the toes. They were perfect. In fact, they were the only pair of shoes that Mavis owned which actually fit.

Of course she couldn't wear them in front of Mother. And if Gwen saw them she'd be stuffing her big fat feet in them until the stitching burst. Mavis waited until the next Sunday then wore her old ones as far as the third paddock. She hid them behind a rock. Her feet slipped into the new boots like butter; she walked with eyes glued downward, admiring the shine and blackness, the way the top hugged her ankle, making the little blue hollow there look finely boned.

It was hard to tell what would constitute Doing The Right Thing. The problem was that everybody seemed to like Frank, even Mother. It was that photo of Plain Father McNally, it was like a magic carpet, it put Frank a notch above where he should have been. Mavis was too young then to know that liking someone, and class, position, what Mother called 'provenance'—a word she got from art history but a useful word, one which could be used to classify people as rigidly as buttons, by the same ruthless absolutes—that between the poles of liking someone and what was appropriate, there was a vast and arctic waste. This was Mother's natural habitat. A place called Doing The Right Thing.

Mavis was so busy admiring her boots that she didn't hear them at first. But as she crossed the bridge her father had built so the drovers could get across—it was narrower here, the river, narrow and densely treed, and it was particularly dark under the bridge—she heard a bubbling giggle. A tinkle like brown water running over stones.

They must have heard her, what with the ruckus her boots made on rocks. But they didn't stop what they were doing. So Mavis hid behind a bush and watched.

At first she thought it was Wally Thompson on top of Gwen. But then she saw the man's shirt had ridden up. A cruel white river flowed from the hidden world inside the man's trousers, dragged down below his hips. It disappeared like a fat snake's tail up under the collar, heading toward Frank's heart.

Gwen's legs were parted—nothing unusual there, she was always in trouble for sitting with her legs every which way; once Mother even tied her knees together with a piece of rope. But Gwen's legs were so far apart it looked painful. She looked like a plump wishbone Frank was trying to break. Her dress and her bra were flung to the edge of the water, they were all wet and muddy. Strangely, that was what Mavis was thinking. That those stains would never come out.

Gwen's eyes were closed, her mouth was open. Her face suggested pain. Her breasts spilled out from behind Frank's shoulders. They were large and milky, blue-white, marbled with veins. Maps to a distant place.

Mavis undid the boots as quietly as she could. She crept away to wait. Later she would pretend nothing had happened, she'd take the picture, she'd say yes to Frank's proposal, she'd put the picture in a commemorative silver frame. She did briefly consider throwing those boots in the river, that'd make them jump. But in the long run Mavis couldn't bear to throw away a perfectly good pair of shoes.

'What'd yer want to keep that silly thing for?' Gwen is suddenly standing right behind her, breathing heavily, hot and sour. Even with Gwen's baby elephant walk, Mavis didn't hear her come in. 'Came back for me lamingtons. Those ones you were wrapping. Waste not want not. Gawd, look at that bloody hat!'

Gwen grabs Frank's photo off the mantlepiece and waltzes round with it, trying to make Mavis laugh. She bounces comically on the balls of her enormous feet. But Mavis doesn't find it funny, Gwen's moronic energy, the way she always tries too hard. It is the worst and best thing about her but Mavis could never stand it, certainly can't stand it any more.

'Gwen! Knock it off! Give it here!'

Mavis slaps out, sharp nails connecting with flesh so dense they barely leave a mark. The picture flips and hits the fireplace. Miraculously, the glass doesn't smash.

Perhaps Frank really is made from some indestructible substance. Beyond glass or skin or bone.

chapter 18

It's a couple of hours to sunset, they've come another fifty kilometres down the highway and still no lake. Maybe she got the turn-off wrong; there was never any real sign. Just a gravel road with a certain kink in the elbow. A tree hit by lightning. A funnel-shaped rock.

J got them lost a while back; Ruth fell asleep, and he took a long and pointless detour on a side road, forty K out of their way. Though how he managed this on a completely straight road with no real turn-offs, she's not completely sure; there were only a couple of options to choose from, dirt tracks marked by half kero drum letterboxes, little red flags drooping in the heat.

'You said second left after the third bridge,' he's arguing, 'and that's what I did, took the second turn after that little brook.'

'We don't have brooks, this is Australia. Anyway, all the creeks are dry. That must have been a bore.'

'What's a bore?'

'You are. Stop whingeing and drive.'

It's getting late. Soon the sun will set, colour will heighten, glow the deep technicolour of dying cowboys and men killed down pit. She won't be able to find anything then. She doesn't even know what she's looking for, but it won't be an object. It will be a feeling, a swirl of muddy meaning. Rising from brown water, red dust.

'You'd better go a bit faster, mate. Otherwise we'll be putting the tent up in the dark.'

'Where though? Where are we going to put up a tent?' J looks around nervously, at land spreading flat and blank on every side.

'Told you a hundred times, it's just off this road. There's taps and toilets, all mod cons. Well the woman at the tourist centre said there was. There's taps at least, some barbeques. There was last time I was here.'

'When was that?'

'About twenty years ago.'

'Oh bloody marvellous. It's probably closed down by now.'

'Don't be ridiculous. They don't close down taps. Why would they bother? Stop fussing. We'll be okay.'

'I'm not putting up the tent.'

Ruth can feel it already, her face settling into grim and familiar lines, someone else's face, as if the marks of years and disappointments were already there. A memory in the muscles, in the spartan set of jaw and eye. She pulls J's cap down and squints out grimly. In truth, she's enjoying it. The certainty of saying: it will be there.

J keeps up a worried mutter but finally they see the sign; it's a new glossy one, in modern green metal instead of the old splintered wood, and now, as well as the lake, it offers something called the Dreaming Resort. Have they made topiary, planted a golf course, constructed a mini Harbour Bridge? But then the road turns to dirt like it always did, giving off tough little puffs of dust. She sees these changes are just cosmetic, some half-completed gesture by town planners clutching at straws.

There are modern picnic shelters alright, an information centre, a new kiosk, but everything looks closed. Some of the caravans are still there but they are locked up, wheels replaced by piles of bricks. Mavis sold her van spot after Frank had the stroke; there's a brand-new one there, a modern leviathan the size of a decent house. It's the wrong time of year anyway, it's not Christmas. No-one comes out here now.

Gone too are the old corrugated-iron toilets and in their place are things called 'windy loos'. These are made of extruded green metal in science fiction shapes. Ruth reads the blurb while she's sitting down to piss. This sleek steel object is environmentally friendly and has won awards for design. The wind whistles through all the holes and gaps, and her legs and head are clearly visible at either end. It's a Star Trek version of squatting behind a bush.

Mavis is very proud of this place. In her letters to Ruth, which came with photos of someone's new and ugly baby and snapshots of Mona standing like a dot in an eon of space, Mavis kept talking about how the town was now 'real go ahead'. Mostly this meant sleek new shopping centres with acres of car park and the replacement of all the old milkbars, general stores and haberdashers by Kmarts and fast food outlets and video places offering deals involving chicken and chips. The widening of highways, the installation of roundabouts, the landscaping of verges with regulation greenish-grey shrubs. It will continue until everything in the country looks exactly the same as an outer city suburb. McDonalds growing like fungus, coast to coast.

This place out here took up two or three letters, mainly because Mavis had played a vital and civic-minded role.

'They've made the lake a national park now, you know. The CWA was on the committee. We wrote to our local member. It has sacred sites. The Prime Minister came to open it. They've built picnic shelters and gas barbeques. You can even take tours up where the Abo paintings are.' Mavis couldn't see anything wrong at all. She went on to say how the place had won awards, been commended overseas, how it drew hundreds of people in peak period, how proud she was. She climbed up to the rock caves herself, as an official 'Dreaming Guide'. She memorised the pamphlets and made informative little speeches. She was a well of unwieldy statistics. First this, last that, oldest rock paintings, most artefacts per square inch. She got to wear a uniform and a special Akubra hat.

Ruth can just see Aunt Mavis in one of these loos, her carefully sculpted blonde perm topped off with a cowboy hat at one end, her high heels and light beige stockings sticking out the other. Her face, with its gash of pink lipstick, looking suitably shocked.

The toilets sit at a lonely distance from everything else, in the middle of the dusty rise. You can see everything from here, as from a throne: the dirt sloping down to the caravan site, with its roads and byways like a miniature grid of town; the tin shed where they keep the paddle boats, red, white and green; the kiddies' playground, metal swings glinting on a scorched square of dust. To the left, the twin rock hills, sticking up like boils from inflamed skin. Famous only because they are higher than anything else.

When Ruth was a kid and staying out here at the caravans, she and Mona used to climb up the highest hill. But you didn't do it to find a new perspective. There was a perverse pleasure in arriving to find nothing except greater height and distance; in some ways it was reassuring, that refusal of the picturesque. You were never missing out on anything. It was always just more of the same.

To the right is the old dirt road which came before the highway and which, if you followed it, would bring you to a rocky plateau with no signs or roads or public toilets but full of secret holes and caves. The wind moaning. A lover lost in a honeycomb of rock.

And in the centre of everything, like a dull and sullen secret, the reason why everyone comes. Water. Flat, grey, mysterious. Listening only to its own ancient ache. From this distance it looks shallow, spreading in a great kidney which swells and recedes, in tune with some subterranean logic. An equal and opposite gravity to that of the earth.

When Ruth finally emerges from the spaceship loo, J is looking distraught. He didn't bargain on the harshness or the heat. His idea of camping is jolly songs and marsh-mallows on forks.

'I'm going to have a look around,' she tells him after she's put up the tent. They've claimed a little spot under one of the trees, an official space marked by painted stones and bristling with long-winded signs. They tell you where to put your rubbish and which way you should park your caravan and where you shouldn't light your fire and when and where you should. J reads them carefully, he feels they should stick by the rules. Under those dreadlocks, he's English middle class, through and through.

It's only after she's done it, put the tent up, that Ruth realises the knots she's tied in the peg ropes are the complicated double looped and twice threaded ones taught to her by Uncle Frank. No matter how hard the wind blows or how many times you trip over the tent pegs or how much rain collects in the side flaps, they won't loosen. If you try to untie them from the centre, they just knot over themselves, in equal powers of resistance, again and again. Yet one pull on a secret loop and there it is.

'I'll come along. Just for the stroll.' J sticks his hands in his pockets and looks nervous. At home, with the deros and the punks and the drunks, J is in his element, tough and wiry and capable, squatting over his raggedy treasures, pulling pints and walking with the street swagger, on the balls of his DM feet. Here, though, he looks pale, transplanted, tenuous. Like a cellar vegetable. Or a hothouse flower. Already starting to wilt.

At the shrine to the famous unionists they want five dollars to enter. It is in a small stone house near the kiosk, the only thing open at this time of year. The ghost town on the lake's edge used to be a river port, the free literature tells you, and the paddle steamers could travel all the way up the river, towing barges full of wine and flour, horseshoes and nails. But the river faltered, became unreliable, beaten by drought and the water being diverted upstream. Finally ships were stuck with hulls at pathetic angles, marooned in deep subterranean mud.

Behind the old prison is a little cemetery. There's no sign to identify it, no fence to mark it, just two red dirt roads which wend and criss-cross, seemingly at random,

curling between headstones and then away. As if to pretend
they weren't really leading there at all. The graves themselves are scattered at random across undefined scrub and
earth. But the way they are dotted here and there in sudden
clusters, with some faint logic or weathered symmetry,
means there are probably plots that have lost their markers,
right beneath her feet.

The place hums with heat and light. It's frantic with
flies. This bright starkness is more eerie than fog and mist
at midnight could ever be. Some headstones are just pieces
of corrugated iron with white paint bearing old-fashioned
names. Amelia, Winifred, Edwin and Esther. There's even
a Bathsheba. Names no-one has any more. Others, more
prosperous looking, are hemmed by rusted railings which
serve only to prescribe where weeds should grow. Or perhaps the earth is secretly richer there. That's why they
flourish and burst, in mockery of the wreaths no-one has
placed.

Ruth scours the names, knowing it can't possibly be
there, but it's supersitition; if she finds an Evonne, there'll
be a rhyme or rhythm to it, it will be a secret sign. She
doesn't and anyway most of the headstones are ancient and
illegible, dated 1870, 1895, 1905. They plot the trajectory
of now curable diseases or old mine rockfalls or sudden
bursts of childbirth or the outbreak of something simple
as flu. Nearly all are broken in half. It's like a jigsaw, trying
to guess whose flowery rhyme belongs to who. Some have
been neatly propped on their ruined bases, the top half
pointing sadly to psalms muttering jaggedly through
chipped and splintered teeth. There are bottles smashed
across the cupids, shards glinting on the Italianate saints.
Stone fingers flourish brokenly at sky.

The best one is a little corrugated-iron marker she finds right on the outskirts. It sits with its back turned to the others, looking to the desert, as if preferring to face the truth. It's miraculously whole. All it says is Anne, no surname, twenty-two. Wife of someone.

The inscription says 'Blighted hopes'.

J refuses to go into the mining museum. He hates museums, hates opera, hates libraries. His mother insisted he speak like a BBC announcer and learn the violin. So he leans against a piece of rusting mine machinery and cleans his already immaculate nails.

Old iron implements sit mutely in the weeds near the entrance, baking in slow rays of sun. Ruth sneaks in the back way, wriggling between loose sheets of tin. But she needn't have bothered. The pensioner on duty has nodded off. Dust motes float in the beams of light, falling on the hard hats, drifting like snow through the old woman's hair. A pickaxe here, a shovel there. Those old miners would laugh if they knew these were 'worth a few bob'. Nostalgia is the artery to be quarried, now the minerals have run out. Under glass counters are hunks of rock, old prospecting dishes, a battered hat with a lamp and linotypes from the late 1800s, all courtesy of a benevolent BHP. There are boat hulls and rusting manacles and electric hat contraptions once lashed to the insane. Along with the ancient meat safes and the faded newspapers, the torch helmets and the blurred dead miners in sepia, there are tea towels with pictures of the Sydney Harbour Bridge. And T-shirts shouting hysterically: 'JUST SAY NO TO DRUGS!'.

She's deflated in the end. It's easy to sneer at Sturt pea tea towels and kangaroo wallets, but these stern figures in brown and white, they have paid their dues.

They stand erect and unsmiling outside tin cottages. They are waiting for history to arrive. When it comes it will be sudden. It will leave them receding through a tunnel of unused years. It will be cholera, typhoid, fire, flash flood. The sudden surrender of thrice-gutted earth.

Men stand in unfailing readiness, in unaccustomed daylight, implements in hand. Picks and lamps and shovels, these things give them gravity, they prop them up. Famous yet nameless. Like Frank, known only by tools and deeds.

Inside the dark mouths of doorways, like shadows or sepia ghosts, lurk their absent wives.

'Think I'll walk on up the hill.'

'What, now? It's going to get dark.'

'Won't take long. Why don't you go and have a lie-down?'

J looks dubious but crawls inside the tent. His blond dreads turn bright orange in the glare. He's clutching the present she bought him, one of those shaker things complete with mine shaft. At least J thinks the snowflakes are funny.

She trudges off up the hill.

chapter 19

The town crematorium has an Eftpos machine and cheery posters, like it's a place to book for bus tours out of town. It makes Mavis feel uncomfortable, this breeziness, but she stands her ground.

Twenty years ago she would never have stepped across the threshold of a place like this. But then there are a lot of things she wouldn't have done back then. She wouldn't have let her hair go grey and lifeless, she wouldn't have left the house minus lipstick, she would never have worn ten-dollar discount store shoes. She wouldn't have stopped going to Mass. She wouldn't have had that feeling as she went to cross herself at a drought-stricken font, that the silence Frank had knitted in sly little holes through everything was swelling fit to burst.

She'd gone to the cathedral first. To see Old Father McNally, who used to be Plain Father McNally, but who, with the death of Old Father McNally and the ageing of Young Father McNally into someone who could no longer be called young by any stretch of the jumper, was now called Old Father McNally, plain as that. So old he'd passed the century, hobbling past the finish line like a glue factory nag. So old that the bishop who'd packed him off to purgatory in a barren parish with heat and flies and a demountable church had long ago been recruited to Rome. Plain Father McNally never got there; they just sent him here. Another priest has the parish but they let Old Father McNally moulder on in the presbytery. He sits like a bony black afterthought in the last row at Mass.

The thing is, though, that when Mavis walked through the cathedral door and up the aisle and felt that old airlessness, that emptiness where God should have been, she couldn't do it. Couldn't book Frank in there. Knew Frank would have hated it, her making his peace with that toothless old nag of a God. So she genuflected and hurried out, fluttering through sun slants from stained-glass, through buttery too-golden rays.

'No service?' asks Mr Fitzgerald from behind his computer terminal. This is highly irregular, that someone would come in here and ask to book in. When the person wasn't even officially dead. And someone like Mrs Kelly—he can hardly believe she is there at all. None of this new-fashioned folk mass for Mavis Kelly. No liturgical dancing for her.

Mavis rustles in her purse and draws out the money, a fat wad of it, she has no idea how much these things cost. She doesn't care. She just wants to get rid of the dead weight of things which once had purpose but are now too fragile, too light, like the bones of a bird. The heavy weightlessness of the brown paper and string package under her arm. Those little bones at the police station, so feathery, but in reality weighing an old imperial ton.

She finally found the house money stashed in the tin box under the lemon tree. She went back to the old house when those new people were on holiday, suddenly realising after all these years that she knew Frank better than she thought. The shop had been turned into a junk room, there was grease all over her once sparkling laminex, and Frank's birdbaths had been co-opted into the chook house out back. But she couldn't bring herself to take the box entirely, there was a remnant of the old mystery Frank drew around his shed. Anyway, there was nothing else in the box except that old photo of Plain Father McNally. And a little gold cross, stuffed in a handbag which had seen better days.

She remembered Frank showing Mother that picture the day he first came to ask for work. Frank knocking on Mother's front door when he first turned up at the Goddard place, using that special rat-tatta-tat-tat which was swaggie morse code. Mother's heels tapping angrily up the hallway as she got ready to lecture someone on the evils of shift-lessness, the sinfulness of sloth. But Frank wasn't a swaggie. You could tell by his shoe leather. He was what Mother called a Decent Person Down On His Luck.

He must have had the photo a long time, it was yellowed and tattered and dog-eared from his pocket and from the way he kept folding over the corner, up and down, up and down. He wanted to know where he could find the priest. Said he wanted to look him up. Mother was suddenly flirtatious, suddenly forgiving of Frank's dusty hat brim, his ragged shirt. Because he had in his possession a picture of her brother the priest. Mother told Frank Father had been sent on an important assignment 'on the direct orders of the bishop, no less, to a new parish, a very important parish, quite a big parish, you know'. The way Mother was going on, you would have thought Father McNally was on his way to Rome. Instead of packed off to the middle of nowhere with the flies and sheep and cows. Mother even allowed Frank into her front foyer, usually reserved for proper visitors, and served him lamingtons and sweet black tea. True, they were stale ones from a week ago. And she didn't bring out the best Doulton, like she did with respectable people, with people from town. But Frank was grateful. Frank twirled his hat respectfully at his groin, round and round.

Mavis found something else there too, deep under the lemon tree. Now she has it under her arm. There's something fitting about using the money on this. It's blood money, as her mother used to say.

She wants Fitzgerald to take it right now and burn it, in his big nonholy fire.

'Afraid I can't do that, Mrs Kelly. Not when there's no death certificate. See what I mean?' Fitzgerald looks fearfully at the brown paper package, which seems harmless and even festive, like it might contain a pink jumper or a tin of lamingtons for a favourite niece. But you never know with these Kellys. They'd gone a bit queer.

'Sentimental value, is it? Something of Frank's?'

Mavis shrugs and says she'll be in touch. About the service. When she needs to. There'll be a body then. Just a body. That's all it is. God has floated up somewhere in his storybook clouds, in his fake rays of sunlight, surrounded by chubby cupids playing harps. They all look like Gwen.

Mavis doesn't leave straightaway. She waits in the wood-panelled chapel—modern like those new churches, all stark angles and a plain altar, no gilt or passion purple, not even a proper cross—to watch the early evening service. It's yet another Marconi, heart attack or stroke or rampant diabetes, all that spaghetti turned to white strings of fat. She's vaguely surprised they are in here at all. Must be a Marconi from the lapsed side of things.

The coffin glides, there is a lot of florid Italian-style grieving but Mavis Kelly's eyes are perfectly dry. A Simpson plays the organ. Fitzgerald reads from the Bible, *though I walk in the valley, his staff and his rod.* As the coffin disappears through the curtain, Mavis tries to imagine how she will feel when it is Frank there, moving at a streamlined pace to a nonexistent hell. Frank's gone anyway, she could dance naked round the hospital bed wearing Gwen's beanie. He wouldn't bat an eye.

On the way out, round the back of the Last Rest Funeral Home, where the white tablecloths and non-denominational hymns give way to garbage bins and coffin offcuts and an incinerator where Fitzgerald burns his leaves, Mavis pauses. She fingers the package. She's carried it around for weeks now and with every passing day it gathers gravity even while threatening to float away.

Ruth should be there. Ruth should have a say.

Then just as quickly as she thinks it, in a way built from years of diplomatic praying, prayers like essays where God was a schoolmaster dazzled by fancy footwork, she dismisses the thought. She tried. She rang, twice. She talked to that boyfriend. She said it was urgent. That Ruth should come to the hospital, she should come and see Mavis, as soon as she could. But Ruth couldn't even be bothered to drop in for a cup of tea. It was all on Ruth's own head.

Vonnie's summer dress, her Woolworths comb, her little hankie, flare up brightly and, without an Our Father or even a Prayer of the Faithful, they're gone. She scrapes the ashes into a Fitzgerald's Funeral Service canister she stole from the display near the front door. It is the only thing Mavis has stolen in her life. Bits of Fitzgerald's rubbish are caught up in it but it doesn't matter, it's the thought that counts.

Then she burns the picture of Frank. She's saved the frame of course. Waste Not Want Not. Be Grateful For What We Have Received. Frank's face curls and blackens. Even now those eyes aren't looking at her.

chapter 20

From the bottom the path looks truly treacherous, winding slyly through rock outcrops and sliding slopes of shale. The way is easy at first, a slight incline, feet slipping a little on scrag. Those little rocks, with shiny black bits which chip off into smaller and smaller cubes, they're called something special but Ruth can't remember what. They were used as paperweights and ornaments; Uncle Frank had one in the bedroom, on the old lowboy, to hold down spare notes and change. Ruth used to creep in there and stare at it when he wouldn't talk to her or look at her; it started to infuriate her, anger building in tiny replica. His geometric silence, joined on every side. Nothing could be that perfect. No-one could be that silent for that long.

Before she left for the city she stole it from the bedroom and smashed it to pieces with Frank's old hammer, on the concrete half-painted path. It wasn't worth the effort because it just scattered into tinier and more exquisite pieces, smaller and smaller versions of the same mystery, breaking off again and again.

The incline is getting steeper now and she starts to puff, holding onto boulders for support. Too much sitting in the car. Then she starts to get the rhythm, listening to wind whistle, feeling stones bite through city-bought boots. Boots made for tame footpaths and shopping malls, made to look just like the real thing. But in the end, they are just an empty gesture, thin and elegant, something you hope to get away with. Even her hands, scratched and sore, are city hands. They've never milked oil from engines or wielded a hammer or strung a fence. Held dry earth and let it blow away in the direction of wind.

One foot in front of the other. Hand over muscle. You don't look up or your courage fails. If you look down you fall.

Ruth learnt this lesson the hard way the day Mona dared her to climb to the top. Going up was alright but near the pinnacle Ruth froze. The wind whistled and jeered. Mona teased and prodded and poked. Ruth missed her footing and momentarily the world fell away. Then it reappeared, fragile and harshly solid, all at once. She clung tight to a rock. After a million years of inertia, it felt like it might move. If you fell, nothing here would care.

Mona stood above Ruth on the sharpest apex, balancing easily, jeering, miraculously unafraid. From that angle, fore-shortened, with her long blonde hair hanging and the sun glinting off those mineral-sharp eyes, she looked like an evil angel. Ruth was surely in hell.

After a while Mona got bored, and leaping over cracks and fissures, reached the bottom, pedalling away on her bike. But Ruth was stuck up there for hours, watching sunset turning scrub and hollows red, then blue, then purple-black.

Finally, as the sun died in an uninterrupted line on the horizon, Uncle Frank came walking straight-backed up the hill. As if it required no effort, as if he too was just another piece of straight landscape, vertical not flat. He carried Ruth down like a parcel he had inadvertently forgotten. He didn't say anything. Didn't look her in the eye.

Ruth read once that people's characters can be shaped by their environment. If this theory is true, she is flat, parched, pockmarked with a bitter history. Thrown together hastily out of old bits of tin.

And Frank is a planet lacking water. A little like Mars.

She stops when she's nearly there and rests on the seat provided. The wind is keening, empty breathing too hollow even for a lament. The sun is sinking, it will be getting dark on the way down. But she's caught suddenly by the colours appearing across the plateau, all echoes of the original but with blue and green shadows and faint traces of purple, as if red is breaking up into its constituent parts. She looks and looks, trying to see what Frank and Mum had once seen, to find that beauty under dead layers of skin. But she can't see it. Never could.

There are only these harsh extremes. Flinty, scrubby, closed over, like the afternoon shadow on a face. Hills in the distance, long, flat and female somehow. But those soft flanks turn sharp red close up. Beauty here is always in negative, an alter ego, the shadow of an image burnt upon a rock. And the shadow is just an illusion, a bush cleaving traceries from red. And love is true to itself in such a place: yearning, a perspective endlessly receding, where journeys collapse to a pinpoint. Which is an eye and what it sees.

'There's a point here where you can see the curvature of the earth.'

She can't see it. Perhaps a faint hum of roundness, a haze barely visible to the naked eye. Nothing upon which to remark. It is the silence which intimidates. It demands you listen to it, to the sound of nothing being born, giving birth, over and over again. Water stretches it, closes it over. Rocks bear mute witness to it, stark as certain facts. Earth is flat. Universe is infinite. Horizons can be round.

Then behind her, on a new road they've built which climbs the rock hill, which she hadn't even noticed and which probably brings up Greyhound buses jam-packed with shuttering cameras and packed picnic eskies and koala jumper tourists, voices grating like fingernails across sheer silence: 'Well, me and Alf, we've already *done* the outback', a car drives up. It disgorges women in tracksuits. After all that, she didn't even need to walk.

When Ruth gets to the top of the hill she sees the cave paintings have not escaped the march of modern life. She would have preferred the desert got them, although it will in the end. It's just that the desert will take its time.

The paintings are fenced off by a circle of man-made stone. There's a plaque detailing their geology as if this can explain it all. The paintings are caged by a little wire fence. Like you can mark off what you don't understand. This far, no further. The rest belongs to us. But it's not meant to keep people out. It keeps the unknown in.

The paintings are smaller and more fragile than remembered. Colours are faded, fingers on hands have fallen right away. Those less talented have written over the rest, written over prehistory with a new and empty story, in black texta and red paint: Chris loves Karen. Thommo was here. Suck My Cock. Two of the paintings have been doused and fired. They stand like corpses with the flesh burnt off. Only the frail intent of a finger remains. Pointing to the magic hole.

Ruth tries to crawl inside it, the secret rock. But she's far too big, it's way too late. All she can fit in is her head. She puts her eye to the hole, hoping for a secret frame of reference. But there is only a slice of desert, pinned arbitrarily by an accident of wind. And Frank has already walked off, out of frame and down the years, leaving his boots like mismatched clues at the edge of the lake.

'Come on, we're going. There's nothing here.'

J pokes his head out the flap, incredulous.

'But I just set up the tent!'

'*I* set it up, you can pack it up. Get a move on, it's getting dark.'

Ruth walks back toward the car, listening to J swear and curse as he fiddles and picks, fastidious as a Boy Scout, at Uncle Frank's exquisite mystery, at his incomprehensible perfectly equidistant knots.

the water
underneath

chapter 21

Frank is floating. He can hear the green thrip of machines. He can feel his fingers at the end of his hands. The weight of the sheet on him is light as a girl's summer dress. Now and again a face floats into vision: Mavis, face bare of make-up, looking suddenly old. Gwen grinning, all vacant good cheer. But though Frank's eyes are open, he gives no hint of recognition. He's waiting for one face in particular. He needs to tell her something. He needs to draw her a map. One with no roads or signposts on it. With the secrets and stories under its skin.

Faces swim in and out of focus, they buzz and hover and go away. They whine with aimless velocity, around some empty centre. They are hungry for Frank as so many flies.

The fluorescent light on the ceiling is burning down. They think he can't see it, but he can. It burns a burst of radiance into memory. It's beating down like the sun.

Frank is walking, some place above the ceiling, in the heart of that white and burning light. He's wearing no shirt and wet trousers. Sun licks at the skin on his back. But it won't burn, all the texture there is gone. He knows where he's headed, he doesn't take the road. The road, black and straight and full of logic, is a trick, a thin tightrope over a chasm. It arrives at no truth at all.

Instead he strikes out across secret country, away from the lake, away from Mona hiding in a place where one like her, with hardly a drop of the red clay in her, shouldn't be. Away from the pull of the water. He has no water with him, that's another of the rules. All he has is his shirt, which he dipped in the lake before he left and tied around his waist. This is instead of the plant river man Jacob told him about; if you chewed it, it gave you water, and its leaves gave off moisture which kept you cool. But that plant's gone now, been eaten by all the white-man fish.

Away from the road even the smallest tracks between the spinifex disappear. They are mere accidents, patches of earth slightly depressed. They are false memories of a failing moisture, the scars of useless journeys, of water which ran across earth tight and fierce as a drum. It could gain no foothold, gather no force. It dwindled into spurts of false direction which end in things being lost. It made hard cracks in the earth's skin. You follow them, those false trails, and they lead you nowhere. They double back, frantic for some hope. The path they leave is a snake wound around itself, joined end to end.

The Holy Snake was a trick. Frank knew it but Maudie didn't. It's not the bite of the Snake you should fear, there will be nothing as simple as a lightning bolt when you go to hell. It's the coiling endlessness of the journey, the infinity of travelling never to arrive. These paths are as useless as trying to read the future in the lines of a palm.

Frank stares at his own hands as he walks, holding them before him in that white and burning light. They are strange maps attached to the ends of his world. Their language, faint as breath on a car window, is a spiderweb of journeys taken, journeys failed, journeys never begun. He can't feel them, can't make out the final destination, can't see the meaning, black and definite, rise through blank white skin. He can't believe these heavy capable bits of flesh could be his. But the lines are there, the truth of it, in hieroglyphs and veins branching, in weariness crissing and crossing, hatching deep into his surface, the marks of hammers and scars of effort that grew a skin. Until nothing, not dry earth or blunt metal or shattered glass, could make that skin bleed.

He had tried to construct a life. He'd thought it would keep him safe. The building of sheds, the planting of seeds, the burn of a hundred radiator caps, water bubbling and spitting, trying to make its mark. Nails driven to anchor him and his to the earth. He thought it was solid, those picket fences and tin roofs and orderly paths. The cars collecting in the backyard like journey's end. He thought all the journeys formed a pattern, a map which he would later find himself in. A person in motion defined by where he'd been, where he was going, where he might have been. But the things he built were burdens. Patched together with string and silence, they weighed a ton. When he tried to lean on them, they fell apart, returned to the scrounged bits of rubbish of which they were made. All it took was a sudden wall of water and everything floated away.

He takes nothing with him now. He carries his map with him like a top-heavy snail. He doesn't read the sky, look for signs in stones and earth. She is a feeling. A breath of air marking her own passage. Like the image of a finger pointing to the image that this finger has made.

She's out here somewhere, as invisible and precious as old water, in the faint passage of some secret blood. She carries with her a secret name. He has to tell her about it. And he can only find her by walking, without water or maps or screwdrivers. Into a vast and mapless place.

chapter 22

Fifty kilometres from the lake, on the highway back to town, their brand-new top-of-the-range Commodore breaks down. It sputters, powerful cylinders miss, and then suddenly they are coasting, engineless, only their last forward motion carrying them along. There's not even the faintest decline to induce the semblance of a roll. Nothing about this place will help you. You have to make your own progress, with gauges on empty and dregs of petrol, with jam jar lids and and old chewy and stray bits of string. If you give up, you're a goner. It will get you in the end.

When they left, this car was an oasis, with a name like a spaceship, where travel could be effortless, surrounded by fine velour and a noiseless hum. It ate up old miles and spat them out, like time and distance meant nothing at all. Money can turn what used to be a feat of endurance into something luxurious. Like travelling in a well-appointed lift.

Now, with the engine dead, it's just a car. As unpredictable and fragile as Frank's old trucks. With their holes in the chassis and voracious fuel tanks and wet towels flapping at the windows, in those days the only air-conditioning you had.

J starts swearing, fucking this and fucking that, and Ruth knows he's scared. But because he's been sulking ever since she made him pack up the tent, saying that *she's* the wally, that she bloody well doesn't know what she wants, she lets him stew.

He's propped the bonnet open, he's staring intently inside. What he's hoping to achieve by this Ruth isn't sure. He wouldn't know a spark plug from a dipstick and has never changed a tyre. But she's glad he's occupied, out there beyond the windshield. All the way back, in this artificial womb, he's been huffing and sighing and muttering; he even mentioned his missing dreadlock, another black mark. He must count them, how ridiculous. But she let it go. Now at last there's just silence. And heat growing its skin.

This was about where Uncle Frank broke down that time coming back from the city. Mavis had to take Gwen to a city hosptial, they were coming back by train. Ruth, knew Uncle Frank wouldn't want her to come with him—it was not long after Mum disappeared and his reign of silence had just started then, but she couldn't believe it, didn't know it would go on and on.

She hid under the tarpaulin in the back of the truck. Frank didn't find her there until it was far too late. He didn't go crook. He just plonked her on the passenger seat and kept driving. He didn't say a word.

She knows it was here they broke down because of that funny shaped rock by the side of the road. Strange, in all these miles and miles of distance between the lake and the Settlement, the lake and town, the lake and every day life, if you broke down, it was always here. Like it was the apex of some Bermuda triangle a thousand miles from the sea.

When the fan came loose from the radiator in the old Holden, miles from home, Frank swore. He stood with hands on hips in front of the propped-up bonnet. Ruth stood beside him, unconsciously doing the same. He ignored her, as thoroughly as if she was a rock or post or a tree. At least Frank knew what he was doing when he looked inside a car's stomach. But this time there was nothing he could do, not even one of his usual tricks with a bit of old Juicy Fruit and a rubber hose. The fan had sheared straight through the radiator. It had a hole in it, jagged as a wound. Precious water was bleeding onto the road.

It was over a hundred degrees according to Frank's little key ring thermometer; he always liked to know the exact temperature at any given time. This time it had gone off the dial. Mercury jiggled. Steam bubbled. Frank looked up and down. But the road was empty. As empty as a road can get. Out here you could see for miles and miles.

Frank stayed calm. His face was very red under the old hat. Ruth remembers thinking it was the same colour as the earth, that somehow he and it were of the same inhospitable substance. With hidden springs if only you knew where to dig.

Uncle Frank said, 'Let's hit the road.' But he didn't mean the road; he felt safer off it. He didn't like that straight black ribbon, lulling you into the void of a white man's map. He didn't show it but he was afraid; no water, no cars, it was over a hundred and twenty degrees. Even though his thermometer wasn't working, Frank knew it. He didn't need clocks or fob watches or primus stoves or Redheads. All he needed was skin and eyes and sun.

Frank trudged off through the spinifex carrying the useless radiator. Ruth followed like a squaw. Frank didn't talk to her. They walked for hours. They walked and walked, without water or food or direction, and Ruth was wondering, how on earth does he know where he's going, whether there'll be anything there?

Sure enough, as if by an effort of will, there was a homestead, the only one for miles. It had a windmill, a water tank, some mangy dogs. The woman behind the screen door was holding a baby. She didn't smile or frown. When Frank asked if her husband was about, she shook her head. She looked like every last ounce of juice had been sucked out of her. She lived a life Ruth was beginning to imagine might exist.

Frank asked if Ruth could stay there while he went for help. The woman shrugged. Out of some grim unhappy code she made Ruth sit down with her and her son to a burnt Sunday dinner in the heat. The boy chewed peas to slime. He opened his mouth to show Ruth the result. The woman said, 'Don't.' There was no conviction in it. Ruth chewed and swallowed, chewed and swallowed. The dry metal of fear along with the greasy lamb.

Through the window Ruth could see Uncle Frank trudging toward the road. He had the broken radiator on his back. It looked heavy. But he walked upright. Like a horizon turned on its side. He receded, stiff-backed and implacable, his hat casting a halo on the ground. The burden of Ruth, his responsibility, was incarnate. Across his shoulders. It was heavier than any car part. Heavier than the sheer weight of the sun.

But by the time Frank was a small dot on the horizon,

she had him in perspective. He was just an ordinary man in a too-big world.

'Well that's fucking great. Bloody marvellous. *I* don't know what's wrong with it. Wouldn't have the faintest. Would you?' J's looking around fearfully, at sun setting in bravura crimson, so dramatic a denouement you expect the Statue of Liberty to roll up on the horizon. The End.

'Have we got any water? What are we going to eat?'

J is obviously expecting to settle in for the long haul, to be found dead or dying, to have to eat camel and drink his own urine and carve his initials into a tree. Ruth leans over and hands him the mobile. At least that raises a laugh.

But as J calls the Shell at the Settlement, Ruth knows it can't be that easy. Uncle Frank's battle with bits of tin and crook speedos and half-painted back verandahs, his trick with sticks to make a fire. The way he sniffed air like a dog. The way he could tell water's memory long after it had flowed over ground. How he heralded water, with such faith in storytelling, at its zero gravity, that the mere act of saying something could make it happen. 'Rain.' 'River.' 'Flood.' As if words could hold a moisture all their own.

It can't have been as simple as not having a phone.

chapter 23

The mark is there, hidden under spinifex. No-one but Frank, none of the other boys at the Mission, not even Old Jacob with his weeping sticky eye, would have found it. Just a faint nick. The round push of a heel.

But Frank sees it, he can see it even with his eyes taped shut. He traces the shape of her journey, the tracks of her future, with one finger telling syllables, that dry rosary of earth. Ruined skin absorbs it, that mark which means Frank will be able to find her in all this dust and sun. The toe bulge means she isn't wearing any shoes. Frank isn't either. He ignores the burning. It's useful. He wants his feet to be white, smooth, closed.

The way he knows her is that bump on the bottom of her toe. She dropped a house brick on it one Christmas. Frank bandaged it and held her and rocked her, he wouldn't take her to the hospital no matter how often Mavis told him he should. He wasn't putting her in that white place of sharp instruments, into a place stinking of a white blank death.

When he went to take off the bandages in the morning, they were set hard as a rock. She fainted as he soaked the bandage away, as flesh and blood came with it, turning the bathwater red. He held her and kept pulling, layer by layer, at her ruined skin.

He cut her hula hoop in half and propped it under the bedclothes to keep the weight off, that sheet light as a thin cotton dress. He sat by her all night, telling his necklace of stars. But he'd never known the proper names of them, not really. Maudie didn't tell him, she sank and left him to drown. He just pretended, like he did with Jacob, pretended he knew those shapes and stories, pointing out the saucepan and the archer and the spilt milk across a familiar sky. He had to make do with small bits of the mystery, each one perfectly formed, but no matter how you dismembered it, into ice-cream containers and painted paths and jam jars, into normal life and bits of wilderness, where you wander away from houses and wives and caravans, each piece was always too perfect, always incomplete. And as he sat there all night and talked and listened to her moaning, he knew he was right not to pass this silence on. He couldn't have stood it. Another journey ending in silence. That snake circle leading to a white full stop.

The one he called Von he couldn't help; she was Maudie's, she was his mob. The other one, without any red clay in her, she was a mistake, from when Frank was younger and more stupid, from when he thought that pushing into that fat white flesh might yield a secret, that he could follow some blue-veined milk to a better place. But all he found was the same silence, flattening him under God's heavy hand. And all those times driving in his truck, along dirt roads and highways, into wilderness, into strange towns with strange people in them, looking first for Maudie, and when he couldn't find her, for that crow fella in his black flap dress. Even when he found the crow fella, after tracing his journey across vast tracts of loneliness, like he was tracking a frightened rabbit, his hand trembling on the gun, through country parishes and cities with no sun or moon to steer by, just grey and dirty smog, and into the far reaches of God's dry places, it was useless. When he came across the old bastard huddled in the back of the cathedral, come full circle, like a vulture returning to die, Frank couldn't kill him. Not even then.

When he found Maudie, she wasn't there. He found a grey bed, a black handbag, a little gold cross. Maudie drowned in her earth, long before she was dead. He found his sister though, she was his. And he took her to the white cloud lady, because it wasn't fair to Mavis when he didn't want one of his own. Because Mavis wouldn't understand. Because Frank couldn't tell her. Because he didn't want his sister to drown in silence. And because blood has come full circle. You can never get away.

Frank's been walking for a lifetime now, in heat but not feeling it, through years, not marking them, in sun that can't burn skin already dead. Away from the lake, away from the caravans, away from the road. Until everything, all signs of life have disappeared. No cars, no kero tins of petrol, no sandwiches in plastic, not this time. It was all a Holy Snake trick. Even that little garden where he'd tried to hem wilderness, give it a brightly coloured shape. Those bottles on a windowsill, sparkling their sly water death.

At some point Frank stops, takes off his trousers and leaves them like old snake skin on the ground.

Further on, snagged by a bush, he finds her hair ribbon, the blue one she always wore. Means she isn't wearing a hat. Frank leaves his hanging on a bush. It is the only way to find her, in silence spreading far as the eye can see.

The sun starts to set. The earth is red. But the skin on Frank's back is white. He puts his hands to his mouth and calls her. Her secret name bounces back at him, cracked to broken hemispheres. By red earth. By a blue and indifferent sky.

chapter 24

At the Settlement J refuses to get out of the car. He sits with his hands clenched on the useless wheel. Mechanics tinker under the bonnet and nudge each other and laugh at this Pommie wanker, this skinny long-haired bangle-wearing weirdo who's probably a drug-dealer, a dole bludger, a drug-taking dole-bludging Pommie poof.

'I'm going for a walk.'

'Don't.' J's hand on her arm is surprisingly urgent, leaves red dents when she tries to shake it off. She wants to tell him it's a bit rich this, after the way they've kept it light and cruel all this time. A bit late to want ordinary comfort and to go to water and to expect her to start holding his hand. Like she's someone who wears a frilly apron in private. Like all the time she was really Doris Day. She can't afford it. Not after Uncle Frank.

'Knock it off. I won't be long. File your nails or something.'

'Please. Just stay here.'

'For fuck's sake. Pull yourself together. Don't be such a sook.'

She slams the door and the car judders. She sees J sitting there, looking small and blurry, with his head resting on the wheel. She should go back and give him a hug. But her feet won't let her. They just keep walking toward the bridge.

There's no-one around as Ruth walks up the middle of the main drag. It's Sunday. What do people do here on a Sunday? No lawns to mow, no cars to wash. No cinema to go to, no cafes, no air-conditioning, maybe no TVs. They probably go to the pub. Which is what they would do even early in the day, if it was open, because they couldn't go to Mass. No church. That's one good thing. But there are people around, if she looks closely, at the dark doorways under the falling-down verandahs. Some of them are open a crack; you can see bare feet, the shapeless hems of dresses, the flash of white teeth. They aren't smiling. It's just a slack sort of stare.

Just before the bridge there are some Koori kids. They are drawing circles in the dirt. Their hair is the colour and texture of straw. The boys look up at her and she sees their raggy shorts and their crusty eyes and their old Coca-Cola T-shirts. Ruth and Mona with their bicycles and swing sets, her and J with their mobiles and vacuum sealed car. It isn't fair. But when she turns her back on them someone throws a stone. Cheeky little buggers. Maybe Mavis was right.

The big iron bridge with its black and white flood markers marks the end of the Settlement, the boundary between the safe and the unknown. It spans the slow brown river with a sleek black highway which takes people who have been forced against their will to stop here fast and straight out of town. Away from this place which has only recently been given a proper name.

To Ruth it will always be the Settlement, the place you stop for petrol and where you don't get out of the car. The four mean streets of the place keep running their gauntlet, no bitumen, just dust in little willies which go right up your nose. Each corner has a person in a hat leaning on it. They seem to be the only things holding the place up. By the time the cross-streets get a few hundred metres from the main drag, the roads peter, as if what had been a good idea to start with is too exhausting to complete. On the edge of every street there is nothing but dust and scrub.

But there's the river. There's always the river. No wonder people turn their eyes toward it, away from streets that go nowhere, fast. It runs wide at the horizon, where all eyes look. It comes toward you, it can carry you away. But just before the Settlement, a few kilometres from here but you can just see it, in all this flatness, it chokes to a sob at the sluice. Something older than the cathedral, older than Frank's cave paintings even, has been narrowed by their rules. It worries at the concrete props. It foams like a piss held too long.

Past the obstruction, the river calms, pulling in a long slow breath under the bridge. On the banks are little clumps of people lying under trees.

'Look at them,' Ruth can hear Aunt Mavis saying it, as if Mavis is standing behind her on a kero tin, leaning over her shoulder, shouting through a megaphone and waving a rolled-up *Truth*. 'Shiftless. Lazy. Career drunks. Not worth the water God wasted. Shouldn't be allowed.'

Town people like Mavis never went beyond the Shell. Everyone had to stop of course, it was the last petrol for a hundred miles. But Mavis locked and relocked all the car doors and wound up the windows, even when it was over a hundred degrees. Her fear, grey and soggy and formless, took up all the air. Sitting in the car with Mavis, Ruth was forced to look at things through her tiny keyhole, and from there even the servo looked disreputable, with its grease and oil prints on everything, even the packets of Juicy Fruit Frank brought back. And the heat. And the silence. Deeper, fiercer, emptier here than anywhere else. All the fibro and tin shanties with their boarded-up windows made you feel you were being watched by a blind person. A person who knew exactly where you were.

'They had decent houses. The government paid for them. We paid for them. Decent people with hard-earned money paid for them. And now look at them. Just look what they've done.'

This usually said through a stiff mouth as Mavis snapped open her compact and redid her lippie in the rearview, in preparation for two hours car travel where she wouldn't see a soul. Vowels distorted, constonants falling hollow, everything stained Coral Dawn pink. In the heat of the car on those journeys to the city, Mavis talked on and on, down through the years. She swallowed up all the air. Each word clicked off like a bead on an abacus. The weight at one end tipped things her way.

'Fires lit in lounge rooms. Petrol sniffing. Flyblown babies. Toilets just holes in the ground.' Ruth couldn't remember the rest of it, it was a muttered rosary, a long necklace of greyish-coloured sin. Mavis, punching scone dough on a hundred Saturday afternoons. Indignation rising in vicious puffs. Ruth had to eat it along with the jam and cream.

One time, coming back from the city, they stopped here in the middle of the night. They needed petrol, there wasn't much choice. Mavis and Uncle Frank and Mona and Ruth were in the car. Still taking their Christmas holidays at the old convent by the sea. As if nothing had happened, as if Mum hadn't disappeared. Mavis and Mona were asleep. Mavis was snoring, her dentures giving that rhythmic little click. Spit shining in the streetlight, in a string between her teeth.

Ruth, bleary-eyed, leant her head against the window, feeling the hum and throb of the nozzle in the car. She was trying to stay awake. For Frank. And through the dusty windows, in the yellow glare of a streetlight, she thought she saw her. A thin woman with legs like sticks, in a flowered summer dress. Sitting under the streetlight, under the sparse branches of a tree. Which in hot midday sun would give no shade at all.

She looked like she'd been there for a long time that woman. It was the way she was lying, legs at odd, despairing angles, like she was a puppet someone had been playing with and, tiring of her, had cut the strings, let her fall. Someone had let her flutter there, broken and spindle-shanked, on dry red ground. Around her were sticks of furniture: an old lamp, seatless chairs, a suitcase tied up with string. A man was throwing this stuff out of the doorway of a house. He was yelling at the puppet woman, but through the car window Ruth couldn't hear what he was saying. She could guess though, because as the man chucked down the last chair, the last cardboard box full of empty bottles, he kicked her. Then he dusted his hands off and went back inside.

The woman lay there, limbs all at angles, arms poking out like twigs. A thin cotton dress. And Ruth wanted to tap on the window, jump up and down, yell and scream, Uncle Frank, there she is. Everything will be alright. But Frank was staring hard at the petrol pump and its click of stern knowable numbers, pretending that's all that mattered, that this held the sum of his parts. And when a truck pulled up and some other men piled the woman's furniture on it and then picked her up, like she was a bunch of sticks too, some rubbish the other man had left behind, and carried her to the back of the truck, the light fell on her face. She wasn't tawny coloured, she was too dark, her eyes weren't green. It wasn't Ruth's Mum.

Men threw that collection of sticks which looked like a woman in the back of the truck. And then they drove away.

Ruth just keeps standing there on the bridge, waiting for something to happen. There's that feeling like before a dust storm, a little thrill of grit below the skin. The air has gone grey and airless, after a long slow dusk which slapped viciously to black. Like a broken blind. When a car goes past on its way out to the highway, the wooden boards rumble and a hollow thump starts in the struts. It travels up the iron, through the floorboards, up through Ruth's shins. It even sets up static in the jaw. Maybe this was how Mum felt when she got angry, this rising shudder, until you just had to let it out. You had to walk and walk, further and faster, in the opposite direction, as far and fast as you could.

It looks nice and cool down by the river. But Ruth isn't game. The little clumps of people down there are staring at her. They don't move a muscle. They don't need to. They only need to stare. But she refuses to be frightened. She walks across into what they called the Riverside in the days Mum went drinking here.

She orders a shandy. Shandies are what Mavis always ordered—'Just a dash,' Mavis would say, fluttering at the beer like it was a naughty hand. Ruth would have liked to order a middy, just to shit that ghostly Mavis, but she hates the taste of straight beer. The guy behind the counter looks at her blankly, like she's talking Eskimo, like she's a visitor from Mars. It's getting beyond a joke, this playing dumb crap, so she shows the moron, this much beer, this much lemonade. There are little clumps of Settlement people behind her, they've gone silent, their eyes are boring into her back. But she grits her teeth. She's not going to give in.

Until the old guy sitting next to her prods at her belly and she has to swing around.

'You.' He keeps prodding, moving closer, she can smell the beer on his breath. 'You. You're Not From Here.'

Ruth's thinking, here it comes. The swearing, the jagged bottles, the gangs of drunken men. Mavis told them like Mother Goose stories, just before turning out the light.

'You.' He shakes his finger in her face, like Mavis used to when she was late for tea. 'You shouldn't be here.'

He has long silver hair and a squashed-up nose. But his eyes are keen. His hands don't shake. He wears brand-new boots. The drink has scored his face like too much rain. He has a fifty dollar note in his top pocket. Ruth considers nicking it in the hope of a stray taxi at the Shell.

'Sorry?'

But the old man just keeps muttering and nodding. 'Yep. Telling you now. You're Not From Here.' He's falling off his stool now, almost smothering her, he falls against her and knocks her drink flying and then starts to get angry, starts to swagger and bluster, starts to yell.

'Get out of it. You bugger. You're Not From Here.' The bar man is stepping in, calling the old guy Murray, like the river, when J, looking shit scared, sticks his head through the door.

'Ruth! Get a move on. Car's fixed. We can go.'

So she leaves the old guy sitting there, muttering into his schooner. 'You're Not From Here.' And she gets in the car and they limp back into town.

chapter 25

Frank is calling. Her secret name bounces back like a blow. But Von doesn't hear him. She is too far away. Both in real distance—in the middle of a place with no roads and no trees and no water, nothing from which to construct a map—and in the distant places. And she wouldn't know that name anyway. She only knows the one Frank gave her, the one he made up.

Lily drags a little but the weight is getting lighter all the time. Feet follow each other, there is blood to mark their rise and fall. The blood is red, redder than the earth. But it disappears quickly, as if a finger has pressed into waterlogged skin. Earth drinks her until there is no sign of Von at all.

As she walks, barefooted, bareheaded, carrying Lily like a little dry fish, Von is thinking about the Duke of Gloucester and McGregor and Murrie, about Trevor and the white truck man, about why pain has a different shape when left by different men. As if by towering above you they block out the light, leaving only their hat-shaped silhouettes.

When she got in the white truck, she knew what the driver wanted. But she was thirsty, that's all that mattered. So she let him kiss her and cop a feel. His hands closed around the brown skin of her thigh. It was a small price to pay. She was moving, that's all that mattered, down the long straight road of it, high above the world. She was too weak to walk too far, aware of all the new heaviness. In her thighs, pulling her down. In her head, thoughts like immovable stones. The weight of blood. The flow of breast milk. The water at high tide, swimming her to ground.

She didn't care even when the driver stopped by the roadside and reached over the gear stick and lifted up her dress. She closed her eyes. His hands on her were McGregor's, she could smell the toothpasty spit, the beer and fags like wrong notes in a cathedral hymn. This was what they thought she was, Sister Loyola and Mrs Whelan and Mavis and even Trevor, so she'd do it, even outside the web of rules, she'd keep to where they thought they'd strung her up. They thought she was still hanging there, thin legs akimbo, dress to the wind. Like a saint pegged out to drown. But she was somewhere else, and there were no maps where she was going. No-one could follow, not even Frank.

When the white truck man started to poke her with one finger, down there where she was still sore, she stuck a finger in his eye. Into the white soft place he'd forgotten he had. He yelped and swore and the flat of his hand came swinging. While he was still swearing and lashing, Von jumped out and ran. Down the long straight grim lesson of it, as fast and as hard as she could. Until she couldn't run any more. Until her legs gave out.

Trevor found her there, limping along, only a mile from the Settlement, nearly to Murrie, but Trevor found her first.

He drew up in a angry puff of dust. He dragged her in his truck and slapped her hard across the face. She can't remember what he said. It didn't matter. He called her things. He hit her again. But softer this time, his anger petering dully, like it always did. Ruth crying. Lily whimpering. Von held Lily against her. Lil stopped crying. The baby felt soft and small. Trevor swore and wrenched the steering wheel and the truck slithered and skated, past the white line and back again. But there was nothing to hit. No trees, no people, no cars.

When they got to the weir, just as they'd planned, like everything was still normal, like Trevor could make it normal by just pretending that it was, she told him her milk was gone. It had formed a stinking crust on the top half of her dress. Those blue veins had shrivelled to journey's end. She was glad. Trevor swore and punched the truck door and went to hit her again. But she didn't flinch. He slumped and his hands went loose and then he got back into the truck and headed back. To get Lil's bottle. Back into town.

Von took her shoes off. She wanted to feel the river between her toes. She left them sitting there on the bank; one thong fell in the water and floated away. Von didn't notice but Ruth picked up the other one and held it tight, as tight as she could. She watched her mum fashion a sling from an old bedsheet Dad had left there, for them to sit on, which he kept in the truck to wrap yabbies in or to stuff in the windshield if a stone broke the glass. Von caught Lily like a little fish in the flannelette, tying two corners around her waist and the rest around her neck. She stood straight and tall, taking this weight. This was the way Jacob had told her to do it, how the women from his country did it, so babies wouldn't fall in bad water and drown. Lil was a new weight then, only getting heavier with time.

Von sat Ruth on the river bank. She made her put on her hat.

'You wait for your dad, Ruthie. Won't be long.' She cuffed at Ruth. What should have been affection arrived as a blow to the head. Mum's brown skin against tender scalp, the calluses and rough dryness of it, the bitten fingers ragged at the quick. A hand too much like Uncle Frank's.

Ruth grabbed at Von's hand, tried to keep it with her, but her fingers just got tangled, in the blue ribbon Mum wore in her hair. Her fingernail caught it, a thread tearing off it, tattering away. Then Mum jerked her head, stood up straighter, pulled away. But the blue thread stayed there. Ruth left it there all day.

'Just need to clear the head, Ruthie. Won't be long.'

Ruth watched her mother walk off, following the river, until she was just a black speck pulled along by wide and heavy brownness. They were moving, both the river and Mum. But what Ruth saw was her mum standing still. She was receding in some dry, lonely country she had claimed as her own. It was a blank place, with nothing to distinguish it from anywhere else.

The river kept flowing. Intent on where it was going, on where it might have been. The sky gave distance back like a slap.

Von walked and walked, following the river, flowing slower now, under the bridge. She walked past huddles of drinkers, people caught like old bits of tree around a rock. She didn't want to get snagged like that, she had to keep moving, hard and fast and straight. The river flowed, pulling strongly the other way.

Murrie's house backed onto the river. There was no glass in the windows and the salty, dead fish smell drifted right through the boards and old sheets he'd pinned up at the blank holes, down the dark hallway with its broken floorboards, through the fibro and tin kitchen, up to the room where Murrie should have been sleeping on the bed.

But he wasn't there. The place was empty. It was dark as the black fire holes in Murrie's floor.

Murrie's ute wasn't out front. His bags, his beer, even his bedspread, everything was gone. Only the rubble of a fire left, his old saucepans stacked neatly in the middle of the floor. Only a month or so before but it seemed like a lifetime ago, and it was, Lily's short lifetime, she'd cooked in the old one, saw the rust and dirt in it, but ate baked beans out of it anyway, sharing his spoon.

She lay down in the silence where Murrie should have been. If he was here, he would put his arm round her. He wouldn't be surprised. She would take his hand and rub his palm on her stomach. Only a bit of a bulge there now. A bit of blood to come away.

'Your one, she's Lil,' she would tell him, even said it out loud, a little name falling thin into the space where Murrie was gone. 'I'm coming back tomorrow. Bring some of my things.'

Murrie wouldn't be looking at her, his eyes would be on the light coming through the window, shattering into the colours made by flowered sheets. He'd lined up his old beer bottles there, and the light through the sheets and the bottles split brown glass into rainbows, into drops of yellow

and green and blue. She would tell him she'd named the
baby for the river flowers that bloomed once every fifty
years. She didn't know the real name, Jacob wouldn't tell
her because she came from the wrong place. But she
thought, when she saw Lily's little webby fingers and her
blue, underwater skin, that she was a river baby, so Lily
was the right name they could call her, all those bastards
in the town.

If Murrie was there, he would have pushed into her. It
might have hurt. But Von wouldn't feel it, not really. She
was floating in Murrie's silence. It was vast and soft and
welcoming. Just like Uncle Frank's.

'Where's Murrie?'

'Gone. Back his own country for a while.'

Old Jacob was the only one down by the river then;
everyone else was in the pub. Big drinking time, day after
Christmas, people still drunk from the day before. Von could
hear them, sudden shouts and spurts of laughter, see the
black shapes on the verandah, erupting now and then into
fists and arms and legs. Von hitched Lily up on her back.
The baby was crying, but Von could only hear it from a
distance, a thin whine underneath the sound of the river
rushing through her, the roar of it blotting everything out.

'Yeah? Where?'

Jacob rubbed his nose with the back of his hand and
snot slimed over it like he'd squashed a snail. He spoke as
if she should know what he meant. She just kept looking
at him. He hooked a thumb back along the river. 'Gone.
Maybe two days.'

Even that slight movement, his finger jerking, made him topple over. Old Jacob was drunk. He lay under the tree. He stared at the sky and there was no energy in him, he was flat out under God's hand. Von started walking, looking for Murrie's footprints, for a man walking along a road. But Murrie was a man in a truck. The road he travelled was straight, the tyres hummed and a cool wind blew in the window. He drank a beer and when he got hungry or thirsty he would stop at a Shell. Murrie was a man whistling and tipping his hat forward. He wasn't coming back.

Jacob muttered and closed his eyes. Von sat down beside him, straining to catch his gist. But Jacob's words didn't flow like water, they were too full of holes and muddiness, there were too few to latch onto, just like Uncle Frank's.

'Not your country.' Old Jacob shook his head from side to side and his finger kept stabbing up at her, but missing, stabbing at the sky. 'Not Maudie's country, see? You're not from here.' He just kept saying it over and over, and Von couldn't make head nor tail. 'Quick. You go back to her country. Maudie, she's still back there.'

Jacob was too drunk, too full of holes and mutters, he didn't make sense.

She just kept walking along the river for a while. But that wasn't right. Murrie came from the red clay, all those miles away. So she struck out. Away from the river, away from the road, walking fast.

If Murrie is walking, she can catch him, Von is thinking, if she walks fast enough, far enough, long enough, if she gets away. When the baby cries, Von stops and tries to feed her but it's no good. Her milk has retreated to that strange, lush landscape which inhabited her for a while. Now her tits are flat as empty brown paper bags. They are sandy coloured, dry as this earth.

Von keeps walking, one foot in front of the other. She strikes out away from the road, so Trevor won't find her, so she can feel the earth underneath her feet. Thinks it's Murrie's earth, but it's not. Murrie's a man driving. He's a man in a truck. Driving along a road.

After a while Lily stops crying. Von's feet bleed but she doesn't feel it. She doesn't hear Frank calling, she is too far away. She can't hear the river. All she can hear is the sound of feet hitting earth.

chapter 26

Ruth has been dreaming, an old nightmare of tidal waves and flash floods and drowning, and she wakes sweating, needing a cigarette. It's past midnight. She sits on the verandah in the cool blackness, and underneath her, from the derelict hotel across the road, from behind corrugated iron, she can hear the Smiths playing, a jumped up country boy, over and over, the same song, like the needle's stuck. And over the top of it, a drunken argument, a man and a woman, the woman pleading, the man kicking garbage bins and picking them up and sledging car bonnets, it's getting louder and louder, amplified by height and a too-empty street. You cunt, you fucking cunt. The woman's crying. A slow soft sound that goes on and on.

The phone makes her jump.

'Ruth? It's Auntie Mavis. Ruthie? That you?'

For some reason Mavis is whispering. Probably because it's midnight. Although she lives alone, there's no-one to wake. Ruth stays silent. She listens to Mavis's voice trembling down the wire, as if from a great distance, but

Ruth knows she's probably just across the road. Mavis was always a bit weird about phones. Whispered if it was late, shouted if she had to phone the city. As if you had to yell louder the further away you were.

'Ruth! I know you're there. Answer me this second.'

'Hi. What do you want?'

'Well what do you reckon, Ruth Cook? Why haven't you returned my calls? Why haven't you come to see me? Or your Uncle Frank. He's in the hospital, you know. He's sinking fast.'

'He's probably not my uncle anyway.' Ruth tries to sound bored. 'Mona reckoned Mum was his bastard. And that he was her Dad. It's all bullshit, isn't it? Him being my Uncle Frank.'

Frank the iceberg. Now he's melting. And it won't be her that drowns.

Mavis goes silent. But not for long.

'That's none of your business, missy. What does it matter anyway? He's family, that's the point. I talked to that boyfriend, asked you to call, Does that lout ever do more than grunt? Ruth? Did he tell you I called?'

'Listen, Ruth. Your Uncle Frank . . .' Mavis sounds like she's crying. Ruth can't believe it. It makes her feel embarrassed. Makes her want to hang up and run away.

'You'd better come right this second. Straight to the hospital, do you hear? I'm calling from a pay phone, the money's gone . . .'

'Okay. See you there.'

But she doesn't. She's been waiting for years. Now Frank can wait for her.

. . .

The street is wide as an airstrip, so wide it takes your breath away. The only thing here as big as a child remembers, the only space which hasn't shrunk. The earth too smells familiar, she can't see it properly, but she knows it's red and glinting with minerals, stray quartz pebbles, bits of old beer bottle, scrub and thorns. A fine grit which insinuates into every orifice but in the end wears down to dust.

The gate hangs on its hinge like a broken jaw. In the old days Frank and Mavis would never have let it get like that. But the people who live here now look like what Mavis used to call 'wasters', people who let junk and rubbish pile up in their front yard. Creeping up the driveway, Ruth takes her shoes off so they don't crunch on the drive. Someone's home, up late for here, but the glow is dim, just the fuzzy blue flicker of a TV. The light falls on the junk all over the verandah, the old red verandah now painted an acidic blue. There's a broken air-conditioner, boxes of car tools, piles of yellow newspapers tied up with string. Ruth peers at them, always hopeful. But they are recent, they are not dated 1968.

In the backyard they've put up a new shed to replace Frank's old one but that doesn't matter, he cleaned that out, she didn't expect to find anything there. She knows exactly where the lemon tree was, though, because its roots kept cracking up Frank's path. He tried to fix it, but short of cutting the tree down, there was nothing he could do. Mavis wanted to pave the whole backyard. Easier to clean.

Right next to where the bits of concrete poke up, filled with dirt and old lolly wrappers, she starts to dig. This mess means they aren't gardeners, they wouldn't have dug down this far. At first she can't feel anything and panics, thinking maybe they put down sewerage pipes, found it, chucked it out at the tip. Then her hand touches the edge, sharp metal, cold. She sits there for a while. The padlock isn't a problem; it's rusted right through. Anyway, all she'll find are Frank's blueprints, for the inventions he dissected like an autopsy, looking for his dodgy ticker. Trying to make it start.

Wind is rising. A moon. Then stars. Spread like jewels on a black blanket. But she's not looking at them. She's staring at Frank's secret box.

The padlock comes away easily. Inside is a black hand-bag. Inside that a gold cross. And a fuzzy black and white picture of some priest. He's not smiling, he looks grim and pinched. Like a sad black crow. He has one hand on the handlebars of a motorbike, an old-fashioned one like the ones you see in British movies about the war. On the back it's dated 1939. That's it, no name, no location. Just the picture and the cross.

She stares and stares at it. There must be some way through it, some way to turn it inside out like a sock. To see the unpicked threads, all the sobs and cries and laughter running under that sepia skin. She doesn't understand.

It's not until she throws the handbag at the shed and starts digging, with soft useless city hands, getting dirt under all the nails, breaking them, ripping fingernails to shreds, that she finds it. Way down deep. Far below Uncle Frank's tin box, curled under an old dead root of the lemon tree. It's tiny and tattered but glowing slightly. Just an ordinary blue ribbon, but it's got that little tear in it where the fabric tattered away. And Uncle Frank, he'd buried it. Like an old dog with a bone.

Ruth puts her face up to the stars wheeling on their cold curvature. She doesn't cry. Anger is burning in her like a sharp black spear.

chapter 27

After she tips a disbelieving J out of bed and packs up all their stuff and leaves a cheque in the letterbox for the woman who owns the flat, Ruth drives straight to the hospital. It's late, it's very early, it's two in the morning. Surely Mavis won't be there now. But Frank will. Frank can't get away. He's lying like a blank sheet of paper ready for anyone to write something on, but none of it will be true. Only Frank knows the secrets and he wields his silence like a brick. Ruth's ready though. Anger is wielding her now. She's a black and angry spear.

It drives her fast and furious through the streets of the town, J cursing and dozing against the window, cutting the right-angled corners, burning rubber at the lights. But it doesn't matter, everyone is safe in their little houses, tucked up in bed. Leaving the car at an angle, with the doors open and the engine still running, she uses her anger to drive her feet up the glossy hallway, past the nurses' station where a trim woman in a white dress leaps up, but she's too late, Ruth's too fast.

Mavis jumps a foot when Ruth cannons into Frank's bed.

'Ruth, what on earth . . .' she starts to say, but Ruth is already grabbing at the little canister marked 'Fitzgerald's Funerals' which sits there, like a bowl of grapes, like a hospital gift, next to the newspaper Frank can't read.

'What's this, Mavis?'

Mavis pauses like she's going to tell her some bullshit. But then her face falls, she's gone way too soft.

'Vonnie's underpants.' Even Mavis realises this sounds silly. She snivels into a hankie and tries to sit up straight. 'And her dress. What she was wearing. Don't know why Frank had it, don't want to, doesn't really matter any more.' She sticks her chin out. Ruth would like to punch it, hard. 'In any case, it was mine. Sort of. Well. It was Frank's. And someone had to do something, didn't they? As usual it was me.'

'Bullshit, Mavis. It's mine.'

Ruth imagines they will have a tug of war, Mavis and her, over Frank lying there, white as a sheet. She imagines she will laugh about it later, that it will remind Ruth of her and Mona tugging over Mavis's old slippers, a pink high heel breaking off. But Mavis doesn't move. She's gone soft as putty underneath her girdle, she can't get her breath.

Ruth takes one look at Frank. She sees his hands lying empty on the counterpane, the flat place where his big belly should be. Then she looks at his face. His eyes are open but the face is blank. There's nothing there at all.

When Frank finds Vonnie, he thinks she is just asleep. She is lying on her side in what would have been scant shadow at midday, beneath the bones of a dying tree. Lily is still tied to her back. It's getting dark, but Frank can see her, Frank listened to the old Mission men. He stands very still. His eyes unlace shadows from their origins, he finds and fingers the denser shapes. There is a moon, just breaking. Pale bone through soft dark skin.

Vonnie is still warm from the sun, but only on the surface; underneath she's going cold. The cold indifference is rising up. Lily is dry as dust and much colder; she's shrivelled like a tiny bunch of grapes.

Frank sits beside them all night. He doesn't cry. He doesn't sing. He doesn't know the words. Maudie never told him. He has to make them up. He sings them his silence, the only song he has. He thinks about Maudie and Tommy, remembers Jacob and the message sticks. They travel powerful rivers of dry earth. By dawn they might tell him what to do.

Should he bury her in earth? It isn't red clay, it isn't her country, but it's closer than anything he can find. Lil, she's different. She's a water child, her country is the river and then the lake. She is the baby in Jacob's special story, the one born by a fishing place to the wrong husband, whose mother runs away. She is beautiful; her mother heard a spirit song how the child would live forever, in the plains, in the water, in the wind. But she is killed by the right husband, who is the wrong husband but the right husband for the tribe. Doing The Right Thing. Where the child lies dead there are strange lights and the water of the lake turns to salt. At the spot where they throw her body in the water, flowers grow. This is the flower of blood. A spirit comes from the sky. It pierces the husband as he kneels among the flowers. That spear is the blackness at this flower's heart.

Frank wraps Von up in one half of the bedsheet she was carrying, Lily in the other. He carefully folds Von's dress, her underwear, her hair ribbon. There isn't much. She goes gold coloured and naked into dry cold ground.

Then just before he goes secret water tells him what to do. That tree where Von lay down and died, it's dying too, but it still has a breath of life. Frank kneels down to take it, to save his own. Von never knew that if you dug with a pointed stick below that tree, you could find the roots. And if you chopped those roots up and put them in a bag of river reeds, and blew on the roots to loosen them, you could get a drink. Von didn't know because Frank didn't tell her. He thought his silence would save her, like it saved him.

Water tells him. Can't put Von there, in red dry ground. She's his message stick, she'll write the map and give the warning, across the years. Water, that's what was needed all along. So he digs, and she is born again, dead this time, dusty and gold coloured, out of that wrong bad earth.

After he's done that Frank stands and sniffs. There's rain coming, a lot of it. Maybe enough to cry that river home. Frank sets off to find water. Heading for the river and through days and hours of it, toward the rain. He carries Von on his back, slumped and lolling like Maudie, and Lily in one hand, so light and small and dry. As if she had merely floated up in Von's muddy water and he'd caught her in his net, too late, like a shiny fish. He's heading for the truck. On the way, hours and days of carrying them, he stops and sits, for a lifetime sometimes, crying, lost in a hollow dry place. But his women are getting lighter all the time. And rain is coming. At certain places he stops to collect his hat, his trousers, the boots. The terrible skin of an ordinary life.

He's heading for the lake and the truck, the river and the weir. As he walks, Frank cries and cries. He helps that river along.

'I remember we broke a windscreen here. A semi threw up a stone. He stuffed a towel in the hole and pressed the heel of his hand against the glass. You had to do that to stop it breaking, that old kind of windscreen. It shatters instead of crazes. It can fly in and take out your eye.'

His hand was cut, the skin so old and weathered it was alien. He never noticed the blood dripping from finger down to thumb.

'Oh please.' J is half-asleep, head juddering on the window. 'Do you have to? Can't we just sing songs instead?'

Ruth's been driving and driving, for as long as she can remember, first through town streets in their tidy geometry, then on the Airport Road to the lake. She needs someone to tell the stories to. The stories are miles, with ends and beginnings. Miles tell stories, they string a rope over blackness. Stories can pull you along a road.

'What happened in the end? With the radiator.' J's interested despite himself. It's four in the morning now. Only a secret dance of hand and foot keeps them from the hollow spin of space. 'When the car broke down in the desert? How'd he get out of that?'

'He was picked up by a truck driver who took him into the Settlement. Mavis told me that story. Only story about Frank she ever told. And she was crying. Like it was a warning. That was weird. Frank never said a word. And you know what? Even though it was Sunday and the Shell was shut, he found a little junk shop that was open. He looked through the windows all full of cobwebs and old candlesticks and bits of trash—tea sets, Mavis said, horseshoes, babies' prams, nothing to make you think it might be there. And he found it. Right at the back. Under an old tarp. There was a radiator. It was in perfect working order. Even the serial number was correct.'

'So?' J waits for her to explain.

But she doesn't know. She has never known what the moral to this story is or to any of Frank's stories of wounds and scars and missing pieces, of things lost and sometimes found. Is it that strange things happen, or that effort, hard work, Doing The Right Thing, all this will be rewarded? She doesn't know.

She only knows she is back on this road again like she never left it, keeping to the rules like a mantra for success. At times she feels Frank is peering through the window with her, reeling in the white line of his road. At other times he is the window, obscured and dark with a glassy silence, cobwebbed with an onion skin of junk. Frank is the secret thing she is trying to find, that Von was looking for, walking fast in all the wrong directions. He is the configuration they needed to crack.

J goes to sleep. But Ruth isn't lonely. In the silence, in the hum of a road passing, a story travelling, Frank is with her. He's peering over her shoulder, like she used to his, asking how far is it to go. Listening to her story, travelling her miles, to her country for once. Stories and miles knit together. They make a rug for her knees, a pillow for his head.

As the sun starts to come up on a straight horizon— flat, flat, raw and blueish, with bushes tracing arteries from glare—Frank is there. She drives tirelessly. He doesn't speak.

There is only the glow of the instruments, a road and a moon keeping pace. Ruth plays that old game of pretending the telegraph poles are moving and becomes so convinced it is hard to return to reality, like staring at a pattern which contains a face. Being unable to see at first what will later become all too clear.

Frank's face in profile closed over. His silence, so rare and jagged, glittering invisible in air. She wishes it would get dark again, that there would be no need to look at each other, that silence was full to bursting, that it could mean what it once did. That when she was tired of driving she could lay her head in his trouser lap and not feel him flinch.

She would sleep in the green glow of his dashboard. Feel the secret dance of Frank's feet and hands. Hear his stories thread her vacuum rush like a rope.

epilogue

The dirt road makes you skid sideways. There are corrugations in it which at low speed can shudder you into a spin. The cautious end up in the bushes, wheels spinning uselessly, in a storm of dust. So you don't let it beat you, you floor the accelerator, you give it a go. With heart in mouth and blindly, all you can do is punch it, in a whirl of dust and stones. When you go faster, a pattern reveals itself. It was there all the time. If only you'd known where to look.

A lizard, black and fat, shining like marquisite, sits in the middle of a curve. It refuses to move. The car edges round it, juddering and shuddering, scrub poking viciously, but you don't give up. You round a final swollen curve of water, stop a little way from the vans.

J is still asleep. Ruth leaves him and walks. Past the vans, the barbeques, the shuttered kiosk, the water by the roadside silver, the lake grey then blue then pink. There's no-one around.

But she shuts the gate anyway. She doesn't want to

break the rules. She walks over dead earth at water's edge, crushing water plants with her heels. She stops and takes off her boots and her jeans.

Wading in, feeling the suck of the water, the puckered folds, earth holding her down. She has weight, she is made of earth, she won't float away. She walks and walks, feeling fish flick against white and private skin. Sand is vast and tiny, between water-blenched toes.

At the deepest part, where she can just hold her hands above the water, she gives Mum's dead skin back to the river. The ashes make no stipple, they surrender and dissolve. The thong, the one she has saved ever since she was six, slaps stupidly and floats there, a dull useless Woolworths thing. But the hair ribbon flutters, makes the sheerest shiver, on a skin already closing, turning back. Then it sinks and disappears.

Ruth dives down, down and down, deeper and deeper, to the very centre of her earth. Reeds humming, fish startled, face flattened with the pressure, sun receding. Water swallows her whole. She goes down and down until lungs gasp and water is earth, dark and heavy and flat.

When she comes back up, it's finally raining. Big fat drops of it. She breaks through water both soft and strong. Water fragile as a womb.

*a*cknowledgements

Thanks to Damian Blayney and Sara Lyons for their support and patience during the first draft of this book. Also to Brett Smith, for his unwavering belief in my writing over many years. Finally to my Mum Isabelle for teaching me the value of reading and to my Dad Jack for all his storytelling.

FILM
Sean Condon

'A lot of this sounds like substitution for love, Henry. That you want only to be loved.'

'I'm already loved, and it's fine. What I want is different. What I want is to be...' Henry paused and thought. 'I want an Oscar.'

Dr Wagner laughed, the involuntary sound coming out of his nose. 'What for?' He covered his mouth, but Henry knew he was still smiling.

'Whatever. I don't care. I just *want* one. I want to be in amongst that crowd. The statuette crowd, clutching and thanking and grinning. I want to be envied by other poor idiots like me.'

'I thought you wanted to make films. What you just told me sounds like the sort of superficial longing of somebody flicking through *People* magazine, somebody who—'

'I *used* to want to make films, when I was *young* enough to want to. Now I'd take anything I could get. I'd be happy enough being a measly *actor*.'

Film (2001) 396pp. **** *Film* is the thoroughly entertaining life story of cinephile Henry Powdermaker who, at age eight makes a film that ends his parents' marriage. Follows his strange, extremely indirect path from homewrecker to Hollywood. A very funny, yet oddly moving journey. Memorable characters and sharp, realistic (sometimes surreal) dialogue make this a book that leaps off the page and straight into the heart. Starring Henry Powdermaker, Charles Rocket, Madeleine Ford, Audrey Gillespie and Ethan Vaughan. There are controversial cameos by Quentin Tarantino, Courtney Love, Peter Bogdanovich and many more. Written by Sean Condon, author of *Sean & David's Long Drive* and *Drive Thru America*. Rated PG.

1 86508 436 0

BECOMING MADAME MAO
Anchee Min

'Mao makes her see heaven's grace in his valour. In bed he is impatient, like a tomb robber grabbing gold. She presents herself, the gift of seduction. In the future the couple will do the same to the minds of a billion.'

Madame Mao is the 'white-boned demon', the woman many hold directly responsible for the excesses of the Cultural Revolution.

Moving with assurance from the intimately personal to the broader stage of world history, Anchee Min tells the stirring, erotically charged story of this extraordinary woman. With lush psychological insight, Min penetrates the myth surrounding Madame Mao and creates a finely nuanced, always ambiguous portrait of a woman driven by ambition, betrayal, and a never-to-be-fulfilled need to be loved.

Becoming Madame Mao exists with all the compressed drama and high lyrical poetry of great opera.

1 86508 497 2